The House Without a Key

The House Without a Key

Earl Derr Biggers

MINT EDITIONS

The House Without a Key was first published in 1925.

This edition published by Mint Editions 2021.

ISBN 9781513282060 | E-ISBN 9781513287089

Published by Mint Editions®

MINT
EDITIONS

minteditionbooks.com

Publishing Director: Jennifer Newens
Design & Production: Rachel Lopez Metzger
Project Manager: Micaela Clark
Typesetting: Westchester Publishing Services

Contents

I

Kona Weather

Miss Minerva Winterslip was a Bostonian in good standing, and long past the romantic age. Yet beauty thrilled her still, even the semi-barbaric beauty of a Pacific island. As she walked slowly along the beach she felt the little catch in her throat that sometimes she had known in Symphony Hall, Boston, when her favorite orchestra rose to some new and unexpected height of loveliness.

It was the hour at which she liked Waikiki best, the hour just preceding dinner and the quick tropic darkness. The shadows cast by the tall cocoanut palms lengthened and deepened, the light of the falling sun flamed on Diamond Head and tinted with gold the rollers sweeping in from the coral reef. A few late swimmers, reluctant to depart, dotted those waters whose touch is like the caress of a lover. On the springboard of the nearest float a slim brown girl poised for one delectable instant. What a figure! Miss Minerva, well over fifty herself, felt a mild twinge of envy—youth, youth like an arrow, straight and sure and flying. Like an arrow the slender figure rose, then fell; the perfect dive, silent and clean.

Miss Minerva glanced at the face of the man who walked beside her. But Amos Winterslip was oblivious to beauty; he had made that the first rule of his life. Born in the Islands, he had never known the mainland beyond San Francisco. Yet there could be no doubt about it, he was the New England conscience personified—the New England conscience in a white duck suit.

"Better turn back, Amos," suggested Miss Minerva. "Your dinner's waiting. Thank you so much."

"I'll walk as far as the fence," he said. "When you get tired of Dan and his carryings-on, come to us again. We'll be glad to have you."

"That's kind of you," she answered, in her sharp crisp way. "But I really must go home. Grace is worried about me. Of course, she can't understand. And my conduct is scandalous, I admit. I came over to Honolulu for six weeks, and I've been wandering about these islands for ten months."

"As long as that?"

She nodded. "I can't explain it. Every day I make a solemn vow I'll start packing my trunks—to-morrow."

"And to-morrow never comes," said Amos. "You've been taken in by the tropics. Some people are."

"Weak people, I presume you mean," snapped Miss Minerva. "Well, I've never been weak. Ask anybody on Beacon Street."

He smiled wanly. "It's a strain in the Winterslips," he said. "Supposed to be Puritans, but always sort of yearning toward the lazy latitudes."

"I know," answered Miss Minerva, her eyes on that exotic shore line. "It's what sent so many of them adventuring out of Salem harbor. Those who stayed behind felt that the travelers were seeing things no Winterslip should look at. But they envied them just the same—or maybe for that very reason." She nodded. "A sort of gypsy strain. It's what sent your father over here to set up as a whaler, and got you born so far from home. You know you don't belong here, Amos. You should be living in Milton or Roxbury, carrying a little green bag and popping into a Boston office every morning."

"I've often thought it," he admitted. "And who knows—I might have made something of my life—"

They had come to a barbed-wire fence, an unaccustomed barrier on that friendly shore. It extended well down on to the beach; a wave rushed up and lapped the final post, then receded.

Miss Minerva smiled. "Well, this is where Amos leaves off and Dan begins," she said. "I'll watch my chance and run around the end. Lucky you couldn't build it so it moved with the tide."

"You'll find your luggage in your room at Dan's, I guess," Amos told her. "Remember what I said about—" He broke off suddenly. A stocky, white-clad man had appeared in the garden beyond the barrier, and was moving rapidly toward them. Amos Winterslip stood rigid for a moment, an angry light flaming in his usually dull eyes. "Good-by," he said, and turned.

"Amos!" cried Miss Minerva sharply. He moved on, and she followed. "Amos, what nonsense! How long has it been since you spoke to Dan?"

He paused under an algaroba tree. "Thirty-one years," he said. "Thirty-one years the tenth of last August."

"That's long enough," she told him. "Now, come around that foolish fence of yours, and hold out your hand to him."

"Not me," said Amos. "I guess you don't know Dan, Minerva, and the sort of life he's led. Time and again he's dishonored us all—"

"Why, Dan's regarded as a big man," she protested. "He's respected—"

"And rich," added Amos bitterly. "And I'm poor. Yes, that's the way it often goes in this world. But there's a world to come, and over there I reckon Dan's going to get his."

Hardy soul though she was, Miss Minerva was somewhat frightened by the look of hate on his thin face. She saw the uselessness of further argument. "Good-by, Amos," she said. "I wish I might persuade you to come East some day—" He gave no sign of hearing, but hurried along the white stretch of sand.

When Miss Minerva turned, Dan Winterslip was smiling at her from beyond the fence. "Hello, there," he cried. "Come this side of the wire and enjoy life again. You're mighty welcome."

"How are you, Dan?" She watched her chance with the waves and joined him. He took both her hands in his.

"Glad to see you," he said, and his eyes backed him up. Yes, he did have a way with women. "It's a bit lonely at the old homestead these days. Need a young girl about to brighten things up."

Miss Minerva sniffed. "I've tramped Boston in galoshes too many winters," she reminded him, "to lose my head over talk like that."

"Forget Boston," he urged. "We're all young in Hawaii. Look at me."

She did look at him, wonderingly. He was sixty-three, she knew, but only the mass of wavy white hair overhanging his temples betrayed his age. His face, burned to the deepest bronze by long years of wandering under the Polynesian sun, was without a line or wrinkle. Deep-chested and muscular, he could have passed on the mainland for a man of forty.

"I see my precious brother brought you as far as the dead-line," he remarked as they moved on through the garden. "Sent me his love, I presume?"

"I tried to get him to come round and shake hands," Miss Minerva said.

Dan Winterslip laughed. "Don't deprive poor Amos of his hate for me," he urged. "It's about all he lives for now. Comes over every night and stands under that algaroba tree of his, smoking cigarettes and staring at my house. Know what he's waiting for? He's waiting for the Lord to strike me down for my sins. Well, he's a patient waiter, I'll say that for him."

Miss Minerva did not reply. Dan's great rambling house of many rooms was set in beauty almost too poignant to be borne. She stood, drinking it all in again, the poinciana trees like big crimson umbrellas, the stately golden glow, the gigantic banyans casting purple shadows, her favorite hau tree, seemingly old as time itself, covered with a profusion of yellow blossoms. Loveliest of all were the flowering vines, the bougainvillea burying everything it touched in brick-red splendor. Miss Minerva wondered what her friends who every spring went into sedate ecstasies over the Boston Public Gardens would say if they could see what she saw now. They would be a bit shocked, perhaps, for this was too lurid to be quite respectable. A scarlet background—and a fitting one, no doubt, for Cousin Dan.

They reached the door at the side of the house that led directly into the living-room. Glancing to her right, Miss Minerva caught through the lush foliage glimpses of the iron fence and tall gates that fronted on Kalia Road. Dan opened the door for her, and she stepped inside. Like most apartments of its sort in the Islands, the living-room was walled on but three sides, the fourth was a vast expanse of wire screening. They crossed the polished floor and entered the big hall beyond. Near the front door a Hawaiian woman of uncertain age rose slowly from her chair. She was a huge, high-breasted, dignified specimen of that vanishing race.

"Well, Kamaikui, I'm back," Miss Minerva smiled.

"I make you welcome," the woman said. She was only a servant, but she spoke with the gracious manner of a hostess.

"Same room you had when you first came over, Minerva," Dan Winterslip announced. "Your luggage is there—and a bit of mail that came in on the boat this morning. I didn't trouble to send it up to Amos's. We dine when you're ready."

"I'll not keep you long," she answered, and hurried up the stairs.

Dan Winterslip strolled back to his living-room. He sat down in a rattan chair that had been made especially for him in Hong-Kong, and glanced complacently about at the many evidences of his prosperity. His butler entered, bearing a tray with cocktails.

"Two, Haku?" smiled Winterslip. "The lady is from Boston."

"Yes-s," hissed Haku, and retired soundlessly.

In a moment Miss Minerva came again into the room. She carried a letter in her hand, and she was laughing.

"Dan, this is too absurd," she said.

"What is?"

"I may have told you that they are getting worried about me at home. Because I haven't been able to tear myself away from Honolulu, I mean. Well, they're sending a policeman for me."

"A policeman?" He lifted his bushy eyebrows.

"Yes, it amounts to that. It's not being done openly, of course. Grace writes that John Quincy has six weeks' vacation from the banking house, and has decided to make the trip out here. 'It will give you some one to come home with, my dear,' says Grace. Isn't she subtle?"

"John Quincy Winterslip? That would be Grace's son."

Miss Minerva nodded. "You never met him, did you, Dan? Well, you will, shortly. And he certainly won't approve of you."

"Why not?" Dan Winterslip bristled.

"Because he's proper. He's a dear boy, but oh, so proper. This journey is going to be a great cross for him. He'll start disapproving as he passes Albany, and think of the long weary miles of disapproval he'll have to endure after that."

"Oh, I don't know. He's a Winterslip, isn't he?"

"He is. But the gypsy strain missed him completely. He's a Puritan."

"Poor boy." Dan Winterslip moved toward the tray on which stood the amber-colored drinks. "I suppose he'll stop with Roger in San Francisco. Write him there and tell him I want him to make this house his home while he's in Honolulu."

"That's kind of you, Dan."

"Not at all. I like youth around me—even the Puritan brand. Now that you're going to be apprehended and taken back to civilization, you'd better have one of these cocktails."

"Well," said his guest, "I'm about to exhibit what my brother used to call true Harvard indifference."

"What do you mean?" asked Winterslip.

"I don't mind if I do," twinkled Miss Minerva, lifting a cocktail glass.

Dan Winterslip beamed upon her. "You're a good sport, Minerva," he remarked, as he escorted her across the hall.

"When in Rome," she answered, "I make it a point not to do as the Bostonians do. I fear it would prove a rather thorny path to popularity."

"Precisely."

"Besides, I shall be back in Boston soon. Tramping about to art exhibits and Lowell Lectures, and gradually congealing into senility."

But she was not in Boston now, she reflected, as she sat down at the gleaming table in the dining-room. Before her, properly iced, was a generous slice of papaia, golden yellow and inviting. Somewhere beyond the foliage outside the screens, the ocean murmured restlessly. The dinner would be perfect, she knew, the

Island beef dry and stringy, perhaps, but the fruits and the salad more than atoning.

"Do you expect Barbara soon?" she inquired presently.

Dan Winterslip's face lighted like the beach at sunrise. "Yes, Barbara has graduated. She'll be along any day now. Nice if she and your perfect nephew should hit on the same boat."

"Nice for John Quincy, at any rate," Miss Minerva replied. "We thought Barbara a lively, charming girl when she visited us in the East."

"She's all of that," he agreed proudly. His daughter was his dearest possession. "I tell you, I've missed her. I've been mighty lonesome."

Miss Minerva gave him a shrewd look. "Yes, I've heard rumors," she remarked, "about how lonesome you've been."

He flushed under his tan. "Amos, I suppose?"

"Oh, not only Amos. A great deal of talk, Dan. Really, at your age—"

"What do you mean, my age? I told you we're all young out here." He ate in silence for a moment. "You're a good sport—I said it and I meant it. You must understand that here in the Islands a man may behave a—a bit differently than he would in the Back Bay."

"At that," she smiled, "all men in the Back Bay are not to be trusted. I'm not presuming to rebuke you, Dan. But—for Barbara's sake—why not select as the object of your devotion a woman you could marry?"

"I could marry this one—if we're talking about the same woman."

"The one I refer to," Miss Minerva replied, "is known, rather widely, as the Widow of Waikiki."

"This place is a hotbed of gossip. Arlene Compton is perfectly respectable."

"A former chorus girl I believe."

"Not precisely. An actress—small parts—before she married Lieutenant Compton."

"And a self-made widow."

"Just what do you mean by that?" he flared. His gray eyes glittered.

"I understand that when her husband's aeroplane crashed on Diamond Head, it was because he preferred it that way. She had driven him to it."

"Lies, all lies!" Dan Winterslip cried. "Pardon me, Minerva, but you mustn't believe all you hear on the beach." He was silent for a moment. "What would you say if I told you I proposed to marry this woman?"

"I'm afraid I'd become rather bromidic," she answered gently, "and remind you that there's no fool like an old fool." He did not speak.

"Forgive me, Dan. I'm your first cousin, but a distant relative for all that. It's really none of my business. I wouldn't care—but I like you. And I'm thinking of Barbara—"

He bowed his head. "I know," he said, "Barbara. Well, there's no need to get excited. I haven't said anything to Arlene about marriage. Not yet."

Miss Minerva smiled. "You know, as I get on in years," she remarked, "so many wise old saws begin to strike me as utter nonsense. Particularly that one I just quoted." He looked at her, his eyes friendly again. "This is the best avocado I ever tasted," she added. "But tell me, Dan, are you sure the mango is a food? Seems more like a spring tonic to me."

By the time they finished dinner the topic of Arlene Compton was forgotten and Dan had completely regained his good nature. They had coffee on his veranda—or, in Island parlance, lanai—which opened off one end of the living-room. This was of generous size, screened on three sides and stretching far down on to the white beach. Outside the brief tropic dusk dimmed the bright colors of Waikiki.

"No breeze stirring," said Miss Minerva.

"The trades have died," Dan answered. He referred to the beneficent winds which—save at rare, uncomfortable intervals—blow across the Islands out of the cool northeast. "I'm afraid we're in for a stretch of Kona weather."

"I hope not," Miss Minerva said.

"It saps the life right out of me nowadays," he told her, and sank into a chair. "That about being young, Minerva—it's a little bluff I'm fond of."

She smiled gently. "Even youth finds the Kona hard to endure," she comforted. "I remember when I was here before—in the 'eighties. I was only nineteen, but the memory of the sick wind lingers still."

"I missed you then, Minerva."

"Yes. You were off somewhere in the South Seas."

"But I heard about you when I came back. That you were tall and blonde and lovely, and nowhere near so prim as they feared you were going to be. A wonderful figure, they said—but you've got that yet."

She flushed, but smiled still. "Hush, Dan. We don't talk that way where I come from."

"The 'eighties," he sighed. "Hawaii was Hawaii then. Unspoiled, a land of opera bouffe, with old Kalakaua sitting on his golden throne."

"I remember him," Miss Minerva said. "Grand parties at the palace. And the afternoons when he sat with his disreputable friends on the royal lanai, and the Royal Hawaiian Band played at his feet, and he haughtily tossed them royal pennies. It was such a colorful, naive spot then, Dan."

"It's been ruined," he complained sadly. "Too much aping of the mainland. Too much of your damned mechanical civilization— automobiles, phonographs, radios—bah! And yet—and yet, Minerva— away down underneath there are deep dark waters flowing still."

She nodded, and they sat for a moment busy with their memories. Presently Dan Winterslip snapped on a small reading light at his side. "I'll just glance at the evening paper, if you don't mind."

"Oh, do," urged Miss Minerva.

She was glad of a moment without talk. For this, after all, was the time she loved Waikiki best. So brief, this tropic dusk, so quick the coming of the soft alluring night. The carpet of the waters, apple-green by day, crimson and gold at sunset, was a deep purple now. On top of that extinct volcano called Diamond Head a yellow eye was winking, as though to hint there might still be fire beneath. Three miles down, the harbor lights began to twinkle, and out toward the reef the lanterns of Japanese sampans glowed intermittently. Beyond, in the roadstead, loomed the battered hulk of an old brig slowly moving toward the channel entrance. Always, out there, a ship or two, in from the East with a cargo of spice or tea or ivory, or eastward bound with a load of tractor salesmen. Ships of all sorts, the spic and span liner and the rakish tramp, ships from Melbourne and Seattle, New York and Yokohama, Tahiti and Rio, any port on the seven seas. For this was Honolulu, the Crossroads of the Pacific—the glamorous crossroads where, they said, in time all paths crossed again. Miss Minerva sighed.

She was conscious of a quick movement on Dan's part. She turned and looked at him. He had laid the paper on his knee, and was staring straight ahead. That bluff about being young—no good now. For his face was old, old.

"Why, Dan—" she said.

"I—I'm wondering, Minerva," he began slowly. "Tell me again about that nephew of yours."

She was surprised, but hid it. "John Quincy?" she said. "He's just the usual thing, for Boston. Conventional. His whole life has been planned for him, from the cradle to the grave. So far he's walked the line. The inevitable preparatory school, Harvard, the proper clubs, the family banking house—even gone and got himself engaged to the very girl his mother would have picked for him. There have been times when I hoped he might kick over—the war—but no, he came back and got meekly into the old rut."

"Then he's reliable—steady?"

Miss Minerva smiled. "Dan, compared with that boy, Gibraltar wobbles occasionally."

"Discreet, I take it?"

"He invented discretion. That's what I'm telling you. I love him—but a little bit of recklessness now and then—However, I'm afraid it's too late now. John Quincy is nearly thirty."

Dan Winterslip was on his feet, his manner that of a man who had made an important decision. Beyond the bamboo curtain that hung in the door leading to the living-room a light appeared. "Haku!" Winterslip called. The Japanese servant came swiftly.

"Haku, tell the chauffeur—quick—the big car! I must get to the dock before the PRESIDENT TYLER sails for San Francisco. Wikiwiki!"

The servant disappeared into the living-room, and Winterslip followed. Somewhat puzzled, Miss Minerva sat for a moment, then rose and pushed aside the curtain. "Are you sailing, Dan?" she asked.

He was seated at his desk, writing hurriedly. "No, no—just a note—I must get it off on that boat—"

There was an air of suppressed excitement about him. Miss Minerva stepped over the threshold into the living-room. In another moment Haku appeared with an announcement that was unnecessary, for the engine of an automobile was humming in the drive. Dan Winterslip took his hat from Haku. "Make yourself at home, Minerva—I'll be back shortly," he cried, and rushed out.

Some business matter, no doubt. Miss Minerva strolled aimlessly about the big airy room, pausing finally before the portrait of Jedediah Winterslip, the father of Dan and Amos, and her uncle. Dan had had it painted from a photograph after the old man's death; it was the work of an artist whose forte was reputed to be landscapes—oh it must assuredly have been landscapes, Miss Minerva thought. But even so there was no mistaking the power and personality of this New Englander who had set up in Honolulu as a whaler. The only time she had seen him, in the 'eighties, he had been broken and old, mourning his lost fortune, which had gone with his ships in an Arctic disaster a short time before.

Well, Dan had brought the family back, Miss Minerva reflected. Won again that lost fortune and much more. There were queer rumors about his methods—but so there were about the methods of Bostonians who had never strayed from home. A charming fellow, whatever his past. Miss Minerva sat down at the grand piano and played a few old familiar bars—The Beautiful Blue Danube. Her thoughts went back to the 'eighties.

Dan Winterslip was thinking of the 'eighties too as his car sped townward along Kalakaua Avenue. But it was the present that concerned him when they reached the dock and he ran, panting a little, through a dim pier-shed toward the gangplank of the PRESIDENT TYLER. He had no time to spare, the ship was on the point of sailing. Since it was a through boat from the Orient it left without the ceremonies that attend the departure of a liner plying only between Honolulu and the mainland. Even so, there were cries of "Aloha," some hearty and some tremulous, most of the travelers were bedecked with leis, and a confused little crowd milled about the foot of the plank.

Dan Winterslip pushed his way forward and ran up the sharp incline. As he reached the dock he encountered an old acquaintance, Hepworth, the second officer.

"You're the man I'm looking for," he cried.

"How are you, sir," Hepworth said. "I didn't see your name on the list."

"No, I'm not sailing. I'm here to ask a favor."

"Glad to oblige, Mr. Winterslip."

Winterslip thrust a letter into his hand. "You know my cousin Roger in 'Frisco. Please give him that—him and no one else—as soon after you land as you possibly can. I'm too late for the mail—and I prefer this way anyhow. I'll be mighty grateful."

"Don't mention it—you've been very kind to me and I'll be only too happy—I'm afraid you'll have to go ashore, sir. Just a minute, there—" He took Winterslip's arm and gently urged him back on to the plank. The instant Dan's feet touched the dock, the plank was drawn up behind him.

For a moment he stood, held by the fascination an Islander always feels at sight of a ship outward bound. Then he turned and walked slowly through the pier-shed. Ahead of him he caught a glimpse of a slender lithe figure which he recognized at once as that of Dick Kaohla, the grandson of Kamaikui. He quickened his pace and joined the boy.

"Hello, Dick," he said.

EARL DERR BIGGERS

"Hello." The brown face was sullen, unfriendly.

"You haven't been to see me for a long time," Dan Winterslip said. "Everything all right?"

"Sure," replied Kaohla. "Sure it's all right." They reached the street, and the boy turned quickly away. "Good night," he muttered.

Dan Winterslip stood for a moment, thoughtfully looking after him. Then he got into the car. "No hurry now," he remarked to the chauffeur.

When he reappeared in his living-room, Miss Minerva glanced up from the book she was reading. "Were you in time, Dan?" she asked.

"Just made it," he told her.

"Good," she said, rising. "I'll take my book and go up-stairs. Pleasant dreams."

He waited until she reached the door before he spoke. "Ah—Minerva—don't trouble to write your nephew about stopping here."

"No, Dan?" she said, puzzled again.

"No. I've attended to the invitation myself. Good night."

"Oh—good night," she answered, and left him.

Alone in the great room, he paced restlessly back and forth over the polished floor. In a moment he went out on to the lanai, and found the newspaper he had been reading earlier in the evening. He brought it back to the living-room and tried to finish it, but something seemed to trouble him. His eyes kept straying—straying—with a sharp exclamation he tore one corner from the shipping page, savagely ripped the fragment to bits.

Again he got up and wandered about. He had intended paying a call down the beach, but that quiet presence in the room above—Boston in its more tolerant guise but Boston still—gave him pause.

He returned to the lanai. There, under a mosquito netting, was the cot where he preferred to sleep; his dressing-room was near at hand. However, it was too early for bed. He stepped through the door on to the beach. Unmistakable, the soft treacherous breath of the Kona fanned his cheek—the "sick wind" that would pile the breakers high along the coast and blight temporarily this Island paradise. There was no moon, the stars that usually seemed so friendly and so close were now obscured. The black water rolled in like a threat. He stood staring out into the dark—out there to the crossroads where paths always crossed again. If you gave them time—if you only gave them time—

As he turned back, his eyes went to the algaroba tree beyond the wire, and he saw the yellow flare of a match. His brother Amos. He had a sudden friendly feeling for Amos, he wanted to go over and talk to him, talk of the far days when they played together on this beach. No use, he knew. He sighed, and the screen door of the lanai banged behind him—the screen door without a lock in a land where locks are few.

Tired, he sat in the dark to think. His face was turned toward the curtain of bamboo between him and the living-room. On that curtain a shadow appeared, was motionless a second, then vanished. He caught his breath—again the shadow. "Who's there?" he called.

A huge brown arm was thrust through the bamboo. A friendly brown face was framed there.

"Your fruit I put on the table," said Kamaikui. "I go to bed now."

"Of course. Go ahead. Good night."

The woman withdrew. Dan Winterslip was furious with himself. What was the matter with him, anyhow? He who had fought his way through unspeakable terrors in the early days—nervous—on edge—

"Getting old," he muttered. "No, by heaven—it's the Kona. That's it. The Kona. I'll be all right when the trades blow again."

When the trades blew again! He wondered. Here at the crossroads one could not be sure.

II

THE HIGH HAT

John Quincy Winterslip walked aboard the ferry at Oakland feeling rather limp and weary. For more than six days he had been marooned on sleepers—his pause at Chicago had been but a flitting from one train to another—and he was fed up. Seeing America first—that was what he had been doing. And what an appalling lot of it there was! He felt that for an eternity he had been staring at endless plains, dotted here and there by unesthetic houses the inmates of which had unquestionably never heard a symphony concert.

Ahead of him ambled a porter, bearing his two suitcases, his golf clubs and his hat-box. One of the man's hands was gone—chewed off, no doubt, in some amiable frontier scuffle. In its place he wore a steel hook. Well, no one could question the value of a steel hook to a man in the porter's profession. But how quaint—and western!

The boy indicated a spot by the rail on the forward deck, and the porter began to unload. Carefully selecting the man's good hand, John Quincy dropped into it a tip so generous as to result in a touching of hook to cap in a weird salute. The object of this attention sank down amid his elaborate trappings, removed the straw hat from his perspiring head, and tried to figure out just what had happened to him.

Three thousand miles from Beacon Street, and two thousand miles still to go! Why, he inquired sourly of his usually pleasant self, had he ever agreed to make this absurd expedition into heathen country? Here it was late June, Boston was at its best. Tennis at Longwood, long mild evenings in a single shell on the Charles, weekends and golf with Agatha Parker at Magnolia. And if one must travel, there was Paris. He hadn't seen Paris in two years and had been rather planning a quick run over, when his mother had put this preposterous notion into his head.

Preposterous—it was all of that. Traveling five thousand miles just as a gentle hint to Aunt Minerva to return to her calm, well-ordered life behind purple window-panes on Beacon Street. And was there any chance that his strong-minded relative would take the hint? Not one in a thousand. Aunt Minerva was accustomed to do as she pleased—he had an uncomfortable, shocked recollection of one occasion when she had said she would do as she damn well pleased.

John Quincy wished he was back. He wished he was crossing Boston Common to his office on State Street, there to put out a new issue of bonds. He was not yet a member of the firm—that was an honor accorded only to Winterslips who were bald and a little stooped—but his heart was in his work. He put out a bond issue with loving apprehension, waiting for the verdict as a playwright waits behind the scenes on a first night. Would those First Mortgage Sixes go over big, or would they flop at his feet?

The hoarse boom of a ferry whistle recalled John Quincy to his present unbelievable location on the map. The boat began to move. He was dimly conscious of a young person of feminine gender who came and sat at his side. Away from the slip and out into the harbor the ferry carried John Quincy, and he suddenly sat up and took notice, for he was never blind to beauty, no matter where he encountered it.

And he was encountering beauty now. The morning air was keen and dry and bright. Spread out before him was that harbor which is like a tired navigator's dream come true. They passed Goat Island, and he heard the faint echo of a bugle; he saw Tamalpais lifting its proud head toward the sparkling sky, he turned, and there was San Francisco scattered blithely over its many hills.

The ferry plowed on, and John Quincy sat very still. A forest of masts and steam funnels—here was the water-front that had supplied the atmosphere for those romantic tales that held him spellbound when he was a boy at school—a quiet young Winterslip whom the gypsy strain had missed. Now he could distinguish a bark from Antwerp, a great liner from the Orient, a five-masted schooner that was reminiscent of those supposedly forgotten stories. Ships from the Treaty Ports, ships from cocoanut islands in southern seas. A picture as intriguing and colorful as a back drop in a theater—but far more real.

Suddenly John Quincy stood up. A puzzled look had come into his calm gray eyes. "I—I don't understand," he murmured.

He was startled by the sound of his own voice. He hadn't intended to speak aloud. In order not to appear too utterly silly, he looked around for some one to whom he might pretend he had addressed that remark. There was no one about—except the young person who was obviously feminine and therefore not to be informally accosted.

John Quincy looked down at her. Spanish or something like that, blue-black hair, dark eyes that were alight now with the amusement she was striving to hide, a delicate oval face tanned a deep brown. He looked again at the harbor—beauty all about the boat, and beauty on it. Much better than traveling on trains!

The girl looked up at John Quincy. She saw a big, broad-shouldered young man with a face as innocent as a child's. A bit of friendliness, she decided instantly, would not be misunderstood.

"I beg your pardon," she said.

"Oh—I—I'm sorry," he stammered. "I didn't mean—I spoke without intending—I said I didn't understand—"

"You didn't understand what?"

"A most amazing thing has happened," he continued. He sat down, and waved his hand toward the harbor. "I've been here before."

She looked perplexed. "Lots of people have," she admitted.

"But—you see—I mean—I've never been here before."

She moved away from him. "Lots of people haven't." She admitted that, too.

John Quincy took a deep breath. What was this discussion he had got into, anyhow? He had a quick impulse to lift his hat gallantly and walk away, letting the whole matter drop. But no, he came of a race that sees things through.

"I'm from Boston," he said.

"Oh," said the girl. That explained everything.

"And what I'm trying to make clear—although of course there's no reason why I should have dragged you into it—"

"None whatever," she smiled. "But go on."

"Until a few days ago I was never west of New York, never in my whole life, you understand. Been about New England a bit, and abroad a few times, but the West—"

"I know. It didn't interest you."

"I wouldn't say that," protested John Quincy with careful politeness. "But there was such a lot of it—exploring it seemed a hopeless undertaking. And then—the family thought I ought to go, you see—so I rode and rode on trains and was—you'll pardon me—a bit bored. Now—I come into this harbor, I look around me, and I get the oddest feeling. I feel that I've been here before."

The girl's face was sympathetic. "Other people have had that experience," she told him. "Choice souls, they are. You've been a long time coming, but you're home at last." She held out a slim brown hand. "Welcome to your city," she said.

John Quincy solemnly shook hands. "Oh, no," he corrected gently. "Boston's my city. I belong there, naturally. But this—this is familiar." He glanced northward at the low hills sheltering the Valley of the Moon, then back at San Francisco. "Yes, I seem to have known my way about here once. Astonishing, isn't it?"

"Perhaps—some of your ancestors—"

"That's true. My grandfather came out here when he was a young man. He went home again—but his brothers stayed. It's the son of one of them I'm going to visit in Honolulu."

"Oh—you're going on to Honolulu?"

"To-morrow morning. Have you ever been there?"

"Ye—es." Her dark eyes were serious. "See—there are the locks— that's where the East begins. The real East. And Telegraph Hill—" she pointed; no one in Boston ever points, but she was so lovely John Quincy overlooked it—"and Russian Hill and the Fairmont on Nob Hill."

"Life must be full of ups and downs," he ventured lightly. "Tell me about Honolulu. Sort of a wild place, I imagine?"

She laughed. "I'll let you discover for yourself how wild it is," she told him. "Practically all the leading families came originally from your beloved New England. 'Puritans with a touch of sun,' my father calls them. He's clever, my father," she added, in an odd childish tone that was wistful and at the same time challenging.

"I'm sure of it," said John Quincy heartily. They were approaching the Ferry Building and other passengers crowded about them. "I'd help you with that suitcase of yours, but I've got all this truck. If we could find a porter—"

"Don't bother," she answered. "I can manage very well." She was staring down at John Quincy's hat box. "I—I suppose there's a silk hat in there?" she inquired.

"Naturally," replied John Quincy.

She laughed—a rich, deep-throated laugh. John Quincy stiffened slightly. "Oh, forgive me," she cried. "But—a silk hat in Hawaii!"

John Quincy stood erect. The girl had laughed at a Winterslip. He filled his lungs with the air sweeping in from the open spaces, the broad open spaces where men are men. A weird reckless feeling came over him. He stooped, picked up the hat box, and tossed it calmly over the rail. It bobbed indignantly away. The crowd closed in, not wishing to miss any further exhibition of madness.

"That's that," said John Quincy quietly.

"Oh," gasped the girl, "you shouldn't have done it!"

And indeed, he shouldn't. The box was an expensive one, the gift of his admiring mother at Christmas. And the topper inside, worn in the gloaming along the water side of Beacon Street, had been known to add a touch of distinction even to that distinguished scene.

"Why not?" asked John Quincy. "The confounded thing's been a nuisance ever since I left home. And besides we do look ridiculous at times, don't we? We easterners? A silk hat in the tropics! I might have been mistaken for a missionary." He began to gather up his luggage. "Shan't need a porter any more," he announced gaily. "I say—it was awfully kind of you—letting me talk to you like that."

"It was fun," she told him. "I hope you're going to like us out here. We're so eager to be liked, you know. It's almost pathetic."

"Well," smiled John Quincy, "I've met only one Californian to date. But—"

"Yes?"

"So far, so good!"

"Oh, thank you." She moved away.

"Please—just a moment," called John Quincy. "I hope—I mean, I wish—"

But the crowd surged between them. He saw her dark eyes smiling at him and then, irrevocably as the hat, she drifted from his sight.

III

Midnight on Russian Hill

A Few Moments later John Quincy stepped ashore in San Francisco. He had taken not more than three steps across the floor of the Ferry Building when a dapper Japanese chauffeur pushed through the crowd and singling out the easterner with what seemed uncanny perspicacity, took complete charge of him.

Roger Winterslip, the chauffeur announced, was too busy to meet ferries, but had sent word that the boy was to go up to the house and after establishing himself comfortably there, join his host for lunch down-town. Gratified to feel solid ground once more beneath his feet, John Quincy followed the chauffeur to the street. San Francisco glittered under the morning sun.

"I always thought this was a foggy town," John Quincy said.

The Japanese grinned. "Maybe fog will come, maybe it will not. Just now one time maybe it will not. Please." He held open the car door.

Through bright streets where life appeared to flow with a pleasant rhythm, they bowled along. Beside the curbs stood the colorful carts of the flower venders, unnecessarily painting the lily of existence. Weary traveler though he was, John Quincy took in with every breath a fresh supply of energy. New ambitions stirred within him; bigger, better bond issues than ever before seemed ridiculously easy of attainment.

Roger Winterslip had not been among those lured to suburban life down the peninsula; he resided in bachelor solitude on Nob Hill. It was an ancient, battered house viewed from without, but within, John Quincy found, were all known comforts. A bent old Chinese man showed him his room and his heart leaped up when he beheld, at last, a veritable bath.

At one o'clock he sought out the office where his relative carried on, with conspicuous success, his business as an engineer and builder. Roger proved a short florid man in his late fifties.

"Hello, son," he cried cordially. "How's Boston?"

"Every one is quite well," said John Quincy. "You're being extremely kind—"

"Nonsense. It's a pleasure to see you. Come along."

He took John Quincy to a famous club for lunch. In the grill he pointed out several well-known writers. The boy was not unduly impressed, for Longfellow, Whittier and Lowell were not among them. Nevertheless it was a pleasant place, the service perfect, the food of an excellence rare on the codfish coast.

"And what," asked Roger presently, "do you think of San Francisco?"

"I like it," John Quincy said simply.

"No? Do you really mean that?" Roger beamed. "Well, it's the sort of place that ought to appeal to a New Englander. It's had a history, brief, but believe me, my boy, one crowded hour of glorious life. It's sophisticated, knowing, subtle. Contrast it with other cities—for instance, take Los Angeles—"

He was off on a favorite topic and he talked well.

"Writers," he said at last, "are for ever comparing cities to women. San Francisco is the woman you don't tell the folks at home an awful lot about. Not that she wasn't perfectly proper—I don't mean that—but her stockings were just a little thinner and her laugh a little gayer—people might misunderstand. Besides, the memory is too precious to talk about. Hello."

A tall, lean, handsome Englishman was crossing the grill on his way out. "Cope! Cope, my dear fellow!" Roger sped after him and dragged him back. "I knew you at once," he was saying, "though it must be more than forty years since I last saw you."

The Britisher dropped into a chair. He smiled a wry smile. "My dear old chap," he said. "Not so literal, if you don't mind."

"Rot!" protested Roger. "What do years matter? This is a young cousin of mine, John Quincy Winterslip, of Boston. Ah—er—just what is your title now?"

"Captain. I'm in the Admiralty."

"Really? Captain Arthur Temple Cope, John Quincy." Roger turned to the Englishman. "You were a midshipman, I believe, when we met in Honolulu. I was talking to Dan about you not a year ago—"

An expression of intense dislike crossed the captain's face. "Ah, yes, Dan. Alive and prospering, I presume?"

"Oh, yes," answered Roger.

"Isn't it damnable," remarked Cope, "how the wicked thrive?"

An uncomfortable silence fell. John Quincy was familiar with the frankness of Englishmen, but he was none the less annoyed by this open display of hostility toward his prospective host. After all, Dan's last name was Winterslip.

"Ah—er—have a cigarette," suggested Roger.

"Thank you—have one of mine," said Cope, taking out a silver case. "Virginia tobacco, though they are put up in Piccadilly. No? And you, sir—" He held the case before John Quincy, who refused a bit stiffly.

The captain nonchalantly lighted up. "I beg your pardon—what I said about your cousin," he began. "But really, you know—"

"No matter," said Roger cordially. "Tell me what you're doing here."

"On my way to Hawaii," explained the captain. "Sailing at three to-day on the Australian boat. A bit of a job for the Admiralty. From Honolulu I drop down to the Fanning Group—a little flock of islands that belongs to us," he added with a fine paternal air.

"A possible coaling station," smiled Roger.

"My dear fellow—the precise nature of my mission is, of course, a secret." Captain Cope looked suddenly at John Quincy. "By the way, I once knew a very charming girl from Boston. A relative of yours, no doubt."

"A—a girl," repeated John Quincy, puzzled.

"Minerva Winterslip."

"Why," said John Quincy, amazed, "you mean my Aunt Minerva."

The captain smiled. "She was no one's aunt in those days," he said. "Nothing auntish about her. But that was in Honolulu in the 'eighties—we'd put in there on the old wooden Reliance—the poor unlucky ship was limping home crippled from Samoa. Your aunt was visiting at that port—there were dances at the palace, swimming parties—ah, me, to be young again."

"Minerva's in Honolulu now," Roger told him.

"No—really?"

"Yes. She's stopping with Dan."

"With Dan." The captain was silent for a moment. "Her husband—"

"Minerva never married," Roger explained.

"Amazing," said the captain. He blew a ring of smoke toward the paneled ceiling. "The more shame to the men of Boston. My time is hardly my own, but I shall hope to look in on her." He rose. "This was a bit of luck—meeting you again, old chap. I'm due aboard the boat very shortly—you understand, of course." He bowed to them both, and departed.

"Fine fellow," Roger said, staring after him. "Frank and British, but a splendid chap."

"I wasn't especially pleased," John Quincy admitted, "by the way he spoke of Cousin Dan."

Roger laughed. "Better get used to it," he advised. "Dan is not passionately beloved. He's climbed high, you know, and he's trampled down a few on his way up. By the way, he wants you to do an errand for him here in San Francisco."

"Me!" cried John Quincy. "An errand?"

"Yes. You ought to feel flattered. Dan doesn't trust everybody. However, it's something that must wait until dark."

"Until dark," repeated the puzzled young man from Boston.

"Precisely. In the meantime I propose to show you about town."

"But—you're busy. I couldn't think of taking you away—"

Roger laid his hand on John Quincy's shoulder. "My boy, no westerner is ever too busy to show a man from the East about his city. I've been looking forward to this chance for weeks. And since you insist on sailing tomorrow at ten, we must make the most of our time."

Roger proved an adept at making the most of one's time in San Francisco. After an exhilarating afternoon of motoring over the town and the surrounding country, he brought John Quincy back to the house at six, urging him to dress quickly for a dinner of which he apparently had great hopes.

The boy's trunk was in his room, and as he put on a dinner coat he looked forward with lively anticipation to a bit of San Francisco night life in Roger's company. When he came down-stairs his host was waiting, a distinguished figure in his dinner clothes, and they set out blithely through the gathering dusk.

"Little place I want you to try," Roger explained as they sat down at a table in a restaurant that was outwardly of no special note. "Afterward we'll look in on that musical show at the Columbia."

The restaurant more than justified Roger's hopes of it. John Quincy began to glow with a warm friendly feeling for all the world, particularly this city by the western gate. He did not think of himself as a stranger here. He wasn't a stranger, anyhow. The sensation he had first experienced in the harbor returned to him. He had been here before, he was treading old familiar ground. In far, forgotten, happy times he had known the life of this city's streets. Strange, but true. He spoke to Roger about it.

Roger smiled. "A Winterslip, after all," he said. "And they told me you were just a sort of—of Puritan survival. My father used to know that sensation you speak of, only he felt it whenever he entered a new town. Might be something in reincarnation, after all."

"Nonsense," said John Quincy.

"Probably. Just the blood of the roaming Winterslips in your veins." He leaned across the table. "How would you like to come to San Francisco to live?"

"Wha—what?" asked John Quincy, startled.

"I'm getting along in years, and I'm all alone. Lots of financial details in my office—take you in there and let you look after them. Make it worth your while."

"No, no, thank you," said John Quincy firmly. "I belong back east. Besides, I could never persuade Agatha to come out here."

"Agatha who?"

"Agatha Parker—the girl I'm engaged to—in a way. Been sort of understood between us for several years. No," he added, "I guess I'd better stay where I belong."

Roger Winterslip looked his disappointment. "Probably had," he admitted. "I fancy no girl with that name would follow you here. Though a girl worth having will follow her man anywhere—but no matter." He studied John Quincy keenly for a moment. "I must have been wrong about you, anyhow."

John Quincy felt a sudden resentment. "Just what do you mean by that?" he inquired.

"In the old days," Roger said, "Winterslips were the stuff of which pioneers are made. They didn't cling to the apron-strings of civilization. They got up some fine morning and nonchalantly strolled off beyond the horizon. They lived—but there, you're of another generation. You can't understand."

"Why can't I?" demanded John Quincy.

"Because the same old rut has evidently been good enough for you. You've never known a thrill. Or have you? Have you ever forgot to go to bed because of some utterly silly reason—because, for example, you were young and the moon was shining on a beach lapped by southern seas? Have you ever lied like a gentleman to protect a woman not worth the trouble? Ever made love to the wrong girl?"

"Of course not," said John Quincy stiffly.

"Ever run for your life through crooked streets in the rowdy quarter of a strange town? Ever fought with a ship's officer—the old-fashioned kind with fists like flying hams? Ever gone out on a man hunt and when you got your quarry cornered, leaped upon him with no weapon but your bare hands? Have you ever—"

"The type of person you describe," John Quincy cut in, "is hardly admirable."

"Probably not," Roger agreed. "And yet—those are incidents from my own past, my boy." He regarded John Quincy sadly. "Yes, I must have been wrong about you. A Puritan survival after all."

John Quincy deigned no reply. There was an odd light in the older man's eyes—was Roger secretly laughing at him? He appeared to be, and the boy resented it.

But he forgot to be resentful at the revue, which proved to be witty and gay, and Roger and he emerged from the theater at eleven the best of friends again. As they stepped into Roger's car, the older man gave the chauffeur an address on Russian Hill.

"Dan's San Francisco house," he explained, as he climbed in after John Quincy. "He comes over about two months each year, and keeps a place here. Got more money than I have."

Dan's San Francisco house? "Oh," said John Quincy, "the errand you mentioned?"

Roger nodded. "Yes." He snapped on a light in the top of the limousine, and took an envelope from his pocket. "Read this letter. It was delivered to me two days ago by the Second Officer of the President Tyler."

John Quincy removed a sheet of note paper from the envelope. The message appeared to be rather hastily scrawled.

"Dear Roger," he read. "You can do me a great service— you and that discreet lad from Boston who is to stop over with you on his way out here. First of all, give John Quincy my regards and tell him that he must make my house his home while he is in the Islands. I'll be delighted to have him.

"About the errand. You have a key to my house on Russian Hill. Go up there—better go at night when the caretaker's not likely to be around. The lights are off, but you'll find candles in the pantry. In the store room on the top floor is an old brown trunk. Locked, probably—mash the lock if it is. In the lower section you'll find a battered strong box made of ohia wood and bound with copper. Initials on it—T.M.B.

"Wrap it up and take it away. It's rather an armful, but you can manage it. Have John Quincy conceal it in his luggage and some dark night when the ship's about half-way over, I want him to take it on deck and quietly drop it overboard. Tell him to be sure nobody sees him. That's all. But send me a guarded cable when you get the box, and tell him to send me a radio when the Pacific has it at last. I'll sleep better then.

"Not a word, Roger. Not a word to any one. You'll understand. Sometimes the dead past needs a bit of help in burying its dead.

Your Cousin Dan

Solemnly John Quincy handed the letter back into Roger's keeping. The older man thoughtfully tore it to bits and tossed them through the car window open beside him. "Well," said John Quincy. "Well—" A fitting comment eluded him.

"Simple enough," smiled Roger. "If we can help poor old Dan to sleep better as easily as that, we must do it, eh?"

"I—I suppose so," John Quincy agreed.

They had climbed Russian Hill, and were speeding along a deserted avenue lined by imposing mansions. Roger leaned forward. "Go on to the corner," he said to the chauffeur. "We can walk back," he explained to John Quincy. "Best not to leave the car before the house. Might excite suspicion."

Still John Quincy had no comment to make. They alighted at the corner and walked slowly back along the avenue. In front of a big stone house, Roger paused. He looked carefully in all directions, then ran with surprising speed up the steps. "Come on," he called softly.

John Quincy came. Roger unlocked the door and they stepped into a dark vestibule. Beyond that, darker still, was a huge hall, the dim suggestion of a grand staircase. Here and there an article of furniture, shrouded in white, stood like a ghost, marooned but patient. Roger took out a box of matches.

"Meant to bring a flashlight," he said, "but I clean forgot. Wait here—I'll hunt those candles in the pantry."

He went off into the dark. John Quincy took a few cautious steps. He was about to sit down on a chair—but it was like sitting on the lap of a ghost. He changed his mind, stood in the middle of the floor, waited. Quiet, deathly quiet. The black had swallowed Roger, with not so much as a gurgle.

After what seemed an age, Roger returned, bearing two lighted candles. One each, he explained. John Quincy took his, held it high. The flickering yellow flame accentuated the shadows, was really of small help.

Roger led the way up the grand staircase, then up a narrower flight. At the foot of still another flight, in a stuffy passage on the third floor, he halted.

"Here we are," he said. "This leads to the storage room under the roof. By gad, I'm getting too old for this sort of thing. I meant to bring a chisel to use on that lock. I know where the tools are—I'll be gone only a minute. You go on up and locate the trunk."

"All—all right," answered John Quincy.

Again Roger left him. John Quincy hesitated. Something about a deserted house at midnight to dismay the stoutest heart—but nonsense! He was a grown man. He smiled, and started up the narrow stair. High above his head the yellow light of the candle flickered on the brown rafters of the unfinished store room.

He reached the top of the stairs, and paused. Gloom, gloom everywhere. Odd how floor boards will creak even when no one is moving over them. One was creaking back of him now.

He was about to turn when a hand reached from behind and knocked the candle out of his grasp. It rolled on the floor, extinguished.

This was downright rude! "See here," cried John Quincy, "wh—who are you?"

A bit of moonlight struggled in through a far window, and suddenly between John Quincy and that distant light there loomed the determined figure of a man. Something told the boy he had better get ready, but where he came from one had a moment or two for preparation. He had none here. A fist shot out and found his face, and John Quincy Winterslip of Boston went down amid the rubbish of a San Francisco attic. He heard, for a second, the crash of planets in collision, and then the clatter of large feet on the stairs. After that, he was alone with the debris.

He got up, thoroughly angry, and began brushing off the dinner coat that had been his tailor's pride. Roger arrived. "Who was that?" he demanded breathlessly. "Somebody went down the back stairs to the kitchen. Who was it?"

"How should I know?" inquired John Quincy with pardonable peevishness. "He didn't introduce himself to me." His cheek was stinging; he put his handkerchief to it and noted in the light of Roger's candle that it was red when it came away. "He wore a ring," added John Quincy. "Damned bad taste!"

"Hit you, eh?" inquired Roger.

"I'll say he did."

"Look!" Roger cried. He pointed. "The trunk-lock smashed." He went over to investigate. "And the box is gone. Poor old Dan!"

John Quincy continued to brush himself off. Poor old Dan's plight gave him a vast pain, a pain which had nothing to do with his throbbing jaw. A fine nerve poor old Dan had to ask a complete stranger to offer his face for punishment in a dusty attic at midnight. What was it all about, anyhow?

Roger continued his search. "No use," he announced. "The box is gone, that's plain. Come on, we'll go down-stairs and look about. There's your candle on the floor."

John Quincy picked up the candle and relighted it from Roger's flame. Silently they went below. The outer door of the kitchen stood open. "Left that way," said Roger. "And see"—he pointed to a window with a broken pane—"that's where he came in."

"How about the police?" suggested John Quincy.

Roger stared at him. "The police? I should say not! Where's your discretion, my boy? This is not a police matter. I'll have a new glass put in that window to-morrow. Come on—we might as well go home. We've failed."

The note of reproof in his voice angered John Quincy anew. They left the extinguished candles on a table in the hall, and returned to the street.

"Well, I'll have to cable Dan," Roger said, as they walked toward the corner. "I'm afraid he'll be terribly upset by this. It won't tend to endear you to him, either."

"I can struggle along," said John Quincy, "without his affection."

"If you could only have held that fellow till I came—"

"Look here," said John Quincy, "I was taken unawares. How could I know that I was going up against the heavyweight champion in that attic? He came at me out of the dark—and I'm not in condition—"

"No offense, my boy," Roger put in.

"I see my mistake," went on John Quincy. "I should have trained for this trip out here. A stiff course in a gymnasium. But don't worry. The next lad that makes a pass at me will find a different target. I'll do a daily three dozen and I'll take boxing lessons. From now on until I get home, I'll be expecting the worst."

Roger laughed. "That's a nasty cut on your cheek," he remarked. "We'd better stop at this drug store and have it dressed."

A solicitous drug clerk ministered to John Quincy with iodine, cotton and court plaster, and he reentered the limousine bearing honorably the scar of battle. The drive to Nob Hill was devoid of light chatter.

Just inside the door of Roger's house, a whirlwind in a gay gown descended upon them. "Barbara!" Roger said. "Where did you come from?"

"Hello, old dear," she cried, kissing him. "I motored up from Burlingame. Spending the night with you—I'm sailing on the President Tyler in the morning. Is this John Quincy?"

"Cousin John," smiled Roger. "He deserves a kiss, too. He's had a bad evening."

The girl moved swiftly toward the defenseless John Quincy. Again he was unprepared, and this time it was his other cheek that suffered, though not unpleasantly. "Just by way of welcome," Barbara laughed. She was blonde and slender. John Quincy thought he had never seen so much energy imprisoned in so slight a form. "I hear you're bound for the Islands?" she said.

"To-morrow," John Quincy answered. "On your boat."

"Splendid!" she cried. "When did you get in?"

"John Quincy came this morning," Roger told her.

"And he's had a bad evening?" the girl said. "How lucky I came along. Where are you taking us, Roger?"

John Quincy stared. Taking them? At this hour?

"I'll be getting along up-stairs," he ventured.

"Why, it's just after twelve," said Barbara. "Lots of places open. You dance, don't you? Let me show you San Francisco. Roger's a dear old thing—we'll let him pay the checks."

"Well—I—I—" stammered John Quincy. His cheek was throbbing and he thought longingly of that bed in the room up-stairs. What a place, this West!

"Come along!" The girl was humming a gay little tune. All vivacity, all life. Rather pleasant sort at that. John Quincy took up his hat.

Roger's chauffeur had lingered a moment before the house to inspect his engine. When he saw them coming down the steps, he looked as though he rather wished he hadn't. But escape was impossible; he climbed to his place behind the wheel.

"Where to, Barbara?" Roger asked. "Tait's?"

"Not Tait's," she answered. "I've just come from there."

"What! I thought you motored in from Burlingame?"

"So I did—at five. I've traveled a bit since then. How about some chop-suey for this Boston boy?"

Good lord, John Quincy thought. Was there anything in the world he wanted less? No matter. Barbara took him among the Chinese.

He didn't give a hang about the Chinese. Nor the Mexicans, whose restaurants interested the girl next. At the moment, he was unsympathetic toward Italy. And even toward France. But he struggled on the international round, affronting his digestion with queer dishes, and dancing thousands of miles with the slim Barbara in his arms. After scrambled eggs at a place called Pete's Fashion, she consented to call it an evening.

As John Quincy staggered into Roger's house, the great clock in the hall was striking three. The girl was still alert and sparkling. John Quincy hastily concealed a yawn.

"All wrong to come home so early," she cried. "But we'll have a dance or two on the boat. By the way, I've been wanting to ask. What does it mean? The injured cheek?"

"Why—er—I—" John Quincy remarked. Over the girl's shoulder he saw Roger violently shaking his head. "Oh, that," said John Quincy, lightly touching the wound. "That's where the West begins. Good night. I've had a bully time." And at last he got up-stairs.

He stood for a moment at his bedroom window, gazing down at the torchlight procession of the streets through this amazing city. He was a little dazed. That soft warm presence close by his side in the car—pleasant, very pleasant. Remarkable girls out here. Different!

Beyond shone the harbor lights. That other girl—wonderful eyes she had. Just because she had laughed at him, his treasured hat box floated now forlorn on those dark waters. He yawned again. Better be careful. Mustn't be so easily influenced. No telling where it would end.

IV

A FRIEND OF TIM'S

It was another of those mornings on which the fog maybe did not come. Roger and his guests were in the limousine again; it seemed to John Quincy that they had left it only a few minutes before. So it must have seemed to the chauffeur too as, sleepy-eyed, he hurried them toward the water-front.

"By the way, John Quincy," Roger said, "you'll want to change your money before you go aboard."

John Quincy gathered his wandering thoughts. "Oh, yes, of course," he answered.

Roger smiled. "Just what sort of money would you like to change it for?" he inquired.

"Why—" began John Quincy. He stopped. "Why, I always thought—"

"Don't pay any attention to Roger," Barbara laughed. "He's spoofing you." She was fresh and blooming, a little matter like three A.M. made no difference to her. "Only about one person out of a thousand in this country knows that Hawaii is a part of the United States, and the fact annoys us deeply over in the Islands. Dear old Roger was trying to get you in wrong with me by enrolling you among the nine hundred and ninety-nine."

"Almost did it, too," chuckled Roger.

"Nonsense," said Barbara. "John Quincy is too intelligent. He's not like that congressman who wrote a letter to 'the American Consul at Honolulu'."

"Did one of them do that?" smiled John Quincy.

"He certainly did. We almost gave up the struggle after that. Then there was the senator who came out on a junket, and began a speech with: 'When I get home to my country—' Some one in the audience shouted: 'You're there now, you big stiff!' It wasn't elegant, of course, but it expressed our feeling perfectly. Oh, we're touchy, John Quincy."

"Don't blame you a bit," he told her. "I'll be very careful what I say."

They had reached the Embarcadero, and the car halted before one of the piers. The chauffeur descended and began to gather up the baggage.

Roger and John Quincy took a share of it, and they traversed the pier-shed to the gangplank.

"Get along to your office, Roger," Barbara said.

"No hurry," he answered. "I'll go aboard with you, of course."

Amid the confusion of the deck, a party of girls swept down on Barbara, pretty lively girls of the California brand. John Quincy learned with some regret that they were there only to see Barbara off. A big broad-shouldered man in white pushed his way through the crowd.

"Hello there!" he called to Barbara.

"Hello, Harry," she answered. "You know Roger, don't you? John Quincy, this is an old friend of mine, Harry Jennison."

Mr. Jennison was extremely good-looking, his face was deeply tanned by the Island sun, his hair blond and wavy, his gray eyes amused and cynical. Altogether, he was the type of man women look at twice and never forget; John Quincy felt himself at once supplanted in the eyes of Barbara's friends.

Jennison seized the boy's hand in a firm grip. "Sailing too, Mr. Winterslip?" he inquired. "That's good. Between us we ought to be able to keep this young woman entertained."

The shore call sounded, and the confusion increased. Along the deck came a little old lady, followed by a Chinese woman servant. They walked briskly, and the crowd gave way before them.

"Hello—this is luck," cried Roger. "Madame Maynard—just a moment. I want you to meet a cousin of mine from Boston." He introduced John Quincy. "I give him into your charge. Couldn't find a better guide, philosopher and friend for him if I combed the Islands."

The old lady glanced at John Quincy. Her black eyes snapped. "Another Winterslip, eh?" she said. "Hawaii's all cluttered up with 'em now. Well, the more the merrier. I know your aunt."

"Stick close to her, John Quincy," Roger admonished.

She shook her head. "I'm a million years old," she protested. "The boys don't stick so close any more. They like 'em younger. However, I'll keep my eye on him. My good eye. Well, Roger, run over some time." And she moved away.

"A grand soul," said Roger, smiling after her. "You'll like her. Old missionary family, and her word's law over there."

"Who's this Jennison?" asked John Quincy.

"Him?" Roger glanced over to where Mr. Jennison stood, the center of an admiring feminine group. "Oh, he's Dan's lawyer. One of the leading citizens of Honolulu, I believe. John J. Adonis himself, isn't he?" An officer appeared, herding the reluctant throng toward the gangplank. "I'll have to leave you, John Quincy. A pleasant journey. When you come through on your way home, give me a few more days to try to convince you on my San Francisco offer."

John Quincy laughed. "You've been mighty kind."

"Not at all." Roger shook his hand warmly. "Take care of yourself over there. Hawaii's a little too much like Heaven to be altogether safe. So long, my boy, so long."

He moved away. John Quincy saw him kiss Barbara affectionately and with her friends join the slow procession ashore.

The young man from Boston stepped to the rail. Several hundred voices were calling admonitions, promises, farewells. With that holiday spirit so alien to John Quincy's experience, those ashore were throwing confetti. The streamers grew in number, making a tangle of color, a last frail bond with the land. The gangplank was taken up; clumsily the PRESIDENT TYLER began to draw away from the pier. On the topmost deck a band was playing—Aloha-oe, the sweetest, most melancholy song of good-by ever written. John Quincy was amazed to feel a lump rising in his throat.

The frail, gay-colored bond was breaking now. A thin veined hand at John Quincy's side waved a handkerchief. He turned to find Mrs. Maynard. There were tears on her cheeks.

"Silly old woman," she said. "Sailed away from this town a hundred and twenty-eight times. Actual count—I keep a diary. Cried every time. What about? I don't know."

The ship was well out in the harbor now. Barbara came along, Jennison trailing her. The girl's eyes were wet.

"An emotional lot, we Islanders," said the old lady. She put her arm about the girl's slim waist. "Here's another one of 'em. Living way off the way we do, any good-by at all—it saddens us." She and Barbara moved on down the deck.

Jennison stopped. His eyes were quite dry. "First trip out?" he inquired.

"Oh, yes," replied John Quincy.

"Hope you'll like us," Jennison said. "Not Massachusetts, of course, but we'll do our best to make you feel at home. It's a way we have with strangers."

"I'm sure I shall have a bully time," John Quincy remarked. But he felt somewhat depressed. Three thousand miles from Beacon Street—

and moving on! He waved to some one he fancied might be Roger on the dock, and went to find his stateroom.

He learned that he was to share his cabin with two missionaries. One was a tall, gloomy old man with a lemon-colored face—an honored veteran of the foreign field named Upton. The other was a ruddy-cheeked boy whose martyrdom was still before him. John Quincy suggested drawing lots for a choice of berths, but even this mild form of gambling appeared distasteful to those emissaries of the church.

"You boys take the berths," said Upton. "Leave me the couch. I don't sleep well anyhow." His tone was that of one who prefers to suffer.

John Quincy politely objected. After further discussion it was settled that he was to have the upper berth, the old man the lower, and the boy the couch. The Reverend Mr. Upton seemed disappointed. He had played the role of martyr so long he resented seeing any one else in the part.

The Pacific was behaving in a most unfriendly manner, tossing the great ship about as though it were a piece of driftwood. John Quincy decided to dispense with lunch, and spent the afternoon reading in his berth. By evening he felt better, and under the watchful and somewhat disapproving eyes of the missionaries, arrayed himself carefully for dinner.

His name being Winterslip, he had been invited to sit at the captain's table. He found Madame Maynard, serene and twinkling, at the captain's right, Barbara at his left, and Jennison at Barbara's side. It appeared that oddly enough there was an aristocracy of the Islands, and John Quincy, while he thought it quaint there should be such distinctions in an outpost like Hawaii, took his proper place as a matter of course.

Mrs. Maynard chatted brightly of her many trips over this route. Suddenly she turned to Barbara. "How does it happen, my dear," she asked, "that you're not on the college boat?"

"All booked up," Barbara explained.

"Nonsense," said the frank old lady. "You could have got on. But then"—she looked meaningly toward Jennison—"I presume this ship was not without its attractions."

The girl flushed slightly and made no reply.

"What," John Quincy inquired, "is the college boat?"

"So many children from Hawaii at school on the mainland," the old lady explained, "that every June around this time they practically fill a ship. We call it the college boat. This year it's the Matsonia. She left San Francisco to-day at noon."

"I've got a lot of friends aboard her," Barbara said. "I do wish we could beat her in. Captain, what are the chances?"

"Well, that depends," replied the captain cautiously.

"She isn't due until Tuesday morning," Barbara persisted. "Wouldn't it be a lark if you could land us the night before? As a favor to me, Captain."

"When you look at me like that," smiled the officer, "I can only say that I'll make a supreme effort. I'm just as eager as you to make port on Monday—it would mean I could get off to the Orient that much sooner."

"Then it's settled," Barbara beamed.

"It's settled that we'll try," he said. "Of course, if I speed up there's always the chance I may arrive off Honolulu after sundown, and be compelled to lay by until morning. That would be torture for you."

"I'll risk it," Barbara smiled. "Wouldn't dear old dad be pleased if I should burst upon his vision Monday evening?"

"My dear girl," the captain said gallantly, "any man would be pleased to have you burst upon his vision any time."

There was, John Quincy reflected, much in what the captain said. Up to that moment there had been little of the romantic in his relations with girls; he was accustomed to look upon them merely as tennis or golf opponents or a fourth at bridge. Barbara would demand a different classification. There was an enticing gleam in her blue eyes, a hint of the eternal feminine in everything she did or said, and John Quincy was no wooden man. He was glad that when he left the dinner table, she accompanied him.

They went on deck and stood by the rail. Night had fallen, there was no moon, and it seemed to John Quincy that the Pacific was the blackest, angriest ocean he had ever seen. He stood gazing at it gloomily.

"Homesick, John Quincy?" Barbara asked. One of his hands was resting on the rail. She laid her own upon it.

He nodded. "It's a funny thing. I've been abroad a lot, but I never felt like this. When the ship left port this morning, I nearly wept."

"It's not so very funny," she said gently. "This is an alien world you're entering now. Not Boston, John Quincy, nor any other old, civilized place. Not the kind of place where the mind rules. Out here it's the heart that charts our course. People you're fond of do the wildest, most unreasonable things, simply because their minds are sleeping and their hearts are beating fast. Just—just remember, please, John Quincy."

There was an odd note of wistfulness in her voice. Suddenly at their side appeared the white-clad figure of Harry Jennison.

"Coming for a stroll, Barbara?" he inquired.

For a moment she did not reply. Then she nodded. "Yes," she said. And called over her shoulder as she went: "Cheer up, John Quincy."

He watched her go, reluctantly. She might have stayed to assuage his loneliness. But there she walked along the dim deck, close to Jennison's side.

After a time, he sought the smoking-room. It was deserted, but on one of the tables lay a copy of the Boston Transcript. Delighted, John Quincy pounced upon it, as Robinson Crusoe might have pounced on news from home.

The issue was ten days old, but no matter. He turned at once to the financial pages. There it was, like the face of a well-beloved friend, the record of one day's trading on the Stock Exchange. And up in one corner, the advertisement of his own banking house, offering an issue of preferred stock in a Berkshire cotton mill. He read eagerly, but with an odd detached feeling. He was gone, gone from that world, away out here on a black ocean bound for picture-book islands. Islands where, not so long ago, brown tribes had battled, brown kings ruled. There seemed no link with that world back home, those gay-colored streamers of confetti breaking so readily had been a symbol. He was adrift. What sort of port would claim him in the end?

He threw the paper down. The Reverend Mr. Upton entered the smoking-room.

"I left my newspaper here," he explained. "Ah—did you care to look at it?"

"Thank you, I have," John Quincy told him.

The old man picked it up in a great bony hand. "I always buy a Transcript when I get the chance," he said. "It carries me back. You know, I was born in Salem, over seventy years ago."

John Quincy stared at him. "You've been a long time out here?" he asked.

"More than fifty years in the foreign field," answered the old man. "I was one of the first to go to the South Seas. One of the first to carry the torch down there—and a dim torch it was, I'm afraid. Afterward I was transferred to China." John Quincy regarded him with a new

EARL DERR BIGGERS

interest. "By the way, sir," the missionary continued, "I once met another gentleman named Winterslip. Mr. Daniel Winterslip."

"Really?" said John Quincy. "He's a cousin of mine. I'm to visit him in Honolulu."

"Yes? I heard he had returned to Hawaii, and prospered. I met him just once—in the 'eighties, it was, on a lonely island in the Gilbert group. It was—rather a turning point in his life, and I have never forgotten." John Quincy waited to hear more, but the old missionary moved away. "I'll go and enjoy my Transcript," he smiled. "The church news is very competently handled."

John Quincy rose and went aimlessly outside. A dreary scene, the swish of turbulent waters, dim figures aimless as himself, an occasional ship's officer hurrying by. His stateroom opened directly on the deck and he sank into a steamer chair just outside the door.

In the distance he saw his room steward, weaving his way in and out of the cabins under his care. The man was busy with his last duties for the night, refilling water carafes, laying out towels, putting things generally to rights.

"Evening, sir," he said as he entered John Quincy's room. Presently he came and stood in the door, the cabin light at his back. He was a small man with gold-rimmed eye-glasses and a fierce gray pompadour.

"Everything O.K., Mr. Winterslip?" he inquired.

"Yes, Bowker," smiled John Quincy. "Everything's fine."

"That's good," said Bowker. He switched off the cabin light and stepped out on to the deck. "I aim to take particular care of you, sir. Saw your home town on the sailing list. I'm an old Boston man myself."

"Is that so?" said John Quincy cordially. Evidently the Pacific was a Boston suburb.

"Not born there, I don't mean," the man went on. "But a newspaper man there for ten years. It was just after I left the University."

John Quincy started through the dark. "Harvard?" he asked.

"Dublin," said the steward. "Yes, sir—" He laughed an embarrassed little laugh. "You might not think it now, but the University of Dublin, Class of 1901. And after that, for ten years, working in Boston on the Gazette—reporting, copy desk, managing editor for a time. Maybe I bumped into you there—at the Adams House bar, say, on a night before a football game."

"Quite possible," admitted John Quincy. "One bumped into so many people on such occasions."

"Don't I know it?" Mr. Bowker leaned on the rail, in reminiscent mood. "Great times, sir. Those were the good old days when a newspaper man who wasn't tanked up was a reproach to a grand profession. The Gazette was edited mostly from a place called the Arch Inn. We'd bring our copy to the city editor there—he had a regular table—a bit sloppy on top, but his desk. If we had a good story, maybe he'd stand us a cocktail."

John Quincy laughed.

"Happy days," continued the Dublin graduate, with a sigh. "I knew every bartender in Boston well enough to borrow money. Were you ever in that place in the alley back of the Tremont Theater—?"

"Tim's place," suggested John Quincy, recalling an incident of college days.

"Yeah, bo. Now you're talking. I wonder what became of Tim. Say, and there was that place on Boylston—but they're all gone now, of course. An old pal I met in 'Frisco was telling me it would break your heart to see the cobwebs on the mirrors back in Beantown. Gone to the devil, just like my profession. The newspapers go on consolidating, doubling up, combining the best features of both, and an army of good men go on the town. Good men and true, moaning about the vanished days and maybe landing in jobs like this one of mine." He was silent for a moment. "Well, sir, anything I can do for you—as a mutual friend of Tim's—"

"As a friend of Tim's," smiled John Quincy, "I'll not hesitate to mention it."

Sadly Bowker went on down the deck. John Quincy sat lonely again. A couple passed, walking close, talking in low tones. He recognized Jennison and his cousin. "Between us we ought to be able to keep this young woman entertained," Jennison had said. Well, John Quincy reflected, his portion of the entertainment promised to be small.

V

The Blood of the Winterslips

The Days that followed proved that he was right. He seldom had a moment alone with Barbara. When he did, Jennison seemed always to be hovering near by, and he did not long delay making the group a threesome. At first John Quincy resented this, but gradually he began to feel that it didn't matter.

Nothing appeared to matter any more. A great calm had settled over the waters and over John Quincy's soul. The Pacific was one vast sheet of glass, growing a deeper blue with every passing hour. They seemed to be floating in space in a world where nothing ever happened, nothing could happen. Quiet restful days gave way to long brilliant nights. A little walk, a little talk, and that was life.

Sometimes John Quincy chatted with Madame Maynard on the deck. She who had known the Islands so many years had fascinating tales to tell, tales of the monarchy and the missionaries. The boy liked her immensely, she was a New Englander at heart despite her glamourous lifetime in Hawaii.

Bowker, too, he found excellent company. The steward was that rarity even among college graduates, an educated man; there was no topic upon which he could not discourse at length and brilliantly. In John Quincy's steamer trunk were a number of huge imposing volumes—books he had been meaning to tackle long ago, but it was Bowker who read them, not John Quincy.

As the days slipped by, the blue of the water deepened to ultramarine, the air grew heavier and warmer. Underfoot throbbed the engines that were doing their best for Barbara and an early landing. The captain was optimistic, he predicted they would make port late Monday afternoon. But Sunday night a fierce sudden storm swept down upon them, and lashed the ship with a wet fury until dawn. When the captain appeared at luncheon Monday noon, worn by a night on the bridge, he shook his head.

"We've lost our bet, Miss Barbara," he said. "I can't possibly arrive off Honolulu before midnight."

Barbara frowned. "But ships sail at any hour," she reminded him. "I don't see why—if we sent radios ahead—"

"No use," he told her. "The Quarantine people keep early hours. No, I'll have to lay by near the channel entrance until official sunrise—about six. We'll get in ahead of the Matsonia in the morning. That's the best I can offer you."

"You're a dear, anyhow," Barbara smiled. "That old storm wasn't your fault. We'll drown our sorrow to-night with one last glorious dance—a costume party." She turned to Jennison. "I've got the loveliest fancy dress—Marie Antoinette—I wore it at college. What do you say, Harry?"

"Fine!" Jennison answered. "We can all dig up some sort of costume. Let's go."

Barbara hurried off to spread the news. After dinner that evening she appeared, a blonde vision straight from the French Court, avid for dancing. Jennison had rigged up an impromptu pirate dress, and was a striking figure. Most of the other passengers had donned weird outfits; on the Pacific boats a fancy dress party is warmly welcomed and amusingly carried out.

John Quincy took small part in the gaiety, for he still suffered from New England inhibitions. At a little past eleven he drifted into the main saloon and found Madame Maynard seated there alone.

"Hello," she said. "Come to keep me company. I've sworn not to go to bed until I see the light on Diamond Head."

"I'm with you," John Quincy smiled.

"But you ought to be dancing, boy. And you're not in costume."

"No," admitted John Quincy. He paused, seeking an explanation. "A—a fellow can't make a fool of himself in front of a lot of strangers."

"I understand," nodded the old lady. "It's a fine delicacy, too. But rather rare, particularly out this way."

Barbara entered, flushed and vibrant. "Harry's gone to get me a drink," she panted. She sat down beside Mrs. Maynard. "I've been looking for you, my dear. You know, you haven't read my palm since I was a child. She's simply wonderful—" this to John Quincy. "Can tell you the most amazing things."

Mrs. Maynard vehemently shook her head. "I don't read 'em any more," she said. "Gave it up. As I've grown older, I've come to understand how foolish it is to peer into the future. To-day—that's enough for me. That's all I care to think about."

"Oh, please," the girl pouted.

The old woman took Barbara's slim hand in hers, and studied the palm for a moment. John Quincy thought he saw a shadow cross her face. Again she shook her head.

"Carpe diem," she said. "Which my nephew once translated as 'grab the day.' Dance and be happy to-night, and let's not try to look behind the curtain. It doesn't pay, my dear. Take an old woman's word for that."

Harry Jennison appeared in the door. "Oh, here you are," he said. "I've got your drink waiting in the smoking-room."

"I'm coming," the girl said, and went. The old woman stared after her. "Poor Barbara," she murmured. "Her mother's life was none too happy, either—"

"You saw something in her hand—" John Quincy suggested.

"No matter," the old lady snapped. "There's trouble waiting for us all, if we look far enough ahead. Now, let's go on deck. It's getting on toward midnight."

She led him out to the starboard rail. A solitary light, like a star, gleamed in the distance. Land, land at last. "Diamond Head?" John Quincy asked.

"No," she said. "That's the beacon on Makapuu Point. We shall have to round Koko Head before we sight Honolulu." She stood for a moment by the rail, one frail hand resting upon it. "But that's Oahu," she said gently. "That's home. A sweet land, boy. Too sweet, I often think. I hope you'll like it."

"I'm sure I shall," replied John Quincy gallantly.

"Let's sit down here." They found deck chairs. "Yes, a dear land," she went on. "But we're all sorts, in Hawaii—just as it is the whole world over—honest folks and rascals. From the four corners of the globe men come to us—often because they were no longer welcome at home. We offer them a paradise, and some repay us by becoming good citizens, while others rot away. I often think it will take a lot of stamina to make good in Heaven—and Hawaii is the same."

The tall emaciated figure of the Reverend Mr. Upton appeared before them. He bowed. "Good evening, Madame. You're nearly home."

"Yes," she said. "Glad of it, too."

He turned to John Quincy. "You'll be seeing Dan Winterslip in the morning, young man."

"I expect I shall," John Quincy replied.

"Just ask him if he recalls that day on Apiang Island in the 'eighties. The Reverend Frank Upton."

"Of course," replied John Quincy. "But you haven't told me much about it, you know."

"No, I haven't." The missionary dropped into a chair. "I don't like to reveal any secrets about a man's past," he said. "However, I understand that the story of Dan Winterslip's early life has always been known in Honolulu." He glanced toward Madame Maynard.

"Dan was no saint," she remarked. "We all know that."

He crossed his thin legs. "As a matter of fact, I'm very proud of my meeting with Dan Winterslip," he went on. "I feel that in my humble way I persuaded him to change his course—for the better."

"Humph," said the old lady. She was dubious, evidently.

John Quincy was not altogether pleased at the turn the conversation had taken. He did not care to have the name of a Winterslip thus bandied about. But to his annoyance, the Reverend Mr. Upton was continuing.

"It was in the 'eighties, as I told you," said the missionary. "I had a lonely station on Apiang, in the Gilbert group. One morning a brig anchored just beyond the reef, and a boat came ashore. Of course, I joined the procession of natives down to the beach to meet it. I saw few enough men of my own race.

"There was a ruffianly crew aboard, in charge of a dapper, rather handsome young white man. And I saw, even before they beached her, midway in the boat, a long pine box.

"The white man introduced himself. He said he was First Officer Winterslip, of the brig Maid of Shiloh. And when he mentioned the name of the ship, of course I knew at once. Knew her unsavory trade and history. He hurried on to say that their captain had died the day before, and they had brought him ashore to bury him on land. It had been the man's last wish.

"Well." The Reverend Mr. Upton stared at the distant shore line of Oahu. "I looked over at that rough pine box—four Malay sailors were carrying it ashore. 'So Tom Brade's in there,' I said. Young Winterslip nodded. 'He's in there, right enough,' he answered. And I knew I was looking on at the final scene in the career of a famous character of the South Seas, a callous brute who knew no law, a pirate and adventurer, the master of the notorious Maid of Shiloh. Tom Brade, the blackbirder."

"Blackbirder?" queried John Quincy.

The missionary smiled. "Ah, yes—you come from Boston. A blackbirder, my boy, is a shipping-master who furnishes contract labor to the plantations at so much a head. It's pretty well wiped out now, but in the 'eighties! A horrible business—the curse of God was on it. Sometimes the laborers came willingly. Sometimes. But mostly they came at the point of a knife or the muzzle of a gun. A bloody, brutal business.

"Winterslip and his men went up the beach and began to dig a grave under a cocoanut palm. I followed. I offered to say a prayer. Winterslip laughed—not much use, he said. But there on that bright morning under the palm I consigned to God the soul of a man who had so much to answer for. Winterslip agreed to come to my house for lunch. He told me that save for a recruiting agent who had remained aboard the brig, he was now the only white man on the ship.

"During lunch, I talked to him. He was so young—I discovered this was his first trip. 'It's no trade for you,' I told him. And after a time, he agreed with me. He said he had two hundred blacks under the hatches that he must deliver to a plantation over in the Kingsmill group, and that after he'd done that, he was through. 'I'll take the Maid back to Sydney, Dominie,' he promised, 'and turn her over. Then I'm pau. I'm going home to Honolulu.'"

The Reverend Mr. Upton rose slowly. "I learned later that he kept his word," he finished. "Yes, Dan Winterslip went home, and the South Seas saw him no more. I've always been a little proud of my part in that decision. I've had few rewards. It's not everywhere that the missionaries have prospered in a worldly way—as they did in Hawaii." He glanced at Madame Maynard. "But I've had satisfactions. And one of them arose from that meeting on the shore of Apiang. It's long past my bed hour—I must say good night."

He moved away. John Quincy sat turning this horror over and over in his mind. A Winterslip in the blackbirding business! That was pretty. He wished he was back on Beacon Street.

"Sweet little dig for me," the old lady was muttering indignantly. "That about the missionaries in Hawaii. And he needn't be so cocky. If Dan Winterslip dropped blackbirding, it was only because he'd found something more profitable, I fancy." She stood up suddenly. "At last," she said.

John Quincy rose and stood beside her. Far away a faint yellow eye was winking. For a moment the old lady did not speak.

"Well, that's that," she said finally, in a low voice. "I've seen Diamond Head again. Good night, my boy."

"Good night," John Quincy answered.

He stood alone by the rail. The pace of the PRESIDENT TYLER was slowing perceptibly. The moon came from behind a cloud, crept back again. A sort of unholy calm was settling over the hot, airless, deep blue world. The boy felt a strange restlessness in his heart.

He ascended to the boat deck, seeking a breath of air. There, in a secluded spot, he came upon Barbara and Jennison—and stopped, shocked. His cousin was in the man's arms, and their bizarre costumes added a weird touch to the scene. They did not see John Quincy, for in their world at that moment there were only two. Their lips were crushed together, fiercely—

John Quincy fled. Good lord! He had kissed a girl or two himself, but it had been nothing like that.

He went to the rail outside his stateroom. Well, what of it? Barbara was nothing to him; a cousin, yes, but one who seemed to belong to an alien race. He had sensed that she was in love with Jennison; this was no surprise. Why did he feel that frustrated pang deep in his heart? He was engaged to Agatha Parker.

He gripped the rail, and sought to see again Agatha's aristocratic face. But it was blurred, indistinct. All Boston was blurred in his memory. The blood of the roaming Winterslips, the blood that led on to blackbirding and hot breathless kisses in the tropic night—was it flowing in his veins too? Oh, lord—he should have stayed at home where he belonged.

Bowker, the steward, came along. "Well, here we are," he said. "We'll anchor in twelve fathoms and wait for the pilot and the doctor in the morning. I heard they'd been having Kona weather out this way, but I imagine this is the tail end of it. There'll be a moon shortly, and by dawn the old trades will be on the job again, God bless them."

John Quincy did not speak. "I've returned all your books, sir," the steward went on, "except that one by Adams on Revolutionary New England. It's a mighty interesting work. I intend to finish it to-night, so I can give it to you before you go ashore."

"Oh, that's all right," John Quincy said. He pointed to dim harbor lights in the distance. "Honolulu's over there, I take it."

"Yeah—several miles away. A dead town, sir. They roll up the sidewalks at nine. And let me give you a tip. Keep away from the okolehau."

"The what?" asked John Quincy.

EARL DERR BIGGERS

"The okolehau. A drink they sell out here."

"What's it made of?"

"There," said Bowker, "you have the plot for a big mystery story. What is it made of? Judging by the smell, of nothing very lovely. A few gulps, and you hit the ceiling of eternity. But oh, boy—when you drop! Keep off it, sir. I'm speaking as one who knows."

"I'll keep off it," John Quincy promised.

Bowker disappeared. John Quincy remained by the rail, that restless feeling growing momentarily. The moon was hidden still, the ship crept along through the muggy darkness. He peered across the black waters toward the strange land that awaited him.

Somewhere over there, Dan Winterslip waited for him too. Dan Winterslip, blood relative of the Boston Winterslips, and ex-blackbirder. For the first time, the boy wished he had struck first in that dark attic in San Francisco, wished he had got that strong box and cast it overboard in the night. Who could say what new scandal, what fresh blot on the honored name of Winterslip, might have been averted had he been quicker with his fists?

As John Quincy turned and entered his cabin, he made a firm resolution. He would linger but briefly at this, his journey's end. A few days to get his breath, perhaps, and then he would set out again for Boston. And Aunt Minerva would go with him, whether she wanted to or not.

VI

Beyond the Bamboo Curtain

Had John Quincy been able to see his Aunt Minerva at that moment, he would not have been so sure that he could persuade her to fall in with his plans. He would, indeed, have been profoundly shocked at the picture presented by his supposedly staid and dignified relative.

For Miss Minerva was sitting on a grass mat in a fragrant garden in the Hawaiian quarter of Honolulu. Pale golden Chinese lanterns, inscribed with scarlet letters, hung above her head. Her neck was garlanded with ropes of buff ginger blossoms twined with maile. The sleepy, sensuous music of ukulele and steel guitar rose on the midnight air and before her, in a cleared space under the date palms, Hawaiian boys and girls were performing a dance she would not be able to describe in great detail when she got back to Beacon Street.

Miss Minerva was, in her quiet way, very happy. One of the ambitions of her life had been realized, and she was present at a luau, or native Hawaiian feast. Few white people are privileged to attend this intimate ceremony, but Honolulu friends had been invited on this occasion, and had asked her to go with them. At first she had thought she must refuse, for Dan was expecting Barbara and John Quincy on Monday afternoon. When on Monday evening he had informed her that the PRESIDENT TYLER would not land its passengers until the next day, she had hastened to the telephone and asked to reconsider her refusal.

And she was glad she had. Before her, on another mat, lay the remnants of a dinner unique in her experience. Dan had called her a good sport, and she had this evening proved him to be correct. Without a qualm she had faced the queer food wrapped in brown bundles, she had tasted everything, poi served in individual calabashes, chicken stewed in cocoanut milk, squid and shrimps, limu, or sea-weed, even raw fish. She would dream tonight!

Now the feasting had given way to the dance. The moonlight was tracing lacy patterns on the lawn, the plaintive wail of the music rose ever louder, the Hawaiian young people, bashful at first in the presence of strangers, were bashful no longer. Miss Minerva closed her eyes and leaned back against the trunk of a tall palm. Even in Hawaiian love songs there is a note of hopeless melancholy; it touched her emotions as no symphony ever could. A curtain was lifted and she was looking into the past, the primitive, barbaric past of these Islands in the days before the white men came.

A long, heart-breaking crescendo, and the music stopped, the swaying bodies of the dancers were momentarily still. It seemed to Miss Minerva's friends an opportune moment to depart. They entered the house and in the stuffy little parlor, took leave of their brown, smiling host and hostess. The baby whose arrival in the world was the inspiration for the luau awoke for a second and smiled at them too. Outside in the narrow street their car was waiting.

Through silent, deserted Honolulu they motored toward Waikiki. As they passed the Judiciary Building on King Street, the clock in the tower struck the hour of one. She had not been out so late, Miss Minerva reflected, since that night when a visiting company sang Parsifal at the Boston Opera House.

The iron gates that guarded the drive at Dan's house were closed. Leaving the car at the curb, Miss Minerva bade her friends good night and started up the walk toward the front door. The evening had thrilled her, and she moved with the long confident stride of youth. Dan's scarlet garden was shrouded in darkness, for the moon, which had been playing an in-and-out game with the fast-moving clouds all evening, was again obscured. Exotic odors assailed her nostrils; she heard all about her the soft intriguing noises of the tropic night. She really should get to bed, she knew, but with a happy truant feeling she turned from the front walk and went to the side of the house for a last look at the breakers.

She stood there under a poinciana tree near the door leading into Dan's living-room. For nearly two weeks the Kona wind had prevailed, but now on her cheek, she thought she felt the first kindly breath of the trades. Very wide awake, she stared out at the dim foaming lines of surf between the shore and the coral reef. Her mind strayed back to the Honolulu she had known in Kalakaua's day, to that era when the Islands were so naive, so colorful—unspoiled. Ruined now, Dan had said, ruined by a damned mechanical civilization. "But away down underneath, Minerva, there are deep dark waters flowing still."

The moon came out, touching with silver the waters at the crossroads, then was lost again under fleecy clouds. With a little sigh that was perhaps for her lost youth and the 'eighties, Miss Minerva pushed open the unlocked door leading into the great living-room, and closed it gently so as not to waken Dan.

An intense darkness engulfed her. But she knew her way across the polished floor and set out confidently, walking on tiptoe. She had gone half-way to the hall door when she stopped, her heart in her mouth. For not five feet away she saw the luminous dial of a watch, and as she stared at it with frightened eyes, it moved.

Not for nothing had Miss Minerva studied restraint through more than fifty years. Many women would have screamed and fainted. Miss Minerva's heart pounded madly, but that was all. Standing very still, she studied that phosphorescent dial. Its movement had been slight, it was now at rest again. A watch worn on some one's wrist. Some one who had been on the point of action, but had now assumed an attitude of cautious waiting.

Well, Miss Minerva grimly asked herself, what was she going to do about it? Should she cry out a sharp: "Who's there?" She was a brave woman, but the foolhardiness of such a course was apparent. She had a vision of that dial flashing nearer, a blow, perhaps strong hands at her throat.

She took a tentative step, and then another. Now, surely, the dial would stir again. But it remained motionless, steady, as though the arm that wore it were rigid at the intruder's side.

Suddenly Miss Minerva realized the situation. The wearer of the watch had forgotten the tell-tale numerals on his wrist, he thought himself hidden in the dark. He was waiting for her to go on through the room. If she made no sound, gave no sign of alarm, she might be safe. Once beyond that bamboo curtain leading into the hall, she could rouse the household.

She was a woman of great will power, but it took all she had to move serenely on her way. She shut her lips tightly and accomplished it, veering a bit from that circle of light that menaced her, looking back at it over her shoulder as she went. After what seemed an eternity the bamboo curtain received her, she was through it, she was on the stairs. But it seemed to her that never again would she be able to look at a watch or a clock and find that the hour was anything save twenty minutes past one!

When she was half-way up the stairs, she recalled that it had been her intention to snap on the lights in the lower hall. She did not turn back, nor did she search for the switch at the head of the stairs. Instead, she went hastily on into her room, and just as though she had been an ordinary woman, she closed her door and dropped down, trembling a little, on a chair.

But she was no ordinary woman, and in two seconds she was up and had reopened her door. Her sudden terror was evaporating; she felt her heart beat in a strong regular rhythm again. Action was required of her now, calm confident action; she was a Winterslip and she was ready.

The servants' quarters were in a wing over the kitchen; she went there at once and knocked on the first door she came to. She knocked once, then again, and finally the head of a very sleepy Japanese man appeared.

"Haku," said Miss Minerva, "there is some one in the living-room. You must go down and investigate at once."

He stared at her, seeming unable to comprehend.

"We must go down," amended Miss Minerva.

He disappeared, and Miss Minerva waited impatiently. Where was her nerve, she wondered, why hadn't she seen this through alone? At home, no doubt, she could have managed it, but here there was something strange and terrifying in the very air. The moonlight poured in through a small window beside her, forming a bright square at her feet. Haku reappeared, wearing a gaudy kimono that he often sported on the beach.

Another door opened suddenly, and Miss Minerva started. Bah! What ailed her, anyhow, she wondered. It was only Kamaikui, standing there a massive figure in the dim doorway, a bronze statue clad in a holoku.

"Some one in the living-room," Miss Minerva explained again. "I saw him as I came through."

Kamaikui made no reply, but joined the odd little procession. In the upper hall Haku switched on the lights, both up-stairs and down. At the head of the stairs there was a brief pause—then Miss Minerva took her rightful place at the head of the line. She descended with a firm step, courageous and competent, Boston at its best. After her followed a stolid little Japanese man in a kimono gay with passionate poppies, and a Polynesian woman who wore the fearful Mother Hubbard of the missionaries as though it were a robe of state.

In the lower hall Miss Minerva did not hesitate. She pushed on through the bamboo curtain and her hand—it trembled ever so slightly—

found the electric switch and flooded the living-room with light. She heard the crackle of bamboo behind her as her strange companions followed where she led. She stood looking curiously about her.

There was no one in sight, no sign of any disturbance, and it suddenly occurred to Miss Minerva that perhaps she was behaving in a rather silly fashion. After all, she had neither seen nor heard a living thing. The illuminated dial of a watch that moved a little—might it not have been a figment of her imagination? She had experienced a stirring evening. Then, too, she remembered, there had been that small glass of okolehau. A potent concoction!

Kamaikui and Haku were looking at her with the inquiring eyes of little children. Had she roused them for a fool's errand? Her cheeks flushed slightly. Certainly in this big brilliant room, furnished with magnificent native woods and green with many potted ferns, everything seemed proper and in order.

"I—I may have been mistaken," she said in a low voice. "I was quite sure—but there's no sign of anything wrong. Mr. Winterslip has not been resting well of late. If he should be asleep we won't waken him."

She went to the door leading on to the lanai and pushed aside the curtain. Bright moonlight outside revealed most of the veranda's furnishings, and here, too, all seemed well. "Dan," Miss Minerva called softly. "Dan. Are you awake?"

No answer. Miss Minerva was certain now that she was making a mountain out of a molehill. She was about to turn back into the living-room when her eyes, grown more accustomed to the semi-darkness, noted a rather startling fact.

Day and night, over Dan's cot in one corner of the lanai, hung a white mosquito netting. It was not there now.

"Come, Haku," Miss Minerva said. "Turn on the light out here."

Haku came, and the green-shaded lamp glowed under his touch. The little lamp by which Dan had been reading his evening paper that night when he had seemed suddenly so disturbed, and rushed off to send a letter to Roger in San Francisco. Miss Minerva stood recalling that incident, she recalled others, because she was very reluctant to turn toward that cot in the corner. She was conscious of Kamaikui brushing by her, and then she heard a low, half-savage moan of fear and sorrow.

Miss Minerva stepped to the cot. The mosquito netting had been torn down as though in some terrific struggle and there, entangled in the meshes of it, she saw Dan Winterslip. He was lying on his left side, and as she stared down at him, one of the harmless little Island lizards ran up his chest and over his shoulder—and left a crimson trail on his white pajamas.

VII

Enter Charlie Chan

Miss Minerva leaned far over, her keen eyes seeking Dan's face. It was turned toward the wall, half buried in the pillow. "Dan," she said brokenly. She put her hand on his cheek. The night air was warm and muggy, but she shivered a little as she drew the hand quickly away. Steady! She must be steady now.

She hurried through the living-room to the hall; the telephone was in a closet under the front stairs. Her fingers were trembling again as she fumbled with the numerals on the dial. She got her number, heard finally an answering voice.

"Amos? Is that you, Amos? This is Minerva. Come over here to Dan's as quickly as you can."

The voice muttered in protest. Miss Minerva cut in on it sharply.

"For God's sake, Amos, forget your silly feud. Your brother is dead."

"Dead?" he repeated dully.

"Murdered, Amos. Will you come now?"

A long silence. What thoughts, Miss Minerva wondered, were passing through the mind of that stern unbending Puritan?

"I'll come," a strange voice said at last. And then, a voice more like that of the Amos she knew: "The police! I'll notify them, and then I'll come right over."

Returning to the hall, Miss Minerva saw that the big front door was closed. Amos would enter that way, she knew, so she went over and opened it. There was, she noted, an imposing lock, but the key had long since been lost and forgotten. Indeed, in all Dan's great house, she could not recall ever having seen a key. In these friendly trusting islands, locked doors were obsolete.

She reentered the living-room. Should she summon a doctor? But no, it was too late, she knew that only too well. And the police—didn't they bring some sort of doctor with them? Suddenly she began to wonder about the police. During all her time in Honolulu she had never given them a thought before. Away off here at the end of the world—did they have policemen? She couldn't remember ever having seen one. Oh, yes—there was that handsome, brown-skinned Hawaiian who stood on a box at the corner of Fort and King Streets, directing traffic with an air that would have become Kamehameha himself. She heard the scrape of a chair being moved on the lanai, and went to the door.

"Nothing is to be touched out here," she said. "Leave it just as it was. You'd better go up-stairs and dress, both of you."

The two frightened servants came into the living-room, and stood there regarding her. They seemed to feel that this terrible affair called for discussion. But what was there to be said? Even in the event of murder, a Winterslip must maintain a certain well-bred aloofness in dealing with servants. Miss Minerva's feeling for them was kindly. She sympathized with their evident grief, but there was, she felt, nothing to discuss.

"After you've dressed," she ordered, "stay within reach. You'll both be wanted."

They went out, Haku in his absurd costume, Kamaikui moaning and muttering in a way that sent shivers up and down Miss Minerva's spine. They left her there alone—with Dan—and she who had always thought herself equal to anything still hesitated about going out on the lanai.

She sat down in a huge chair in the living-room and gazed about her at the trappings of wealth and position that Dan had left for ever now. Poor Dan. Despite all the whispering against him, she had liked him immensely. It is said of many—usually with small reason—that their lives would make an interesting book. It had been said of Dan, and in his case it was true. What a book his life would have made—and how promptly it would have been barred for all time from the shelves of the Boston Public Library! For Dan had lived life to the full, made his own laws, fought his battles without mercy, prospered and had his way. Dallied often along forbidden paths, they said, but his smile had been so friendly and his voice so full of cheer—always until these last two weeks.

Ever since that night he sent the letter to Roger, he had seemed a different man. There were lines for the first time in his face, a weary apprehensive look in his gray eyes. And how furious he had been when, last Wednesday, he received a cable from Roger. What was in that message, Miss Minerva wondered; what were those few typewritten words that had caused him to fly into such a rage and set him to pacing the floor with tigerish step?

She thought of him as she had seen him last—he had seemed rather pathetic to her then. When the news came that the President Tyler could not dock until morning, and that Barbara—

Miss Minerva stopped. For the first time she thought of Barbara. She thought of a sprightly, vivacious girl as yet untouched by sorrow—and of the morning's homecoming. Tears came into her eyes, and it was through a mist she saw the bamboo curtain that led into the hall pushed aside, and the thin white face of Amos framed there.

Amos entered, walking gingerly, for he was treading ground he had sworn his feet should never touch. He paused before Miss Minerva.

"What's this?" he said. "What's all this?"

She nodded toward the lanai, and he went out there. After what seemed a long time, he reappeared. His shoulders drooped wearily and his watery eyes were staring.

"Stabbed through the heart," he muttered. He stood for a moment regarding his father's picture on the wall. "The wages of sin is death," he added, as though to old Jedediah Winterslip.

"Yes, Amos," said Miss Minerva sharply. "I expected we should hear that from you. And there's another one you may have heard—judge not that ye be not judged. Further than that, we'll waste no time moralizing. Dan is dead, and I for one am sorry."

"Sorry!" repeated Amos drearily. "How about me? My brother—my young brother—I taught him to walk on this very beach—"

"Yes." Miss Minerva looked at him keenly. "I wonder. Well, Dan's gone. Some one has killed him. He was one of us—a Winterslip. What are we going to do about it?"

"I've notified the police," said Amos.

"Then why aren't they here? In Boston by this time—but then, I know this isn't Boston. Stabbed, you say. Was there any sign of a weapon?"

"None whatever, that I could see."

"How about that Malay kris on the table out there? The one Dan used as a paper cutter?"

"I didn't notice," Amos replied. "This is a strange house to me, Minerva."

"So it is." Miss Minerva rose and started for the lanai. She was her old competent self again. At that moment a loud knock sounded on the screen door at the front of the house. Presently there were voices in the hall, and Haku ushered three men into the living-room. Though evidently police, they were all in plain clothes. One of them, a tall, angular Yankee with the look of a sailing master about him, stepped forward.

"I'm Hallet," he said. "Captain of Detectives. You're Mr. Amos Winterslip, I believe?"

EARL DERR BIGGERS

"I am," Amos answered. He introduced Miss Minerva. Captain Hallet gave her a casual nod; this was man's business and he disliked having a woman involved.

"Dan Winterslip, you said," he remarked, turning back to Amos. "That's a great pity. Where is he?"

Amos indicated the lanai. "Come, Doctor," Hallet said, and went through the curtain, followed by the smaller of the two men.

As they went out, the third man stepped farther into the room, and Miss Minerva gave a little gasp of astonishment as she looked at him. In those warm islands thin men were the rule, but here was a striking exception. He was very fat indeed, yet he walked with the light dainty step of a woman. His cheeks were as chubby as a baby's, his skin ivory tinted, his black hair close-cropped, his amber eyes slanting. As he passed Miss Minerva he bowed with a courtesy encountered all too rarely in a work-a-day world, then moved on after Hallet.

"Amos!" cried Miss Minerva. "That man—why he—"

"Charlie Chan," Amos explained. "I'm glad they brought him. He's the best detective on the force."

"But—he's Chinese!"

"Of course."

Miss Minerva sank into a chair. Ah, yes, they had policemen out here, after all.

In a few moments Hallet came briskly back into the living-room. "Look here," he said. "The doctor tells me Mr. Winterslip has been dead a very short while. I don't want your evidence just yet—but if either of you can give me some idea as to the hour when this thing happened—"

"I can give you a rather definite idea," said Miss Minerva calmly. "It happened just previous to twenty minutes past one. Say about one fifteen."

Hallet stared at her. "You're sure of that?"

"I ought to be. I got the time from the wrist watch of the person who committed the murder."

"What! You saw him!"

"I didn't say that. I said I saw his wrist watch."

Hallet frowned. "I'll get that straight later," he said. "Just now I propose to comb this part of town. Where's the telephone?"

Miss Minerva pointed it out to him, and heard him in earnest conversation with a man at headquarters named Tom. Tom's job, it seemed, was to muster all available men and search Honolulu, particularly the Waikiki district, rounding up any suspicious characters. He was also to have on hand, awaiting his chief's return, the passenger lists of all ships that had made port at Honolulu during the past week.

Hallet returned to the living-room. He took a stand directly in front of Miss Minerva. "Now," he began, "you didn't see the murderer, but you saw his wrist watch. I'm a great believer in taking things in an orderly fashion. You're a stranger here. From Boston, I believe?"

"I am," snapped Miss Minerva.

"Stopping in this house?"

"Precisely."

"Anybody here besides you and Mr. Winterslip?"

Miss Minerva's eyes flashed. "The servants," she said. "And I would like to call your attention to the fact that I am Dan Winterslip's first cousin."

"Oh, sure—no offense. He has a daughter, hasn't he?"

"Miss Barbara is on her way home from college. Her ship will dock in the morning."

"I see. Just you and Winterslip. You're going to be an important witness."

"It will be a novel experience, at any rate," she remarked.

"I dare say. Now, go back—" Miss Minerva glared at him—it was a glare that had frightened guards on the Cambridge subway. He brushed it aside. "You understand that I haven't time for please, Miss Winterslip. Go back and describe last evening in this house."

"I was here only until eight-thirty," she told him, "when I went to a luau with some friends. Previous to that, Mr. Winterslip dined at his usual hour and we chatted for a time on the lanai."

"Did he seem to have anything on his mind?"

"Well, he has appeared a bit upset—"

"Wait a minute!" The captain took out a note-book. "Want to put down some of this. Been upset, has he? For how long?"

"For the past two weeks. Let me think—just two weeks ago to-night—or rather, last night—he and I were sitting on the lanai, and he was reading the evening paper. Something in it seemed to disturb him. He got up, wrote a note to his cousin Roger in San Francisco, and took it down for a friend aboard the PRESIDENT TYLER to deliver. From that moment he appeared restless and unhappy."

"Go on. This may be important."

"Last Wednesday morning he received a cable from Roger that infuriated him."

EARL DERR BIGGERS

"A cable. What was in it?"

"It was not addressed to me," said Miss Minerva haughtily.

"Well, that's all right. We'll dig it up. Now, about last night. Did he act more upset than ever?"

"He did. But that may have been due to the fact he had hoped his daughter's ship would dock yesterday afternoon, and had learned it could not land its passengers until this morning."

"I see. You said you was only here until eight-thirty?"

"I did not," replied Miss Minerva coldly. "I said I was here only until eight-thirty."

"Same thing."

"Well, hardly."

"I'm not here to talk grammar," Hallet said sharply. "Did anything occur—anything out of the ordinary—before you left?"

"No. Wait a moment. Some one called Mr. Winterslip on the telephone while he was at dinner. I couldn't help overhearing the conversation."

"Good for you!" She glared at him again. "Repeat it."

"I heard Mr. Winterslip say: 'Hello, Egan. What—you're not coming over? Oh, yes you are. I want to see you. I insist on it. Come about eleven. I want to see you.' That was, at least, the import of his remarks."

"Did he seem excited?"

"He raised his voice above the ordinary tone."

"Ah, yes." The captain stared at his note-book. "Must have been Jim Egan, who runs this God-forsaken Reef and Palm Hotel down the beach." He turned to Amos. "Was Egan a friend of your brother?"

"I don't know," said Amos.

"You see, Amos was not a friend of his brother, either," explained Miss Minerva. "There was an old feud between them. Speaking for myself, I never heard Dan mention Egan, and he certainly never came to the house while I was here."

Hallet nodded. "Well, you left at eight-thirty. Now tell us where you went and when you got back. And all about the wrist watch."

Miss Minerva rapidly sketched her evening at the luau. She described her return to Dan's living-room, her adventure in the dark—the luminous dial that waited for her to pass.

"I wish you'd seen more," Hallet complained. "Too many people wear wrist watches."

"Probably not many," said Miss Minerva, "wear a wrist watch like that one."

"Oh. It had some distinguishing mark?"

"It certainly did. The numerals were illuminated, and stood out clearly—with an exception. The figure 2 was very dim—practically obliterated."

He looked at her admiringly. "Well, you certainly had your wits about you."

"That's a habit I formed early in life," replied Miss Minerva. "And old habits are hard to break."

He smiled, and asked her to continue. She told of rousing the two servants and, finally, of the gruesome discovery on the lanai.

"But it was Mr. Amos," Hallet said, "who called the station."

"Yes. I telephoned him at once, and he offered to attend to that."

Hallet turned to Amos. "How long did it take you to reach here, Mr. Winterslip?" he inquired.

"Not more than ten minutes," said Amos.

"You could dress and get here in that time?"

Amos hesitated. "I—I did not need to dress," he explained. "I hadn't gone to bed."

Hallet regarded him with a new interest. "Half past one—and you were still up?"

"I—I don't sleep very well," said Amos. "I'm up till all hours."

"I see. You weren't on friendly terms with your brother? An old quarrel between you?"

"No particular quarrel. I didn't approve of his manner of living, and we went separate ways."

"And stopped speaking to each other, eh?"

"Yes. That was the situation," Amos admitted.

"Humph." For a moment the captain stared at Amos, and Miss Minerva stared at him too. Amos! It flashed through her mind that Amos had been a long time alone out there on the lanai before the arrival of the police.

"Those two servants who came down-stairs with you, Miss Winterslip," Hallet said. "I'll see them now. The others can go over until morning."

Haku and Kamaikui appeared, frightened and wide-eyed. Haku had nothing to tell, he had been sleeping soundly from nine until the moment Miss Minerva knocked on his door. He swore it. But Kamaikui had something to contribute.

"I come here with fruit." She pointed to a basket on the table. "On lanai out there are talking—Mr. Dan, a man, a woman. Oh, very much angry."

"What time was that?" Hallet asked.

"Ten o'clock I think."

"Did you recognize any voice except your master's?"

Miss Minerva thought the woman hesitated a second. "No. I do not."

"Anything else?"

"Yes. Maybe eleven o'clock. I am sitting close to window up-stairs. More talking on lanai. Mr. Dan and other man. Not so much angry this time."

"At eleven, eh? Do you know Mr. Jim Egan?"

"I have seen him."

"Could you say if it was his voice?"

"I could not say."

"All right. You two can go now." He turned to Miss Minerva and Amos. "We'll see what Charlie has dug up out here," he said, and led the way to the lanai.

The huge Chinese man knelt, a grotesque figure, by a table. He rose laboriously as they entered.

"Find the knife, Charlie?" the captain asked.

Chan shook his head. "No knife are present in neighborhood of crime," he announced.

"On that table," Miss Minerva began, "there was a Malay kris, used as a paper cutter—"

The Chinese man nodded, and lifted the kris from the desk. "Same remains here still," he said, "untouched, unsullied. Person who killed carried individual weapon."

"How about finger-prints?" asked Hallet.

"Considering from recent discovery," Chan replied, "search for finger-prints are hopeless one." He held out a pudgy hand, in the palm of which lay a small pearl button. "Torn from kid's glove," he elucidated. "Aged trick of criminal mind. No finger-prints."

"Is that all you've got?" asked his chief.

"Most sincere endeavors," said Chan, "have revealed not much. However, I might mention this." He took up a leather-bound book from the table. "Here are written names of visitors who have enjoyed hospitality of the house. A guest book is, I believe, the term. You will find that one of the earlier pages has been ruthlessly torn out. When I make discovery the volume are lying open at that locality."

Captain Hallet took the book in his thin hand. "All right, Charlie," he said. "This is your case."

The slant eyes blinked with pleasure. "Most interesting," murmured Chan.

Hallet tapped the note-book in his pocket. "I've got a few facts here for you—we'll run over them later." He stood for a moment, staring about the lanai. "I must say we seem a little shy on clues. A button torn from a glove, a page ripped from a guest book. And a wrist watch with an illuminated dial on which the figure 2 was damaged." Chan's little eyes widened at mention of that. "Not much, Charlie, so far."

"Maybe more to come," suggested Chan. "Who knows it?"

"We'll go along now," Hallet continued. He turned to Miss Minerva and Amos. "I guess you folks would like a little rest. We'll have to trouble you again to-morrow."

Miss Minerva faced Chan. "The person who did this must be apprehended," she said firmly.

He looked at her sleepily. "What is to be, will be," he replied in a high, sing-song voice.

"I know—that's your Confucius," she snapped. "But it's a do-nothing doctrine, and I don't approve of it."

A faint smile flickered over Chan's face. "Do not fear," he said. "The fates are busy, and man may do much to assist. I promise you there will be no do-nothing here." He came closer. "Humbly asking pardon to mention it, I detect in your eyes slight flame of hostility. Quench it, if you will be so kind. Friendly cooperation are essential between us." Despite his girth, he managed a deep bow. "Wishing you good morning," he added, and followed Hallet.

Miss Minerva turned weakly to Amos. "Well, of all things—"

"Don't you worry about Charlie," Amos said. "He has a reputation for getting his man. Now you go to bed. I'll stay here and notify the—the proper people."

"Well, I will lie down for a little while," Miss Minerva said. "I shall have to go early to the dock. Poor Barbara! And there's John Quincy coming too." A grim smile crossed her face. "I'm afraid John Quincy won't approve of this."

She saw from her bedroom window that the night was breaking, the rakish cocoanut palms and the hau tree were wrapped in a gray mist.

Changing her dress for a kimono, she lay down under the mosquito netting on the bed. She slept but briefly, however, and presently was at her window again. Day had come, the mist had lifted, and it was a rose and emerald world that sparkled before her tired eyes.

The freshness of that scene revivified her. The trades were blowing now—poor Dan, he had so longed for their return. The night, she saw, had worked its magic on the blossoms of the hau tree, transformed them from yellow to a rich mahogany; through the morning they would drop one by one upon the sand. In a distant algaroba a flock of myna birds screamed at the new day. A party of swimmers appeared from a neighboring cottage and plunged gaily into the surf.

A gentle knock sounded on the door, and Kamaikui entered. She placed a small object in Miss Minerva's hand.

Miss Minerva looked down. She saw a quaint old piece of jewelry, a brooch. Against a background of onyx stood the outline of a tree, with emeralds forming the leaves, rubies the fruit, and a frost of diamonds over all.

"What is this, Kamaikui?" she asked.

"Many, many years Mr. Dan have that. One month ago he gives it to a woman down the beach."

Miss Minerva's eyes narrowed. "To the woman they call the Widow of Waikiki?"

"To her, yes."

"How do you happen to have it, Kamaikui?"

"I pick it up from floor of lanai. Before policemen come."

"Very good." Miss Minerva nodded. "Say nothing of this, Kamaikui. I will attend to the matter."

"Yes. Of course." The woman went out.

Miss Minerva sat very still, staring down at that odd bit of jewelry in her hand. It must date back to the 'eighties, at least.

Close above the house sounded the loud whir of an aeroplane. Miss Minerva turned again to the window. A young lieutenant in the air service, in love with a sweet girl on the beach, was accustomed to serenade her thus every morning at dawn. His thoughtfulness was not appreciated by many innocent bystanders, but Miss Minerva's eyes were sympathetic as she watched him sweep exultantly out, far out, over the harbor.

Youth and love, the beginning of life. And on that cot down on the lanai, Dan—and the end.

VIII

STEAMER DAY

Out in the harbor, by the channel entrance, the PRESIDENT TYLER stood motionless as Diamond Head, and from his post near the rail outside his stateroom, John Quincy Winterslip took his first look at Honolulu. He had no feeling of having been here before; this was an alien land. Several miles away he saw the line of piers and unlovely warehouses that marked the water-front; beyond that lay a vast expanse of brilliant green pierced here and there by the top of a modest skyscraper. Back of the city a range of mountains stood on guard, peaks of crystal blue against the azure sky.

A trim little launch from Quarantine chugged importantly up to the big liner's side, and a doctor in a khaki uniform ran briskly up the accommodation ladder to the deck not far from where the boy stood. John Quincy wondered at the man's vitality. He felt like a spent force himself. The air was moist and heavy, the breeze the ship had stirred in moving gone for ever. The flood of energy that had swept over him in San Francisco was but a happy memory now. He leaned wearily on the rail, staring at the bright tropical landscape before him—and not seeing it at all.

He saw instead a quiet, well-furnished Boston office where at this very moment the typewriters were clicking amiably and the stock ticker was busily writing the story of another day. In a few hours—there was a considerable difference of time—the market would close and the men he knew would be piling into automobiles and heading for the nearest country club. A round of golf, then a calm, perfectly served dinner, and after that a quiet evening with a book. Life running along as it was meant to go, without rude interruption or disturbing incident; life devoid of ohia wood boxes, attic encounters, unwillingly-witnessed love scenes, cousins with blackbirding pasts. Suddenly John Quincy remembered, this was the morning when he must look Dan Winterslip in the eye and tell him he had been a bit dilatory with his fists. Oh, well—he straightened resolutely—the sooner that was done, the better.

Harry Jennison came along the deck, smiling and vigorous, clad in spotless white from head to foot. "Here we are," he cried. "On the threshold of paradise!"

"Think so?" said John Quincy.

"Know it," Jennison answered. "Only place in the world, these islands. You remember what Mark Twain said—"

"Ever visited Boston?" John Quincy cut in.

"Once," replied Jennison briefly. "That's Punch Bowl Hill back of the town—and Tantalus beyond. Take you up to the summit some day—wonderful view. See that tallest building? The Van Patten Trust Company—my office is on the top floor. Only drawback about getting home—I'll have to go to work again."

"I don't see how any one can work in this climate," John Quincy said.

"Oh, well, we take it easy. Can't manage the pace of you mainland people. Every now and then some go-getter from the States comes out here and tries to hustle us." He laughed. "He dies of disgust and we bury him in a leisurely way. Been down to breakfast?"

John Quincy accompanied him to the dining saloon. Madame Maynard and Barbara were at the table. The old lady's cheeks were flushed and her eyes sparkled; Barbara, too, was in her gayest mood. The excitement of coming home had made her very happy—or was her happiness all due to that? John Quincy noted her smile of greeting for Jennison, and rather wished he knew less than he did.

"Prepare for a thrill, John Quincy," the girl said. "Landing in Hawaii is like landing nowhere else on the globe. Of course, this is a through boat, and it isn't welcomed as the Matson liners are. But there'll be a crowd waiting for the Matsonia this morning, and we'll steal a little of her aloha."

"A little of her what?" inquired John Quincy.

"Aloha—meaning loving welcome. You shall have all my leis, John Quincy. Just to show you how glad Honolulu is you've come at last."

The boy turned to Madame Maynard. "I suppose this is an old story to you?"

"Bless you, my boy," she said. "It's always new. A hundred and twenty-eight times—yet I'm as thrilled as though I were coming home from college." She sighed. "A hundred and twenty-eight times. So many of those who once hung leis about my neck are gone for ever now. They'll not be waiting for me—not on this dock."

"None of that," Barbara chided. "Only happy thoughts this morning. It's steamer day."

Nobody seemed hungry, and breakfast was a sketchy affair. John Quincy returned to his cabin to find Bowker strapping up his luggage.

"I guess you're all ready, sir," said the steward. "I finished that book last night, and you'll find it in your suit-case. We'll be moving on to the dock shortly. All good luck to you—and don't forget about the okolehau."

"It's graven on my memory," smiled John Quincy. "Here—this is for you."

Bowker glanced at the bank-note and pocketed it. "You're mighty kind, sir," he remarked feelingly. "That will sort of balance up the dollar each I'll get from those two missionaries when we reach China—if I'm lucky. Of course, it's rather distasteful to me to accept anything. From a friend of Tim's, you know."

"Oh, that's for value received," said John Quincy, and followed Bowker on deck.

"There she is," announced Bowker, pausing by the rail. "Honolulu. The South Seas with a collar on, driving a Ford car. Polynesia with a private still and all the other benefits of the white man's civilization. We'll go out at eight to-night, thank heaven."

"Paradise doesn't appeal to you," suggested John Quincy.

"No. Nor any other of these bright-colored lands my poor old feet must tread. I'm getting fed up, sir." He came closer. "I want to hang my hat somewhere and leave it there. I want to buy a little newspaper in some country town and starve to death on the proceeds of running it. What a happy finish! Well, maybe I can manage it, before long."

"I hope so," said John Quincy.

"I hope so, too," said Bowker. "Here's wishing you a happy time in Honolulu. And one other word of warning—don't linger there."

"I don't intend to," John Quincy assured him.

"That's the talk. It's one of those places—you know—dangerous. Lotus on the menu every day. The first thing you know, you've forgot where you put your trunk. So long, sir."

With a wave of the hand, Tim's friend disappeared down the deck. Amid much confusion, John Quincy took his place in line for the doctor's inspection, passed the careful scrutiny of an immigration official who finally admitted that maybe Boston was in the Union, and was then left to his own devices and his long, long thoughts.

The PRESIDENT TYLER was moving slowly toward the shore. Excited figures scurried about her decks, pausing now and then to stare through lifted glasses at the land. John Quincy perceived that early though the hour was, the pier toward which they were heading was alive with people. Barbara came and stood by his side.

"Poor old dad," she said, "he's been struggling along without me for nine months. This will be a big morning in his life. You'll like dad, John Quincy."

"I'm sure I shall," he answered heartily.

"Dad's one of the finest—" Jennison joined them. "Harry, I meant to tell the steward to take my luggage ashore when we land."

"I told him," Jennison said. "I tipped him, too."

"Thanks," the girl replied. "I was so excited, I forgot."

She leaned eagerly over the rail, peering at the dock. Her eyes were shining. "I don't see him yet," she said. They were near enough now to hear the voices of those ashore, gay voices calling flippant greetings. The big ship edged gingerly closer.

"There's Aunt Minerva," cried John Quincy suddenly. That little touch of home in the throng was very pleasant. "Is that your father with her?" He indicated a tall anemic man at Minerva's side.

"I don't see—where—" Barbara began. "Oh—that—why, that's Uncle Amos!"

"Oh, is that Amos?" remarked John Quincy, without interest. But Barbara had gripped his arm, and as he turned he saw a wild alarm in her eyes.

"What do you suppose that means?" she cried. "I don't see dad. I don't see him anywhere."

"Oh, he's in that crowd somewhere—"

"No, no—you don't understand! Uncle Amos! I'm—I'm frightened."

John Quincy didn't gather what it was all about, and there was no time to find out. Jennison was pushing ahead through the crowd, making a path for Barbara, and the boy meekly brought up the rear. They were among the first down the plank. Miss Minerva and Amos were waiting at the foot.

"My dear." Miss Minerva put her arms about the girl and kissed her gently. She turned to John Quincy. "Well, here you are—"

There was something lacking in this welcome. John Quincy sensed it at once.

"Where's dad?" Barbara cried.

"I'll explain in the car—" Miss Minerva began.

"No, now! Now! I must know now!"

The crowd was surging about them, calling happy greetings, the Royal Hawaiian Band was playing a gay tune, carnival was in the air.

"Your father is dead, my dear," said Miss Minerva.

John Quincy saw the girl's slim figure sway gently, but it was Harry Jennison's strong arm that caught her.

For a moment she stood, with Jennison's arm about her. "All right," she said. "I'm ready to go home." And walked like a true Winterslip toward the street.

Amos melted away into the crowd, but Jennison accompanied them to the car. "I'll go out with you," he said to Barbara. She did not seem to hear. The four of them entered the limousine, and in another moment the happy clamor of steamer day was left behind.

No one spoke. The curtains of the car were drawn, but a warm streak of sunlight fell across John Quincy's knees. He was a little dazed. Shocking, this news about Cousin Dan. Must have died suddenly— but no doubt that was how things always happened out this way. He glanced at the white stricken face of the girl beside him, and because of her his heart was heavy.

She laid her cold hand on his. "It's not the welcome I promised you, John Quincy," she said softly.

"Why, my dear girl, I don't matter now."

No other word was spoken on the journey, and when they reached Dan's house, Barbara and Miss Minerva went immediately up-stairs. Jennison disappeared through a doorway at the left; evidently he knew his way about. Haku volunteered to show John Quincy his quarters, so he followed Haku to the second floor.

When his bags were unpacked, John Quincy went down-stairs again. Miss Minerva was waiting for him in the living-room. From beyond the bamboo curtain leading to the lanai came the sound of men's voices, mumbling and indistinct.

"Well," said John Quincy, "how have you been?"

"Never better," his aunt assured him.

"Mother's been rather worried about you. She'd begun to think you were never coming home."

"I've begun to think it myself," Miss Minerva replied.

He stared at her. "Some of those bonds you left with me have matured. I haven't known just what you wanted me to do about them."

"What," inquired Miss Minerva, "is a bond?"

That sort of wild reckless talk never did make a hit with John Quincy. "It's about time somebody came out here and brought you to your senses," he remarked.

"Think so?" said his aunt.

A sound up-stairs recalled John Quincy to the situation. "This was rather sudden—Cousin Dan's death?" he inquired.

"Amazingly so."

"Well, it seems to me that it would be rather an intrusion—our staying on here now. We ought to go home in a few days. I'd better see about reservations—"

"You needn't trouble," snapped Miss Minerva. "I'll not stir from here until I see the person who did this brought to justice."

"The person who did what?" asked John Quincy.

"The person who murdered Cousin Dan," said Miss Minerva.

John Quincy's jaw dropped. His face registered a wide variety of emotions. "Good lord!" he gasped.

"Oh, you needn't be so shocked," said his aunt. "The Winterslip family will still go on."

"Well, I'm not surprised," remarked John Quincy, "when I stop to think. The things I've learned about Cousin Dan. It's a wonder to me—"

"That will do," said Miss Minerva. "You're talking like Amos, and that's no compliment. You didn't know Dan. I did—and I liked him. I'm going to stay here and do all I can to help run down the murderer. And so are you."

"Pardon me. I am not."

"Don't contradict. I intend you shall take an active part in the investigation. The police are rather informal in a small place like this. They'll welcome your help."

"My help! I'm no detective. What's happened to you, anyhow? Why should you want me to go round hobnobbing with policemen—"

"For the simple reason that if we're not careful some rather unpleasant scandal may come out of this. If you're on the ground you may be able to avert needless publicity. For Barbara's sake."

"No, thank you," said John Quincy. "I'm leaving for Boston in three days, and so are you. Pack your trunks."

Miss Minerva laughed. "I've heard your father talk like that," she told him. "But I never knew him to gain anything by it in the end. Come out on the lanai and I'll introduce you to a few policemen."

John Quincy received this invitation with the contemptuous silence he thought it deserved. But while he was lavishing on it his best contempt, the bamboo curtain parted and the policemen came to him. Jennison was with them.

"Good morning, Captain Hallet," said Miss Minerva brightly. "May I present my nephew, Mr. John Quincy Winterslip of Boston."

"I'm very anxious to meet Mr. John Quincy Winterslip," the captain replied.

"How do you do," said John Quincy. His heart sank. They'd drag him into this affair if they could.

"And this, John Quincy," went on Miss Minerva, "is Mr. Charles Chan, of the Honolulu detective force."

John Quincy had thought himself prepared for anything, but— "Mr.—Mr. Chan," he gasped.

"Mere words," said Chan, "can not express my unlimitable delight in meeting a representative of the ancient civilization of Boston."

Harry Jennison spoke. "This is an appalling business, Miss Winterslip," he said. "As perhaps you know, I was your cousin's lawyer. I was also his friend. Therefore I hope you won't think I am intruding if I show a keen interest in what is going forward here."

"Not at all," Miss Minerva assured him. "We shall need all the help we can get."

Captain Hallet had taken a paper from his pocket. He faced John Quincy.

"Young man," he began, "I said I wanted to meet you. Last night Miss Winterslip told me of a cablegram received by the dead man about a week ago, which she said angered him greatly. I happen to have a copy of that message, turned over to me by the cable people. I'll read it to you:

"John Quincy Sailing On President Tyler Stop Owing To Unfortunate Accident He Leaves Here With Empty Hands. Signed Roger Winterslip."

"Yes?" said John Quincy haughtily.

"Explain that, if you will."

John Quincy stiffened. "The matter was strictly private," he said. "A family affair."

Captain Hallet glared at him. "You're mistaken," he replied. "Nothing that concerns Mr. Dan Winterslip is private now. Tell me what that cable meant, and be quick about it. I'm busy this morning."

John Quincy glared back. The man didn't seem to realize to whom he was talking. "I've already said—" he began.

"John Quincy," snapped Miss Minerva. "Do as you're told!"

Oh, well, if she wanted family secrets aired in public! Reluctantly John Quincy explained about Dan Winterslip's letter, and the misadventure in the attic of Dan's San Francisco house.

"An ohia wood box bound with copper," repeated the captain. "Initials on it, T.M.B. Got that, Charlie?"

"It is written in the book," said Chan.

"Any idea what was in that box?" asked Hallet.

"Not the slightest," John Quincy told him.

Hallet turned to Miss Minerva. "You knew nothing about this?" She assured him she did not. "Well," he continued, "one thing more and we'll go along. We've been making a thorough search of the premises by daylight—without much success, I'm sorry to say. However, by the cement walk just outside that door"—he pointed to the screen door leading from the living-room into the garden—"Charlie made a discovery."

Chan stepped forward, holding a small white object in the palm of his hand.

"One-half cigarette, incompletely consumed," he announced. "Very recent, not weather stained. It are of the brand denominated Corsican, assembled in London and smoked habitually by Englishmen."

Hallet again addressed Miss Minerva. "Did Dan Winterslip smoke cigarettes?"

"He did not," she replied. "Cigars and a pipe, but never cigarettes."

"You were the only other person living here."

"I haven't acquired the cigarette habit," snapped Miss Minerva. "Though undoubtedly it's not too late yet."

"The servants, perhaps?" went on Hallet.

"Some of the servants may smoke cigarettes, but hardly of this quality. I take it these are not on sale in Honolulu?"

"They're not," said the captain. "But Charlie tells me they're put up in air-tight tins and shipped to Englishmen the world over. Well, stow that away, Charlie." The Chinese man tenderly placed the half cigarette, incompletely consumed, in his pocketbook. "I'm going on down the beach now to have a little talk with Mr. Jim Egan," the captain added.

"I'll go with you," Jennison offered. "I may be able to supply a link or two there."

"Sure, come along," Hallet replied cordially.

"Captain Hallet," put in Miss Minerva, "it is my wish that some member of the family keep in touch with what you are doing, in order that we may give you all the aid we can. My nephew would like to accompany you—"

"Pardon me," said John Quincy coldly, "you're quite wrong. I have no intention of joining the police force."

"Well, just as you say," remarked Hallet. He turned to Miss Minerva. "I'm relying on you, at any rate. You've got a good mind. Anybody can see that."

"Thank you," she said.

"As good as a man's," he added.

"Oh, now you've spoiled it. Good morning."

The three men went through the screen door into the bright sunshine of the garden. John Quincy was aware that he was not in high favor with his aunt.

"I'll go up and change," he said uncomfortably. "We'll talk things over later—"

He went into the hall. At the foot of the stairs he paused.

From above came a low, heart-breaking moan of anguish. Barbara. Poor Barbara, who had been so happy less than an hour ago.

John Quincy felt his head go hot, the blood pound in his temples. How dare any one strike down a Winterslip! How dare any one inflict this grief on his Cousin Barbara! He clenched his fists and stood for a moment, feeling that he, too, could kill.

Action—he must have action! He rushed through the living-room, past the astonished Miss Minerva. In the drive stood a car, the three men were already in it.

"Wait a minute," called John Quincy. "I'm going with you."

"Hop in," said Captain Hallet.

The car rolled down the drive and out on to the hot asphalt of Kalia Road. John Quincy sat erect, his eyes flashing, by the side of a huge grinning Chinese man.

IX

At the Reef and Palm

They reached Kalakaua Avenue and swerving sharply to the right, Captain Hallet stepped on the gas. Since the car was without a top, John Quincy was getting an unrestricted view of this land that lay at his journey's end. As a small boy squirming about on the hard pew in the First Unitarian Church, he had heard much of Heaven, and his youthful imagination had pictured it as something like this. A warm, rather languid country freshly painted in the gaudiest colors available.

Creamy white clouds wrapped the tops of the distant mountains, and their slopes were bright with tropical foliage. John Quincy heard near at hand the low monotone of breakers lapping the shore. Occasionally he caught a glimpse of apple-green water and a dazzling white stretch of sand. "Oh, Waikiki! Oh, scene of peace—" What was the rest of that poem his Aunt Minerva had quoted in her last letter—the one in which she had announced that she was staying on indefinitely. "And looking down from tum-tum skies, the angels smile on Waikiki." Sentimental, but sentiment was one of Hawaii's chief exports. One had only to look at the place to understand and forgive.

John Quincy had not delayed for a hat, and the sun was beating down fiercely on his brown head. Charlie Chan glanced at him.

"Humbly begging pardon," he remarked, "would say it is unadvisable to venture forth without headgear. Especially since you are a malihini."

"A what?"

"The term carries no offense. Malihini—stranger, newcomer."

"Oh." John Quincy looked at him curiously. "Are you a malihini?"

"Not in the least," grinned Chan. "I am kamaaina—old-timer. Pursuing the truth further, I have been twenty-five years in the Islands."

They passed a huge hotel, and presently John Quincy saw Diamond Head standing an impressive guardian at the far end of that lovely curving beach. A little farther along the captain drew up to the curb and the four men alighted. On the other side of a dilapidated fence was a garden that might have been Eden at its best.

Entering past a gate that hung sorrowfully on one hinge they walked up a dirt path and in a moment a ramshackle old building came into view. They were approaching it on an angle, and John Quincy saw that the greater part of it extended out over the water. The tottering structure was of two stories, with double-decked balconies on both sides and the rear. It had rather an air about it; once, no doubt, it had been worthy to stand in this setting. Flowering vines clambered over it in a friendly endeavor to hide its imperfections from the world.

"Some day," announced Charlie Chan solemnly, "those rafters underneath will disintegrate and the Reef and Palm Hotel will descend into the sea with a most horrid gurgle."

As they drew nearer, it seemed to John Quincy that Chan's prophecy might come true at any moment. They paused at the foot of a crumbling stair that led to the front door, and as they did so a man emerged hurriedly from the Reef and Palm. His once white clothes were yellowed, his face lined, his eyes tired and disillusioned. But about him, as about the hotel, hung the suggestion of a distinguished past.

"Mr. Egan," said Captain Hallet promptly.

"Oh—how are you?" the man replied, with an accent that recalled to John Quincy's mind his meeting with Captain Arthur Temple Cope.

"We want to talk to you," announced Hallet brusquely.

A shadow crossed Egan's face. "I'm frightfully sorry," he said, "but I have a most important engagement, and I'm late as it is. Some other time—"

"Now!" cut in Hallet. The word shot through the morning like a rocket. He started up the steps.

"Impossible," said Egan. He did not raise his voice. "Nothing on earth could keep me from the dock this morning—"

The captain of detectives seized his arm. "Come inside!" he ordered.

Egan's face flushed. "Take your hand off me, damn you! By what right—"

"You watch your step, Egan," advised Hallet angrily. "You know why I'm here."

"I do not."

Hallet stared into the man's face. "Dan Winterslip was murdered last night," he said.

Jim Egan removed his hat, and looked helplessly out toward Kalakaua Avenue. "So I read in the morning paper," he replied. "What has his death to do with me?"

"You were the last person to see him alive," Hallet answered. "Now quit bluffing and come inside."

EARL DERR BIGGERS

Egan cast one final baffled glance at the street, where a trolley bound for the city three miles away was rattling swiftly by. Then he bowed his head and led the way into the hotel.

They entered a huge, poorly furnished public room, deserted save for a woman tourist writing post-cards at a table, and a shabby Japanese clerk lolling behind the desk. "This way," Egan said, and they followed him past the desk and into a small private office. Here all was confusion, dusty piles of magazines and newspapers were everywhere, battered old ledgers lay upon the floor. On the wall hung a portrait of Queen Victoria; many pictures cut from the London illustrated weeklies were tacked up haphazardly. Jennison spread a newspaper carefully over the window-sill and sat down there. Egan cleared chairs for Hallet, Chan and John Quincy, and himself took his place before an ancient roll-top desk.

"If you will be brief, Captain," he suggested, "I might still have time—" He glanced at a clock above the desk.

"Forget that," advised Hallet sharply. His manner was considerably different from that he employed in the house of a leading citizen like Dan Winterslip. "Let's get to business." He turned to Chan. "Got your book, Charlie?"

"Preparations are complete," replied Chan, his pencil poised.

"All right." Hallet drew his chair closer to the desk. "Now Egan, you come through and come clean. I know that last night about seven-thirty you called up Dan Winterslip and tried to slide out of an appointment you had made with him. I know that he refused to let you off, and insisted on seeing you at eleven. About that time, you went to his house. You and he had a rather excited talk. At one-twenty-five Winterslip was found dead. Murdered, Egan! Now give me your end of it."

Jim Egan ran his fingers through his curly, close-cropped hair—straw-colored once, but now mostly gray. "That's all quite true," he said. "Do—do you mind if I smoke?" He took out a silver case and removed a cigarette. His hand trembled slightly as he applied the match. "I did make an appointment with Winterslip for last night," he continued. "During the course of the day I—I changed my mind. When I called up to tell him so, he insisted on seeing me. He urged me to come at eleven, and I went."

"Who let you in?" Hallet asked.

"Winterslip was waiting in the garden when I came. We went inside—"

Hallet glanced at the cigarette in Egan's hand. "By the door leading directly into the living-room?" he asked.

"No," said Egan. "By the big door at the front of the house. Winterslip took me out on his lanai, and we had a bit of a chat regarding the—the business that had brought me. About half an hour later, I came away. When I left, Winterslip was alive and well—in good spirits, too. Smiling, as a matter of fact."

"By what door did you leave?"

"The front door—the one I'd entered by."

"I see." Hallet looked at him thoughtfully for a moment. "You went back later, perhaps."

"I did not," said Egan promptly. "I came directly here and went to bed."

"Who saw you?"

"No one. My clerk goes off duty at eleven. The hotel is open, but there is no one in charge. My patronage is—not large."

"You came here at eleven-thirty and went to bed," Hallet said. "But no one saw you. Tell me, were you well acquainted with Dan Winterslip?"

Egan shook his head. "In the twenty-three years I've been in Honolulu, I had never spoken to him until I called him on the telephone yesterday morning."

"Humph." Hallet leaned back in his chair and spoke in a more amiable tone. "As a younger man, I believe you traveled a lot?"

"I drifted about a bit," Egan admitted. "I was just eighteen when I left England—"

"At your family's suggestion," smiled the captain.

"What's that to you?" Egan flared.

"Where did you go?"

"Australia. I ranched it for a time—and later I worked in Melbourne."

"What doing?" persisted Hallet.

"In—in a bank."

"A bank, eh? And then—"

"The South Seas. Just—wandering about—I was restless—"

"Beach-combing, eh?"

Egan flushed. "I may have been on my uppers at times, but damn it—"

"Wait a minute," Hallet cut in. "What I want to know is—those years you were drifting about—did you by any chance run into Dan Winterslip?"

"I—I might have."

"What sort of an answer is that! Yes or no?"

"Well, as a matter of fact, I did," Egan admitted. "Just once—in Melbourne. But it was a quite unimportant meeting. So unimportant Winterslip had completely forgotten it."

"But you hadn't. And yesterday morning, after twenty-three years' silence between you, you called him on the telephone. On rather sudden business."

"I did."

Hallet came closer. "All right, Egan. We've reached the important part of your story. What was that business?"

A tense silence fell in the little office as they awaited Egan's answer. The Englishman looked Hallet calmly in the eye. "I can't tell you that," he said.

Hallet's face reddened. "Oh, yes, you can. And you're going to."

"Never," answered Egan, without raising his voice.

The captain glared at him. "You don't seem to realize your position."

"I realize it perfectly."

"If you and I were alone—"

"I won't tell you under any circumstances, Hallet."

"Maybe you'll tell the prosecutor—"

"Look here," cried Egan wearily. "Why must I say it over and over? I'll tell nobody my business with Winterslip. Nobody, understand?" He crushed the half-smoked cigarette savagely down on to a tray at his side.

John Quincy saw Hallet nod to Chan. He saw Chan's pudgy little hand go out and seize the remnant of cigarette. A happy grin spread over the Oriental's fat face. He handed the stub to his chief.

"Corsican brand!" he cried triumphantly.

"Ah, yes," said Hallet. "This your usual smoke?"

A startled look crossed Egan's tired face. "No, it's not," he said.

"It's a make that's not on sale in the Islands, I believe?"

"No, I fancy it isn't."

Captain Hallet held out his hand. "Give me your cigarette case, Egan." The Englishman passed it over, and Hallet opened it. "Humph," he said. "You've managed to get hold of a few, haven't you?"

"Yes. They were—given me."

"Is that so? Who gave them to you?"

Egan considered. "I'm afraid I can't tell you that, either," he said.

Hallet's eyes glittered angrily. "Let me give you a few facts," he began. "You called on Dan Winterslip last night, you entered and left by the front door, and you didn't go back. Yet just outside the door leading directly into the living-room, we have found a partly smoked cigarette of this unusual brand. Now will you tell me who gave you these Corsicans?"

"No," said Egan, "I won't."

Hallet slipped the silver cigarette case into his pocket, and stood up. "Very well," he remarked. "I've wasted all the time I intend to here. The district court prosecutor will want to talk to you—"

"Of course," agreed Egan, "I'll come and see him—this afternoon—"

Hallet glared at him. "Quit kidding yourself and get your hat!"

Egan rose too. "Look here," he cried, "I don't like your manner. It's true there are certain matters in connection with Winterslip that I can't discuss, and that's unfortunate. But surely you don't think I killed the man. What motive would I have—"

Jennison rose quickly from his seat on the window-ledge and stepped forward. "Hallet," he said, "there's something I ought to tell you. Two or three years ago Dan Winterslip and I were walking along King Street, and we passed Mr. Egan here. Winterslip nodded toward him. 'I'm afraid of that man, Harry,' he said. I waited to hear more, but he didn't go on, and he wasn't the sort of client one would prompt. 'I'm afraid of that man, Harry.' Just that, and nothing further."

"It's enough," remarked Hallet grimly. "Egan, you're going with me."

Egan's eyes flashed. "Of course," he cried bitterly. "Of course I'm going with you. You're all against me, the whole town is against me, I've been sneered at and belittled for twenty years. Because I was poor. An outcast, my daughter humiliated, not good enough to associate with these New England blue-bloods—these thin-lipped Puritans with a touch of sun—"

At sound of that familiar phrase, John Quincy sat up. Where, where—oh, yes, on the Oakland ferry—

"Never mind that," Hallet was saying. "I'll give you one last chance. Will you tell me what I want to know?"

"I will not," cried Egan.

"All right. Then come along."

"Am I under arrest?" asked Egan.

"I didn't say that," replied Hallet, suddenly cautious. "The investigation is young yet. You are withholding much needed information, and I believe that after you've spent a few hours at the station, you'll change your mind and talk. In fact, I'm sure of it. I haven't any warrant, but your position will be a lot more dignified if you come willingly without one."

Egan considered a moment. "I fancy you're right," he said. "I have certain orders to give the servants, if you don't mind—"

Hallet nodded. "Make it snappy. Charlie will go with you."

Egan and Chan disappeared. The captain, John Quincy and Jennison went out and sat down in the public room. Five minutes passed, ten, fifteen—

Jennison glanced at his watch. "See here, Hallet," he said. "The man's making a monkey of you—"

Hallet reddened, and stood up. At that instant Egan and Chan came down the big-open stairway at one side of the room. Hallet went up to the Englishman.

"Say, Egan—what are you doing? Playing for time?"

Egan smiled. "That's precisely what I'm doing," he replied. "My daughter's coming in this morning on the Matsonia—the boat ought to be at the dock now. She's been at school on the mainland, and I haven't seen her for nine months. You've done me out of the pleasure of meeting her, but in a few minutes—"

"Nothing doing," cried Hallet. "Now you get your hat. I'm pau."

Egan hesitated a moment, then slowly took his battered old straw hat from the desk. The five men walked through the blooming garden toward Hallet's car. As they emerged into the street, a taxi drew up to the curb. Egan ran forward, and the girl John Quincy had last seen at the gateway to San Francisco leaped out into the Englishman's arms.

"Dad—where were you?" she cried.

"Cary, darling," he said. "I was so frightfully sorry—I meant to be at the dock but I was detained. How are you, my dear?"

"I'm fine, dad—but—where are you going?" She looked at Hallet; John Quincy remained discreetly in the background.

"I've—I've a little business in the city, my dear," Egan said. "I'll be home presently, I fancy. If—if I shouldn't be, I leave you in charge."

"Why, dad—"

"Don't worry," he added pleadingly. "That's all I can say now, Cary. Don't worry, my dear." He turned to Hallet. "Shall we go, Captain?"

The two policemen, Jennison and Egan entered the car. John Quincy stepped forward. The girl's big perplexed eyes met his.

"You?" she cried.

"Coming, Mr. Winterslip?" inquired Hallet.

John Quincy smiled at the girl. "You were quite right," he said. "I haven't needed that hat."

She looked up at him. "But you're not wearing any at all. That's hardly wise—"

"Mr. Winterslip!" barked Hallet.

John Quincy turned. "Oh, pardon me, Captain," he said. "I forgot to mention it, but I'm leaving you here. Good-by."

Hallet grunted and started his car. While the girl paid for her taxi out of a tiny purse, John Quincy picked up her suit-case.

"This time," he said, "I insist on carrying it." They stepped through the gateway into the garden that might have been Eden on one of its better days. "You didn't tell me we might meet in Honolulu," the boy remarked.

"I wasn't sure we would." She glanced at the shabby old hotel. "You see, I'm not exactly a social favorite out here." John Quincy could think of no reply, and they mounted the crumbling steps. The public room was quite deserted. "And why have we met?" the girl continued. "I'm fearfully puzzled. What was dad's business with those men? One of them was Captain Hallet—a policeman—"

John Quincy frowned. "I'm not so sure your father wants you to know."

"But I've got to know, that's obvious. Please tell me."

John Quincy relinquished the suit-case, and brought forward a chair. The girl sat down.

"It's this way," he began. "My Cousin Dan was murdered in the night."

Her eyes were tragic. "Oh—poor Barbara!" she cried. That's right, he mustn't forget Barbara. "But dad—oh, go on please—"

"Your father visited Cousin Dan last night at eleven, and he refuses to say why. There are other things he refuses to tell."

She looked up at him, her eyes filled with sudden tears. "I was so happy on the boat," she said. "I knew it couldn't last."

He sat down. "Nonsense. Everything will come out all right. Your father is probably shielding some one—"

She nodded. "Of course. But if he's made up his mind not to talk, he just simply won't talk. He's odd that way. They may keep him down there, and I shall be all alone—"

"Not quite alone," John Quincy told her.

"No, no," she said. "I've warned you. We're not the sort the best people care to know—"

"The more fools they," cut in the boy. "I'm John Quincy Winterslip, of Boston. And you—"

"Carlota Maria Egan," she answered. "You see, my mother was half Portuguese. The other half was Scotch-Irish—my father's English. This is the melting pot out here, you know." She was silent for a moment. "My mother was very beautiful," she added wistfully. "So they tell me—I never knew."

John Quincy was touched. "I thought how beautiful she must have been," he said gently. "That day I met you on the ferry."

The girl dabbed at her eyes with an absurd little handkerchief, and stood up. "Well," she remarked, "this is just another thing that has to be faced. Another call for courage—I must meet it." She smiled. "The lady manager of the Reef and Palm. Can I show you a room?"

"I say, it'll be a rather stiff job, won't it?" John Quincy rose too.

"Oh, I shan't mind. I've helped dad before. Only one thing troubles me—bills and all that. I've no head for arithmetic."

"That's all right—I have," replied John Quincy. He stopped. Wasn't he getting in a little deep?

"How wonderful," the girl said.

"Why, not at all," John Quincy protested. "It's my line, at home." Home! Yes, he had a home, he recalled. "Bonds and interest and all that sort of thing. I'll drop in later in the day to see how you're getting on." He moved away in a mild panic. "I'd better be going now," he added.

"Of course." She followed him to the door. "You're altogether too kind. Shall you be in Honolulu long?"

"That depends," John Quincy said. "I've made up my mind to one thing. I shan't stir from here until this mystery about Cousin Dan is solved. And I'm going to do everything in my power to help in solving it."

"I'm sure you're very clever, too," she told him.

He shook his head. "I wouldn't say that. But I intend to make the effort of my life. I've got a lot of incentives for seeing this affair through." Something else trembled on his tongue. Better not say it. Oh, lord, he was saying it. "You're one of them," he added, and clattered down the stairs.

"Do be careful," called the girl. "Those steps are even worse than they were when I left. Just another thing to be repaired—some day—when our ship comes in."

He left her smiling wistfully in the doorway and hurrying through the garden, stepped out on Kalakaua Avenue. The blazing sun beat down on his defenseless head. Gorgeous trees flaunted scarlet banners along his path, tall cocoanut palms swayed above him at the touch of the friendly trades, not far away rainbow-tinted waters lapped a snowy beach. A sweet land—all of that.

Did he wish that Agatha Parker were there to see it with him? Pursuing the truth further, as Charlie Chan would put it, he did not.

X

A Newspaper Ripped in Anger

When John Quincy got back to the living-room he found Miss Minerva pacing up and down with the light of battle in her eyes. He selected a large, comfortable-looking chair and sank into it.

"Anything the matter?" he inquired. "You seem disturbed."

"I've just been having a lot of pilikia," she announced.

"What's that—another native drink?" he said with interest. "Could I have some too?"

"Pilikia means trouble," she translated. "Several reporters have been here, and you'd hardly credit the questions they asked."

"About Cousin Dan, eh?" John Quincy nodded. "I can imagine."

"However, they got nothing out of me. I took good care of that."

"Go easy," advised John Quincy. "A fellow back home who had a divorce case in his family was telling me that if you're not polite to the newspaper boys they just plain break your heart."

"Don't worry," said Miss Minerva. "I was diplomatic, of course. I think I handled them rather well, under the circumstances. They were the first reporters I'd ever met—though I've had the pleasure of talking with gentlemen from the Transcript. What happened at the Reef and Palm Hotel?"

John Quincy told her—in part.

"Well, I shouldn't be surprised if Egan turned out to be guilty," she commented. "I've made a few inquiries about him this morning, and he doesn't appear to amount to much. A sort of glorified beachcomber."

"Nonsense," objected John Quincy. "Egan's a gentleman. Just because he doesn't happen to have prospered is no reason for condemning him without a hearing."

"He's had a hearing," snapped Miss Minerva. "And it seems he's been mixed up in something he's not precisely proud of. There, I've gone and ended a sentence with a preposition. Probably all this has upset me more than I realize."

John Quincy smiled. "Cousin Dan," he reminded her, "was also mixed up in a few affairs he could hardly have looked back on with pride. No, Aunt Minerva, I feel Hallet is on the wrong trail there. It's just as Egan's daughter said—"

She glanced at him quickly. "Oh—so Egan has a daughter?"

"Yes, and a mighty attractive girl. It's a confounded shame to put this thing on her."

"Humph," said Miss Minerva.

John Quincy glanced at his watch. "Good lord—it's only ten o'clock!" A great calm had settled over the house, there was no sound save the soft lapping of waves on the beach outside. "What, in heaven's name, do you do out here?"

"Oh, you'll become accustomed to it shortly," Miss Minerva answered. "At first, you just sit and think. After a time, you just sit."

"Sounds fascinating," said John Quincy sarcastically.

"That's the odd part of it," his aunt replied, "it is. One of the things you think about, at first, is going home. When you stop thinking, that naturally slips your mind."

"We gathered that," John Quincy told her.

"You'll meet a man on the beach," said Miss Minerva, "who stopped over between boats to have his laundry done. That was twenty years ago, and he's still here."

"Probably they haven't finished his laundry," suggested John Quincy, yawning openly. "Ho, hum. I'm going up to my room to change, and after that I believe I'll write a few letters." He rose with an effort and went to the door. "How's Barbara?" he asked.

Miss Minerva shook her head. "Dan was all the poor child had," she said. "She's taken it rather hard. You won't see her for some time, and when you do—the least said about all this, the better."

"Why, naturally," agreed John Quincy, and went up-stairs.

After he had bathed and put on his whitest, thinnest clothes, he explored the desk that stood near his bed and found it well supplied with note paper. Languidly laying out a sheet, he began to write.

DEAR AGATHA
  Here I am in Honolulu and outside my window I can hear the lazy swish of waters lapping the famous beach of—

Lazy, indeed. John Quincy had a feeling for words. He stopped and stared at an agile little cloud flitting swiftly through the sky—got up from his chair to watch it disappear over Diamond Head. On his

             EARL DERR BIGGERS

way back to the desk he had to pass the bed. What inviting beds they had out here! He lifted the mosquito netting and dropped down for a moment—

Haku hammered on the door at one o'clock, and that was how John Quincy happened to be present at lunch. His aunt was already at the table when he staggered in.

"Cheer up," she smiled. "You'll become acclimated soon. Of course, even then you'll want your nap just after lunch every day."

"I will not," he answered, but there was no conviction in his tone.

"Barbara asked me to tell you how sorry she is not to be with you. She's a sweet girl, John Quincy."

"She's all of that. Give her my love, won't you?"

"Your love?" His aunt looked at him. "Do you mean that? Barbara's only a second cousin—"

He laughed. "Don't waste your time match-making, Aunt Minerva. Some one has already spoken for Barbara."

"Really? Who?"

"Jennison. He seems like a fine fellow, too."

"Handsome, at any rate," Miss Minerva admitted. They ate in silence for a time. "The coroner and his friends were here this morning," said Miss Minerva presently.

"That so?" replied John Quincy. "Any verdict?"

"Not yet. I believe they're to settle on that later. By the way, I'm going down-town immediately after lunch to do some shopping for Barbara. Care to come along?"

"No, thanks," John Quincy said. "I must go up-stairs and finish my letters."

But when he left the luncheon table, he decided the letters could wait. He took a heavy volume with a South Sea title from Dan's library, and went out on to the lanai. Presently Miss Minerva appeared, smartly dressed in white linen.

"I'll return as soon as I'm pau," she announced.

"What is this pau?" John Quincy inquired.

"Pau means finished—through."

"Good lord," John Quincy said. "Aren't there enough words in the English language for you?"

"Oh, I don't know," she answered, "a little Hawaiian sprinkled in makes a pleasant change. And when one reaches my age, John Quincy, one is eager for a change. Good-by."

She left him to his book and the somnolent atmosphere of Dan's lanai. Sometimes he read, colorful tales of other islands farther south. Sometimes he sat and thought. Sometimes he just sat. The blazing afternoon wore on; presently the beach beyond Dan's garden was gay with bathers, sunburned men and girls, pretty girls in brief and alluring costumes. Their cries as they dared the surf were exultant, happy. John Quincy was keen to try these notable waters, but it didn't seem quite the thing—not just yet, with Dan Winterslip lying in that room upstairs.

Miss Minerva reappeared about five, flushed and—though she well knew it was not the thing for one of her standing in the Back Bay—perspiring. She carried an evening paper in her hand.

"Any news?" inquired John Quincy.

She sat down. "Nothing but the coroner's verdict. The usual thing—person or persons unknown. But as I was reading the paper in the car, I had a sudden inspiration."

"Good for you. What was it?"

Haku appeared at the door leading to the living-room. "You ring, miss?" he said.

"I did. Haku, what becomes of the old newspapers in this house?"

"Take and put in a closet beside kitchen," the man told her.

"See if you can find me—no, never mind. I'll look myself."

She followed Haku into the living-room. In a few minutes she returned alone, a newspaper in her hand.

"I have it," she announced triumphantly. "The evening paper of Monday, June sixteenth—the one Dan was reading the night he wrote that letter to Roger. And look, John Quincy—one corner has been torn from the shipping page!"

"Might have been accidental," suggested John Quincy languidly.

"Nonsense!" she said sharply. "It's a clue, that's what it is. The item that disturbed Dan was on that missing corner of the page."

"Might have been, at that," he admitted. "What are you going to do—"

"You're the one that's going to do it," she cut in. "Pull yourself together and go into town. It's two hours until dinner. Give this paper to Captain Hallet—or better still, to Charlie Chan. I am impressed by Mr. Chan's intelligence."

John Quincy laughed. "Damned clever, these Chinese!" he quoted. "You don't mean to say you've fallen for that bunk. They seem clever because they're so different."

"We'll see about that. The chauffeur's gone on an errand for Barbara, but there's a roadster in the garage—"

"Trolley's good enough for me," said John Quincy. "Here, give me the paper."

She explained to him how he was to reach the city, and he got his hat and went. Presently he was on a trolley-car surrounded by representatives of a dozen different races. The melting pot of the Pacific, Carlota Egan had called Honolulu, and the appellation seemed to be correct. John Quincy began to feel a fresh energy, a new interest in life.

The trolley swept over the low swampy land between Waikiki and Honolulu, past rice fields where bent figures toiled patiently in water to their knees, past taro patches, and finally turned on to King Street. Every few moments it paused to take aboard immigrants, Japanese, Chinese, Hawaiians, Portuguese, Philippinos, Koreans, all colors and all creeds. On it went. John Quincy saw great houses set in blooming groves, a Japanese theater flaunting weird posters not far from a Ford service station, then a huge building he recognized as the palace of the monarchy. Finally it entered a district of modern office buildings.

Mr. Kipling was wrong, the boy reflected, East and West could meet. They had.

This impression was confirmed when he left the car at Fort Street and for a moment walked about, a stranger in a strange land. A dusky policeman was directing traffic on the corner, officers of the United States army and navy in spotless duck strolled by, and on the shady side of the street Chinese girls, slim and immaculate in freshly laundered trousers and jackets, were window shopping in the cool of the evening.

"I'm looking for the police station," John Quincy informed a big American with a friendly face.

"Get back on to King Street," the man said. "Go to your right until you come to Bethel, then turn makai—"

"Turn what?"

The man smiled. "A malihini, I take it. Makai means toward the sea. The other direction is mauka—toward the mountains. The police station is at the foot of Bethel, in Kalakaua Hale."

John Quincy thanked him and went on his way. He passed the post-office and was amazed to see that all the lock boxes opened on the street. After a time, he reached the station. A sergeant lounging behind the desk told him that Charlie Chan was at dinner. He suggested the

Alexander Young Hotel or possibly the All American Restaurant on King Street.

The hotel sounded easiest, so John Quincy went there first. In the dim lobby a Chinese house boy wandered aimlessly about with broom and dust pan, a few guests were writing the inevitable post-cards, a Chinese clerk was on duty at the desk. But there was no sign of Chan, either in the lobby or in the dining-room at the left. As John Quincy turned from an inspection of the latter, the elevator door opened and a Britisher in mufti came hurriedly forth. He was followed by a Cockney servant carrying luggage.

"Captain Cope," called John Quincy.

The captain paused. "Hello," he said. "Oh—Mr. Winterslip—how are you?" He turned to the servant. "Buy me an evening paper and an armful of the less offensive-looking magazines." The man hurried off, and Cope again addressed John Quincy. "Delighted to see you, but I'm in a frightful rush. Off to the Fanning Islands in twenty minutes."

"When did you get in?" inquired John Quincy. Not that he really cared.

"Yesterday at noon," said Captain Cope. "Been on the wing ever since. I trust you are enjoying your stop here—but I was forgetting. Fearful news about Dan Winterslip."

"Yes," said John Quincy coolly. Judging by the conversation in that San Francisco club, the blow had not been a severe one for Captain Cope. The servant returned.

"Sorry to run," continued the captain. "But I must be off. The service is a stern taskmaster. My regards to your aunt. Best of luck, my boy."

He disappeared through the wide door, followed by his man. John Quincy reached the street in time to see him rolling off in a big car toward the docks.

Noting the cable office near by, the boy entered and sent two messages, one to his mother and the other to Agatha Parker. He addressed them to Boston, Mass. U.S.A., and was accorded a withering look by the young woman in charge as she crossed out the last three letters. There were only two words in each message, but he returned to the street with the comfortable feeling that his correspondence was now attended to for some time to come.

A few moments later he encountered the All American Restaurant and going inside, found himself the only American in the place. Charlie

Chan was seated alone at a table, and as John Quincy approached, he rose and bowed.

"A very great honor," said Chan. "Is it possible that I can prevail upon you to accept some of this terrible provision?"

"No, thanks," answered John Quincy. "I'm to dine later at the house. I'll sit down for a moment, if I may."

"Quite overwhelmed," bobbed Charlie. He resumed his seat and scowled at something on the plate before him. "Waiter," he said. "Be kind enough to summon the proprietor of this establishment."

The proprietor, a suave little Japanese man, came gliding. He bowed from the waist.

"Is it that you serve here insanitary food?" inquired Chan.

"Please deign to state your complaint," said the Jap.

"This piece of pie is covered with finger-marks," rebuked Chan. "The sight is most disgusting. Kindly remove it and bring me a more hygienic sector."

The Japanese man picked up the offending pastry and carried it away.

"Japanese," remarked Chan, spreading his hands in an eloquent gesture. "Is it proper for me to infer that you come on business connected with the homicide?"

John Quincy smiled. "I do," he said. He took the newspaper from his pocket, pointed out the date and the missing corner. "My aunt felt it might be important," he explained.

"The woman has a brain," said Chan. "I will procure an unmutilated specimen of this issue and compare. The import may be vast."

"You know," remarked John Quincy, "I'd like to work with you on this case, if you'll let me."

"I have only delight," Chan answered. "You arrive from Boston, a city most cultivated, where much more English words are put to employment than are accustomed here. I thrill when you speak. Greatest privilege for me, I would say."

"Have you formed any theory about the crime?" John Quincy asked.

Chan shook his head. "Too early now."

"You have no finger-prints to go on, you said."

Chan shrugged his shoulders. "Does not matter. Finger-prints and other mechanics good in books, in real life not so much so. My experience tell me to think deep about human people. Human passions. Back of murder what, always? Hate, revenge, need to make silent the slain one. Greed for money, maybe. Study human people at all times."

"Sounds reasonable," admitted John Quincy.

"Mostly so," Chan averred. "Enumerate with me the clues we must consider. A guest book devoid of one page. A glove button. A message on the cable. Story of Egan, partly told. Fragment of Corsican cigarette. This newspaper ripped maybe in anger. Watch on living wrist, numeral 2 undistinct."

"Quite a little collection," commented John Quincy.

"Most interesting," admitted Chan. "One by one, we explore. Some cause us to arrive at nowhere. One, maybe two, will not be so unkind. I am believer in Scotland Yard method—follow only essential clue. But it are not the method here. I must follow all, entire."

"The essential clue," repeated John Quincy.

"Sure." Chan scowled at the waiter, for his more hygienic sector had not appeared. "Too early to say here. But I have fondness for the guest book with page omitted. Watch also claims my attention. Odd enough, when we enumerate clues this morning, we pass over watch. Foolish. Very good-looking clue. One large fault, we do not possess it. However, my eyes are sharp to apprehend it."

"I understand," John Quincy said, "that you've been rather successful as a detective."

Chan grinned broadly. "You are educated, maybe you know," he said. "Chinese most psychic people in the world. Sensitives, like film in camera. A look, a laugh, a gesture perhaps. Something go click."

John Quincy was aware of a sudden disturbance at the door of the All American Restaurant. Bowker, the steward, gloriously drunk, was making a noisy entrance. He plunged into the room, followed by a dark, anxious-looking youth.

Embarrassed, John Quincy turned away his face, but to no avail. Bowker was bearing down upon him, waving his arms.

"Well, well, well, well!" he bellowed. "My o' college chum. See you through the window." He leaned heavily on the table. "How you been, o' fellow?"

"I'm all right, thanks," John Quincy said.

The dark young man came up. He was, from his dress, a shore acquaintance of Bowker's. "Look here, Ted," he said. "You've got to be getting along—"

"Jush a minute," cried Bowker. "I want y' to meet Mr. Quincy from Boston. One best fellows God ever made. Mushual friend o' Tim's— you've heard me speak of Tim—"

"Yes—come along," urged the dark young man.

"Not yet. Gotta buy shish boy a lil' drink. What you having, Quincy, o' man?"

"Not a thing," smiled John Quincy. "You warned me against these Island drinks yourself."

"Who—me?" Bowker was hurt. "You're wrong that time, o' man. Don' like to conter—conterdict, but it mush have been somebody else. Not me. Never said a word—"

The young man took his arm. "Come on—you're due on the ship—"

Bowker wrenched away. "Don' paw me," he cried. "Keep your hands off. I'm my own mashter, ain't I? I can speak to an o' friend, can't I? Now, Quincy, o' man—what's yours?"

"I'm sorry," said John Quincy. "Some other time."

Bowker's companion took his arm in a firmer grasp. "You can't buy anything here," he said. "This is a restaurant. You come with me—I know a place—"

"Awright," agreed Bowker. "Now you're talking. Quincy, o' man, you come along—"

"Some other time," John Quincy repeated.

Bowker assumed a look of offended dignity. "Jush as you say," he replied. "Some other time. In Boston, hey? At Tim's place. Only Tim's place is gone." A great grief assailed him. "Tim's gone—dropped out—as though the earth swallowed him up—"

"Yes, yes," said the young man soothingly. "That's too bad. But you come with me."

Submitting at last, Bowker permitted his companion to pilot him to the street. John Quincy looked across at Chan.

"My steward on the PRESIDENT TYLER," he explained. "The worse for wear, isn't he?"

The waiter set a fresh piece of pie before the Chinaman.

"Ah," remarked Chan, "this has a more perfect appearance." He tasted it. "Appearance," he added with a grimace, "are a hellish liar. If you are quite ready to depart—"

In the street Chan halted. "Excuse abrupt departure," he said. "Most honored to work with you. The results will be fascinating, I am sure. For now, good evening."

John Quincy was alone again in that strange town. A sudden homesickness engulfed him. Walking along, he came to a news-cart that was as well supplied with literature as his club reading room. A brisk young man in a cap was in charge.

"Have you the latest Atlantic?" inquired John Quincy.

The young man put a dark brown periodical into his hand. "No," said John Quincy. "This is the June issue. I've seen it."

"July ain't in. I'll save you one, if you say so."

"I wish you would," John Quincy replied. "The name is Winterslip."

He went on to the corner, regretting that July wasn't in. A copy of the Atlantic would have been a sort of link with home, a reminder that Boston still stood. And he felt the need of a link, a reminder.

A trolley-car marked "Waikiki" was approaching. John Quincy hailed it and hopped aboard. Three giggling Japanese girls in bright kimonos drew in their tiny sandaled feet and he slipped past them to a seat.

XI

The Tree of Jewels

Two Hours later, John Quincy rose from the table where he and his aunt had dined together.

"Just to show you how quick I am to learn a new language," he remarked, "I'm quite pau. Now I'm going makai to sit on the lanai, there to forget the pilikia of the day."

Miss Minerva smiled and rose too. "I expect Amos shortly," she said as they crossed the hall. "A family conference seemed advisable, so I've asked him to come over."

"Strange you had to send for him," said John Quincy, lighting a cigarette.

"Not at all," she answered. She explained about the long feud between the brothers.

"Didn't think old Amos had that much fire in him," commented John Quincy, as they found chairs on the lanai. "A rather anemic specimen, judging by the look I had at him this morning. But then, the Winterslips always were good haters."

For a moment they sat in silence. Outside the darkness was deepening rapidly, the tropic darkness that had brought tragedy the night before. John Quincy pointed to a small lizard on the screen.

"Pleasant little beast," he said.

"Oh, they're quite harmless," Miss Minerva told him. "And they eat the mosquitos."

"They do, eh?" The boy slapped his ankle savagely. "Well, there's no accounting for tastes."

Amos arrived presently, looking unusually pale in the half-light. "You asked me to come over, Minerva," he said, as he sat down gingerly on one of Dan Winterslip's Hong-Kong chairs.

"I did. Smoke if you like." Amos lighted a cigarette, which seemed oddly out of place between his thin lips. "I'm sure," Miss Minerva continued, "that we are all determined to bring to justice the person who did this ghastly thing."

"Naturally," said Amos.

"The only drawback," she went on, "is that in the course of the investigation some rather unpleasant facts about Dan's past are likely to be revealed."

"They're bound to be," remarked Amos coldly.

"For Barbara's sake," Miss Minerva said, "I'm intent on seeing that nothing is revealed that is not absolutely essential to the discovery of the murderer. For that reason, I haven't taken the police completely into my confidence."

"What!" cried Amos.

John Quincy stood up. "Now look here, Aunt Minerva—"

"Sit down," snapped his aunt. "Amos, to go back to a talk we had at your house when I was there, Dan was somewhat involved with this woman down the beach. Arlene Compton, I believe she calls herself."

Amos nodded. "Yes, and a worthless lot she is. But Dan wouldn't see it, though I understand his friends pointed it out to him. He talked of marrying her."

"You knew a good deal about Dan, even if you never spoke to him," Miss Minerva went on. "Just what was his status with this woman at the time of his murder—only last night, but it seems ages ago."

"I can't quite tell you that," Amos replied. "I do know that for the past month a malihini named Leatherbee—the black sheep of a good family in Philadelphia, they tell me—has been hanging around the Compton woman, and that Dan resented his presence."

"Humph." Miss Minerva handed to Amos an odd old brooch, a tree of jewels against an onyx background. "Ever see that before, Amos?"

He took it, and nodded. "It's part of a little collection of jewelry Dan brought back from the South Seas in the 'eighties. There were ear-rings and a bracelet, too. He acted rather queerly about those trinkets—never let Barbara's mother or any one else wear them. But he must have got over that idea recently. For I saw this only a few weeks ago."

"Where?" asked Miss Minerva.

"Our office has the renting of the cottage down the beach occupied at present by the Compton woman. She came in not long ago to pay her rent, and she was wearing this brooch." He looked suddenly at Miss Minerva. "Where did you get it?" he demanded.

"Kamaikui gave it to me early this morning," Miss Minerva explained. "She picked it up from the floor of the lanai before the police came."

John Quincy leaped to his feet. "You're all wrong, Aunt Minerva," he cried. "You can't do this sort of thing. You ask the help of the police, and you aren't on the level with them. I'm ashamed of you—"

"Please wait a moment," said his aunt.

"Wait nothing!" he answered. "Give me that brooch. I'm going to turn it over to Chan at once. I couldn't look him in the eye if I didn't."

"We'll turn it over to Chan," said Miss Minerva calmly, "if it seems important. But there is no reason in the world why we should not investigate a bit ourselves before we do so. The woman may have a perfectly logical explanation—"

"Rot!" interrupted John Quincy. "The trouble with you is, you think you're Sherlock Holmes."

"What is your opinion, Amos?" inquired Miss Minerva.

"I'm inclined to agree with John Quincy," Amos said. "You are hardly fair to Captain Hallet. And as for keeping anything dark on account of Barbara—or on anybody's account—that won't be possible, I'm afraid. No getting round it, Minerva, Dan's indiscretions are going to be dragged into the open at last."

She caught the note of satisfaction in his tone, and was nettled by it. "Perhaps. At the same time, it isn't going to do any harm for some member of the family to have a talk with this woman before we consult the police. If she should have a perfectly sincere and genuine explanation—"

"Oh, yes," cut in John Quincy. "She wouldn't have any other kind."

"It won't be so much what she says," persisted Miss Minerva. "It will be in the manner in which she says it. Any intelligent person can see through deceit and falsehood. The only question is, which of us is the intelligent person best fitted to examine her."

"Count me out," said Amos promptly.

"John Quincy?"

The boy considered. He had asked for the privilege of working with Chan, and here, perhaps, was an opportunity to win his respect. But this sounded rather like a woman who would be too much for him.

"No, thanks," he said.

"Very good," replied Miss Minerva, rising. "I'll go myself."

"Oh, no," cried John Quincy, shocked.

"Why not? If none of the men in the family are up to it. As a matter of fact, I welcome the opportunity—"

Amos shook his head. "She'll twist you round her little finger," he predicted.

Miss Minerva smiled grimly. "I should like to see her do it. Will you wait here?"

John Quincy went over and took the brooch from Amos's hand. "Sit down, Aunt Minerva," he said. "I'll see this woman. But I warn you that immediately afterward I shall send for Chan."

"That," his aunt told him, "will be decided at another conference. I'm not so sure, John Quincy, that you are the proper person to go. After all, what experience have you had with women of this type?"

John Quincy was offended. He was a man, and he felt that he could meet and outwit a woman of any type. He said as much.

Amos described the woman's house as a small cottage several hundred yards down the beach, and directed the boy how to get there. John Quincy set out.

Night had fallen over the Island when he reached Kalia Road, a bright silvery night, for the Kona weather was over and the moon traveled a cloudless sky. The scent of plumeria and ginger stole out to him through hedges of flaming hibiscus; the trade winds, blowing across a thousand miles of warm water, still managed a cool touch on his cheek. As he approached what he judged must be the neighborhood of the woman's house, a flock of Indian myna birds in a spreading algaroba screamed loudly, their harsh voices the only note of discord in that peaceful scene.

He had some difficulty locating the cottage, which was almost completely hidden under masses of flowering alamander, its blossoms pale yellow in the moonlight. Before the door, a dark fragrant spot under a heavily laden trellis, he paused uncertainly. A rather delicate errand, this was. But he summoned his courage and knocked.

Only the myna birds replied. John Quincy stood there, growing momentarily more hostile to the Widow of Waikiki. Some huge coarse creature, no doubt, a man's woman, a good fellow at a party—that kind. Then the door opened and the boy got a shock. For the figure outlined against the light was young and slender, and the face, dimly seen, suggested fragile loveliness.

"Is this Mrs. Compton?" he inquired.

"Yeah—I'm Mrs. Compton. What do you want?" John Quincy was sorry she had spoken. For she was, obviously, one of those beauties so prevalent nowadays, the sort whom speech betrays. Her voice recalled the myna birds.

"My name is John Quincy Winterslip." He saw her start. "May I speak with you for a moment?"

"Sure you can. Come in." She led the way along a low narrow passage into a tiny living-room. A pasty-faced young man with stooped shoulders stood by a table, fondling a cocktail shaker.

"Steve," said the woman, "this is Mr. Winterslip. Mr. Leatherbee."

Mr. Leatherbee grunted. "Just in time for a little snifter," he remarked.

"No, thanks," John Quincy said. He saw Mrs. Compton take a smoking cigarette from an ash tray, start to convey it to her lips, then, evidently thinking better of it, crush it on the tray.

"Well," said Mr. Leatherbee, "your poison's ready, Arlene." He proffered a glass.

She shook her head, slightly annoyed. "No."

"No?" Mr. Leatherbee grinned. "The more for little Stevie." He lifted a glass. "Here's looking at you, Mr. Winterslip."

"Say, I guess you're Dan's cousin from Boston," Mrs. Compton remarked. "He was telling me about you." She lowered her voice. "I've been meaning to get over to your place all day. But it was such a shock— it knocked me flat."

"I understand," John Quincy replied. He glanced at Mr. Leatherbee, who seemed not to have heard of prohibition. "My business with you, Mrs. Compton, is private."

Leatherbee stiffened belligerently. But the woman said: "That's all right. Steve was just going."

Steve hesitated a moment, then went. His hostess accompanied him. John Quincy heard the low monotone of their voices in the distance. There was a combined odor of gin and cheap perfume in the air; the boy wondered what his mother would say if she could see him now. A door slammed, and the woman returned.

"Well?" she said. John Quincy perceived that her eyes were hard and knowing, like her voice. He waited for her to sit down, then took a chair facing her.

"You knew my Cousin Dan rather intimately," he suggested.

"I was engaged to him," she answered. John Quincy glanced at her left hand. "He hadn't come across—I mean, he hadn't given me a ring, but it was—you know—understood between us."

"Then his death is a good deal of a blow to you?"

She managed a baby stare, full of pathos. "I'll say it is. Mr. Winterslip was kind to me—he believed in me and trusted me. A lone woman way out here don't get any too much char—kindness."

"When did you see Mr. Winterslip last?"

"Three or four days ago—last Friday evening, I guess it was."

John Quincy frowned. "Wasn't that rather a long stretch?"

She nodded. "I'll tell you the truth. We had a little—misunderstanding. Just a lover's quarrel, you know. Dan sort of objected to Steve hanging around. Not that he'd any reason to—Steve's nothing to me—just a weak kid I used to know when I was trouping. I was on the stage— maybe you heard that."

"Yes," said John Quincy. "You hadn't seen Mr. Winterslip since last Friday. You didn't go to his house last evening?"

"I should say not. I got my reputation to think of—you've no idea how people talk in a place like this—"

John Quincy laid the brooch down upon the table. It sparkled in the lamplight—a reading lamp, though the atmosphere was not in the least literary. The baby stare was startled now. "You recognize that, don't you?" he asked.

"Why—yes—it's—I—"

"Just stick to the truth," said John Quincy, not unkindly. "It's an old piece of jewelry that Mr. Winterslip gave you, I believe."

"Well—"

"You've been seen wearing it, you know."

"Yes, he did give it to me," she admitted. "The only present I ever got from him. I guess from the look of it Mrs. Noah wore it on the Ark. Kinda pretty, though."

"You didn't visit Mr. Winterslip last night," persisted John Quincy. "Yet, strangely enough, this brooch was found on the floor not far from his dead body."

She drew in her breath sharply. "Say—what are you? A cop?" she asked.

"Hardly," John Quincy smiled. "I am here simply to save you, if possible, from the hands of the—er—the cops. If you have any real explanation of this matter, it may not be necessary to call it to the attention of the police."

"Oh!" She smiled. "Say, that's decent of you. Now I will tell you the truth. That about not seeing Dan Winterslip since Friday was bunk. I saw him last night."

"Ah—you did? Where?"

"Right here. Mr. Winterslip gave me that thing about a month ago. Two weeks ago he came to me in a sort of excited way and said he must have it back. It was the only thing he ever give me and I liked it and those emeralds are valuable—so—well, I stalled a while. I said I was having a new clasp put on it. He kept asking for it, and last night he showed up here and said he just had to have it. Said he'd buy me anything in the stores in place of it. I must say he was pretty het up. So I finally turned it over to him and he took it and went away."

"What time was that?"

"About nine-thirty. He was happy and pleasant and he said I could go to a jewelry store this morning and take my pick of the stock." She looked pleadingly at John Quincy. "That's the last I ever saw of him. It's the truth, so help me."

"I wonder," mused John Quincy.

She moved nearer. "Say, you're a nice kid," she said. "The kind I used to meet in Boston when we played there. The kind that's got some consideration for a woman. You ain't going to drag me into this. Think what it would mean—to me."

John Quincy did not speak. He saw there were tears in her eyes. "You've probably heard things about me," she went on, "but they ain't true. You don't know what I been up against out here. An unprotected woman don't have much chance anywhere, but on this beach, where men come drifting in from all over the world—I been friendly, that's my only trouble. I was homesick—oh, God, wasn't I homesick! I was having a good time back there, and then I fell for Bill Compton and came out here with him, and sometimes in the night I'd wake up and remember Broadway was five thousand miles away, and I'd cry so hard I'd wake him. And that made him sore—"

She paused. John Quincy was impressed by the note of true nostalgia in her voice. He was, suddenly, rather sorry for her.

"Then Bill's plane crashed on Diamond Head," she continued, "and I was all alone. And these black sheep along the beach, they knew I was alone—and broke. And I was homesick for Forty-second Street, for the old boardinghouse and the old gang and the Automat and the chewing-gum sign, and try-outs at New Haven. So I gave a few parties just to forget, and people began to talk."

"You might have gone back," John Quincy suggested.

"I know—why didn't I? I been intending to, right along, but every day out here is just like any other day, and somehow you don't get round to picking one out—I been drifting—but honest to God if you keep me out of this I'll go home on the first boat. I'll get me a job, and—and—If you'll only keep me out of it. You got a chance now to wreck my life—it's all up to you—but I know you ain't going to—"

She seized John Quincy's hand in both of hers, and gazed at him pleadingly through her tears. It was the most uncomfortable moment of his life. He looked wildly about the little room, so different from any in the house on Beacon Street. He pulled his hand away.

"I'll—I'll see," he said, rising hastily. "I'll think it over."

"But I can't sleep to-night if I don't know," she told him.

"I'll have to think it over," he repeated. He turned toward the table in time to see the woman's slim hand reach out and seize the bit of jewelry. "I'll take the brooch," he added.

She looked up at him. Suddenly John Quincy knew that she had been acting, that his emotions had been falsely played upon, and he felt again that hot rush of blood to the head, that quick surge of anger, he had experienced in Dan Winterslip's hall. Aunt Minerva had predicted he couldn't handle a woman of this type. Well, he'd show her—he'd show the world. "Give me that brooch," he said coldly.

"It's mine," answered the woman stubbornly.

John Quincy wasted no words; he seized the woman's wrist. She screamed. A door opened behind them.

"What's going on here?" inquired Mr. Leatherbee.

"Oh, I thought you'd left us," said John Quincy.

"Steve! Don't let him have it," cried the woman. Steve moved militantly nearer, but there was a trace of caution in his attitude.

John Quincy laughed. "You stay where you are, Steve," he advised. "Or I'll smash that sallow face of yours." Strange talk for a Winterslip. "Your friend here is trying to hang on to an important bit of evidence in the murder up the beach, and with the utmost reluctance I am forced to use strong-arm methods." The brooch dropped to the floor, he stooped and picked it up. "Well, I guess that's about all," he added. "I'm sorry if you've been homesick, Mrs. Compton, but speaking as a Bostonian, I don't believe Broadway is as glamourous as you picture it. Distance has lent enchantment. Good night."

He let himself out, and found his way to Kalakaua Avenue. He had settled one thing to his own satisfaction; Chan must know about the brooch, and at once. Mrs. Compton's story might be true or not, it certainly needed further investigation by some responsible person.

John Quincy had approached the cottage by way of Kalia Road; he was planning to return to Dan's house along the better lighted avenue.

Having reached that broad expanse of asphalt, however, he realized that the Reef and Palm Hotel was near at hand. There was his promise to Carlota Egan—he had said he would look in on her again to-day. As for Chan, he could telephone him from the hotel. He turned in the direction of the Reef and Palm.

Stumbling through the dark garden, he saw finally the gaunt old hulk of the hotel. Lights of low candle power burned at infrequent intervals on the double-decked veranda. In the huge lobby a few rather shabby-looking guests took their ease. Behind the desk stood—nobody but the Japanese clerk.

John Quincy was directed to a telephone booth, and his keen Bostonian mind required Nipponese aid in mastering the dial system favored by the Honolulu telephone company. At length he got the police station. Chan was out, but the answering voice promised that he would be told to get in touch with Mr. Winterslip immediately on his return.

"How much do I owe you?" inquired John Quincy of the clerk.

"Not a penny," said a voice, and he turned to find Carlota Egan at his elbow. He smiled. This was more like it.

"But I say—you know—I've used your telephone—"

"It's free," she said. "Too many things are free out here. That's why we don't get rich. It was so kind of you to come again."

"Not at all," he protested. He looked about the room. "Your father—"

She glanced at the clerk, and led the way out to the lanai at the side. They went to the far end of it, where they could see the light on Diamond Head, and the silvery waters of the Pacific sweeping in to disappear at last beneath the old Reef and Palm.

"I'm afraid poor dad's having a bad time of it," she said, and her voice broke slightly. "I haven't been able to see him. They're holding him down there—as a witness, I believe. There was some talk of bail, but I didn't listen. We haven't any money—at least, I didn't think we had."

"You didn't think—" he began, puzzled.

She produced a small bit of paper, and put it in his hand. "I want to ask your advice. I've been cleaning up dad's office, and just before you came I ran across that in his desk."

John Quincy stared down at the little pink slip she had given him. By the light of one of the small lamps he saw that it was a check for five thousand dollars, made out to "Bearer" and signed by Dan Winterslip. The date was that of the day before.

"I say, that looks important, doesn't it?" John Quincy said. He handed it back to her, and thought a moment. "By gad—it is important. It seems to me it's pretty conclusive evidence of your father's innocence. If he had that, his business with Cousin Dan must have come to a successful end, and it isn't likely he would—er—do away with the man who signed it and complicate the cashing of it."

The girl's eyes shone. "Just the way I reasoned. But I don't know what to do with it."

"Your father has engaged a lawyer, of course."

"Yes, but a rather poor one. The only kind we can afford. Should I turn this over to him?"

"No—wait a minute. Any chance of seeing your father soon?"

"Yes. It's been arranged I'm to visit him in the morning."

John Quincy nodded. "Better talk with him before you do anything," he advised. He had a sudden recollection of Egan's face when he refused to explain his business with Dan Winterslip. "Take this check with you and ask your father what he wants done with it. Point out to him that it's vital evidence in his favor."

"Yes, I guess that's the best plan," the girl agreed. "Will—will you sit down a moment?"

"Well." John Quincy recalled Miss Minerva waiting impatiently for news. "Just a moment. I want to know how you're getting on. Any big arithmetical problems come up yet?"

She shook her head. "Not yet. It really isn't so bad, the work. We haven't many guests, you know. I could be quite happy—if it weren't for poor dad." She sighed. "Ever since I can remember," she added, "my happiness has had an if in it."

He led her on to speak about herself, there in the calm night by that romantic beach. Through her talk flashed little pictures of her motherless childhood on this exotic shore, of a wearing fight against poverty and her father's bitter struggle to send her to school on the mainland, to give her what he considered her proper place in the world. Here was a girl far different from any he had met on Beacon Street, and John Quincy found pleasure in her talk.

Finally he forced himself to leave. As they walked along the balcony they encountered one of the guests, a meek little man with stooped shoulders. Even at that late hour he wore a bathing suit.

"Any luck, Mr. Saladine?" the girl inquired.

"Luck ith againth me," he lisped, and passed hastily on.

Carlota Egan laughed softly. "Oh, I really shouldn't," she repented at once. "The poor man."

"What's his trouble?" asked John Quincy.

"He's a tourist—a business man," she said. "Des Moines, or some place like that. And he's had the most appalling accident. He's lost his teeth."

"His teeth!" repeated John Quincy.

"Yes. Like so many things in this world, they were false. He got into a battle with a roller out by the second raft, and they disappeared. Since then he spends all his time out there, peering down into the water by day, and diving down and feeling about by night. One of the tragic figures of history," she added.

John Quincy laughed.

"That's the most tragic part of it," the girl continued. "He's the joke of the beach. But he goes on hunting, so serious. Of course, it is serious for him."

They passed through the public room to the front door. Mr. Saladine's tragedy slipped at once from John Quincy's mind.

"Good night," he said. "Don't forget about the check, when you see your father to-morrow. I'll look in on you during the day."

"It was so good of you to come," she said. Her hand was in his. "It has helped me along—tremendously."

"Don't you worry. Happy days are not far off. Happy days without an if. Hold the thought!"

"I'll hold it," she promised.

"We'll both hold it." It came to him that he was also holding her hand. He dropped it hastily. "Good night," he repeated, and fled through the garden.

In the living-room of Dan's house he was surprised to find Miss Minerva and Charlie Chan sitting together, solemnly staring at each other. Chan rose hurriedly at his entrance.

"Hello," said John Quincy. "I see you have a caller."

"Where in the world have you been?" snapped Miss Minerva. Evidently entertaining Chan had got a bit on her nerves.

"Well—I—" John Quincy hesitated.

"Speak out," said Miss Minerva. "Mr. Chan knows everything."

"Most flattering," grinned Chan. "Some things are not entirely well known to me. But about your call on Widow of Waikiki I learn soon after door receives you."

"The devil you did," said John Quincy.

"Simple enough," Chan went on. "Study human people, as I relate to you. Compton lady was friend to Mr. Dan Winterslip. Mr. Leatherbee rival friend. Enter jealous feelings. Since morning both of these people are under watchful regard of Honolulu police. Into the scene, you walk. I am notified and fly to beach."

"Ah—does he also know—" began John Quincy.

"About the brooch?" finished Miss Minerva. "Yes—I've confessed everything. And he's been kind enough to forgive me."

"But not nice thing to do," added Chan. "Humbly begging pardon to mention it. All cards should repose on table when police are called upon."

"Yes," said Miss Minerva, "he forgave me, but I have been gently chided. I have been made to feel, as he puts it, most naughty."

"So sorry," bowed Chan.

"Well, as a matter of fact," said John Quincy, "I was going to tell Mr. Chan the whole story at once." He turned to him. "I've already tried to reach you by telephone at the station. When I left the woman's cottage—"

"Police affairs forbid utmost courtesy," interrupted Chan. "I cut in to remark from the beginning, if you will please do so."

"Oh, yes," smiled John Quincy. "Well, the woman herself let me in, and showed me into her little living-room. When I got there this fellow Leatherbee was mixing cocktails by the table—"

Haku appeared at the door. "Mr. Charlie Chan wanted by telephone," he announced.

Chan apologized and hastened out.

"I intend to tell everything," John Quincy warned his aunt.

"I shan't interfere," she answered. "He has been sitting here looking at me more in sorrow than in anger for the better part of an hour, and I've made up my mind to one thing. I shall have no more secrets from the police."

Chan reentered the room. "As I was saying," John Quincy began, "this fellow Leatherbee was standing by the table, and—"

"Most sorry," said Chan, "but the remainder of that interesting recital is to be told at the station-house."

"At the station-house!" cried John Quincy.

"Precisely the fact. I am presuming you do me the great honor to come with me to that spot. The man Leatherbee is apprehended aboard boat Niagara on verge of sailing to Australia. Woman are also apprehended in act of tearful farewell. Both now relax at police station."

"I thought so," said John Quincy.

"One more amazing fact comes into light," added Chan. "In pocket of Leatherbee is the page ruthlessly extracted from guest book. Kindly procure your hat. Outside I have waiting for me one Ford automobile."

XII

TOM BRADE THE BLACKBRIDER

In Hallet's room at headquarters they found the Captain of Detectives seated grimly behind his desk staring at two reluctant visitors. One of the visitors, Mr. Stephen Leatherbee, stared back with a look of sullen defiance. Mrs. Arlene Compton, late of Broadway and the Automat, was dabbing at her eyes with a tiny handkerchief. John Quincy perceived that she had carelessly allowed tears to play havoc with her make-up.

"Hello, Charlie," said Hallet. "Mr. Winterslip, I'm glad you came along. As you may have heard, we've just pulled this young man off the Niagara. He seemed inclined to leave us. We found this in his pocket."

He put into Chan's hand a time-yellowed page obviously from Dan Winterslip's guest book. John Quincy and Chan bent over it together. The inscription was written in an old-fashioned hand, and the ink was fading fast. It ran:

"In Hawaii all things are perfect, none more so than the hospitality I have enjoyed in this house.—Joseph E. Gleason, 124 Little Bourke Street, Melbourne, Victoria."

John Quincy turned away, shocked. No wonder that page had been ripped out! Evidently Mr. Gleason had not enjoyed the privilege of studying A. S. Hill's book on the principles of rhetoric. How could one thing be more perfect than another?

"Before I take a statement from these people," Hallet was saying, "what's all this about a brooch?"

John Quincy laid the piece of jewelry on the captain's desk. He explained that it had been given Mrs. Compton by Dan Winterslip, and told of its being discovered on the floor of the lanai.

"When was it found?" demanded the captain, glaring his disapproval.

"Most regrettable misunderstanding," put in Chan hastily. "Now completely wiped out. The littlest said, sooner repairs are made. Mr. Winterslip has already tonight examined this woman—"

"Oh, he has, has he!" Hallet turned angrily on John Quincy. "Just who is conducting this case?"

"Well," began John Quincy uncomfortably, "it seemed best to the family—"

"Damn the family!" Hallet exploded. "This affair is in my hands—"

"Please," broke in Chan soothingly. "Waste of time to winnow that out. Already I have boldness to offer suitable rebukes."

"Well, you talked with the woman, then," said Hallet. "What did you get out of her?"

"Say, listen," put in Mrs. Compton. "I want to take back anything I told this bright-eyed boy."

"Lied to him, eh?" said Hallet.

"Why not? What right did he have to question me?" Her voice became wheedling. "I wouldn't lie to a cop," she added.

"You bet your life you wouldn't," Hallet remarked. "Not if you know what's good for you. However, I want to hear what you told this amateur detective. Sometimes lies are significant. Go on, Winterslip."

John Quincy was deeply annoyed. What was this mix-up he had let himself in for, anyhow? He had a notion to rise, and with a cold bow, leave the room. Something told him, however, that he couldn't get away with it.

Very much on his dignity, he repeated the woman's story to him. Winterslip had come to her cottage the night before to make a final appeal for the brooch. On his promise to replace it with something else, she had given it up. He had taken it and left her at nine-thirty.

"That was the last she saw of him," finished John Quincy.

Hallet smiled grimly. "So she told you, at any rate. But she admits she was lying. If you'd had the sense to leave this sort of thing to the proper people—" He wheeled on the woman. "You were lying, weren't you?"

She nodded nonchalantly. "In a way. Dan did leave my cottage at nine-thirty—or a little later. But I went with him—to his house. Oh, it was perfectly proper. Steve went along."

"Oh, yes—Steve." Hallet glanced at Mr. Leatherbee, who did not appear quite the ideal chaperon. "Now, young woman, go back to the beginning. Nothing but the truth."

"So help me," said Mrs. Compton. She attempted a devastating smile. "I wouldn't lie to you, Captain—you know I wouldn't. I realize you're a big man out here, and—"

"Give me your story," cut in Hallet coldly.

"Sure. Dan dropped into my place for a chat last night about nine, and he found Mr. Leatherbee there. He was jealous as sin, Dan was—

honest to God, I don't know why. Me and Steve are just pals—eh, Steve?"

"Pals, that's all," said Steve.

"But anyhow, Dan flew off the handle, and we had one grand blow-up. I tried to explain Steve was just stopping over on his way to Australia, and Dan wants to know what's detaining him. So Steve tells about how he lost all his money at bridge on the boat coming out here. 'Will you move on,' says Dan, 'if I pay your passage?' And Steve answers he will, like a shot. Am I getting this straight, Steve?"

"Absolutely," approved Mr. Leatherbee. "It's just as she says, Captain. Winterslip offered to give—loan me passage money. It was only a loan. And I agreed to sail on the Niagara to-night. He said he had a little cash in his safe at the house, and invited Arlene and me to go back with him—"

"Which we did," said Arlene. "Dan opened the safe and took out a roll of bills. He peeled off three hundred dollars. You didn't often see him in that frame of mind—but as I was saying, he give the money to Steve. Then Steve begins to beef a little—yes, you did, Steve—and wants to know what he's going to do in Australia. Says he don't know a soul down there and he'll just plain starve. Dan was sore at first, then he laughs a nasty little laugh and goes over and tears that there page out of the guest book and gives it to Steve. 'Look him up and tell him you're a friend of mine,' he says. 'Maybe he'll give you a job. The name is Gleason. I've disliked him for twenty years, though he don't know that!'"

"A dirty dig at me," Leatherbee explained. "I took the loan and this Gleason's address and we started to go. Winterslip said he wanted to talk to Arlene, so I came away alone. That was about ten o'clock."

"Where did you go?" Hallet asked.

"I went back to my hotel down-town. I had to pack."

"Back to your hotel, eh? Can you prove it?"

Leatherbee considered. "I don't know. The boy at the desk may remember when I came in, though I didn't stop there for my key—I had it with me. Anyhow, I didn't see Winterslip after that. I just went ahead with my preparations to sail on the Niagara, and I must say you've got your nerve—"

"Never mind that!" Hallet turned to the woman. "And after Leatherbee left—what happened then?"

"Well, Dan started in on that brooch again," she said. "It made me sore, too—I never did like a tight-wad. Besides, my nerves was all on edge. I'm funny that way, rows get me all upset. I like everybody pleasant around me. He went on arguing, so finally I ripped off the brooch and threw it at him, and it rolled away under the table somewhere. Then he said he was sorry, and that was when he offered to replace it with something more up-to-date. The best money could buy—that was what he promised. Pretty soon we was friends again—just as good friends as ever when I came away, about ten-fifteen. His last words was that we'd look round the jewelry stores this morning. I ask you, Captain, is it reasonable to think I'd have anything to do with murdering a man who was in a buying mood like that?"

Hallet laughed. "So you left him at ten-fifteen—and went home alone?"

"I did. And when I saw him last he was alive and well—I'll swear to that on a stack of Bibles as high as the Times Building. Gee, don't I wish I was safe on Broadway to-night!"

Hallet thought for a moment. "Well, we'll look into all this. You can both go—I'm not going to hold you at present. But I expect you both to remain in Honolulu until this affair is cleared up, and I advise you not to try any funny business. You've seen to-night what chance you've got to get away."

"Oh, that's all right." The woman stood, looking her relief. "We've got no reason to beat it, have we, Steve?"

"None in the world," agreed Steve. His facetious manner returned. "Speaking for myself," he added, "innocent is my middle-name."

"Good night, all," said Mrs. Compton, and they went out.

Hallet sat staring at the brooch. "A pretty straight story," he remarked, looking at Chan.

"Nice and neat," grinned the Chinese man.

"If true." Hallet shrugged his shoulders. "Well, for the present, I'm willing to believe it." He turned to John Quincy. "Now, Mr. Winterslip," he said severely, "I want it understood that any other evidence your family digs up—"

"Oh, that's all right," interrupted the boy. "We'll turn it over at once. I've already given to Chan the newspaper my cousin was reading that night he wrote the letter to Roger Winterslip."

Chan took the paper from his pocket. "Such a busy evening," he explained, "the journal was obscure in my mind. Thanks for the recollection." He called to his chief's attention the mutilated corner.

"Look into that," said Hallet.

"Before sleeping," promised Chan. "Mr. Winterslip, we pursue similar paths. The honor of your company in my humble vehicle would pleasure me deeply." Once in the car on the deserted street, he spoke again. "The page ripped from guest book, the brooch lying silent on floor. Both are now followed into presence of immovable stone wall. We sway about, looking for other path."

"Then you think those two were telling the truth?" John Quincy asked.

"As to that, I do not venture to remark," Chan replied.

"How about those psychic powers?" inquired John Quincy.

Chan smiled. "Psychic powers somewhat drowsy just now," he admitted. "Need prodding into wakefulness."

"Look here," said John Quincy, "there's no need for you to take me out to Waikiki. Just drop me on King Street, and I'll get a trolley."

"Making humble suggestion," Chan replied, "is it not possible you will accompany me to newspaper rooms, where we set out on different path?"

John Quincy looked at his watch; it was ten minutes past eleven. "I'll be glad to, Charlie," he said.

Chan beamed with pleasure. "Greatly honored by your friendly manner," he remarked. He turned into a side street. "Newspaper of this nature burst out at evening, very quiet now. Somebody may loiter in rooms, if we have happy luck."

They had just that, for the building of the evening journal was open, and in the city room an elderly man with a green shade over his eyes hammered on a typewriter.

"Hello, Charlie," he said cordially.

"Hello, Pete. Mr. Winterslip of Boston, I have all the honor to present this Pete Mayberry. For many years he explore water-front ferreting for whatever news are hiding there."

The elderly man rose and removed his eye-shade, revealing a pleasant twinkle. He was evidently interested to meet a Winterslip.

"We pursue," continued Chan, "one copy of paper marked June sixteen, present year. If you have no inclination for objecting."

Mayberry laughed. "Go to it, Charlie. You know where the files are."

Chan bowed and disappeared. "Your first appearance out here, Mr. Winterslip?" inquired the newspaper man.

John Quincy nodded. "I've only just got here," he said, "but I can see it's a rather intriguing place."

"You've said it," smiled Mayberry. "Forty-six years ago I came out from Portsmouth, New Hampshire, to visit relatives. I've been in the newspaper game here ever since—most of the time on the water-front. There's a lifework for you!"

"You must have seen some changes," remarked John Quincy inanely.

Mayberry nodded. "For the worse. I knew Honolulu in the glamourous days of its isolation, and I've watched it fade into an eighth carbon copy of Babbittville, U.S.A. The water-front's just a water-front now—but once, my boy! Once it oozed romance at every pore."

Chan returned, carrying a paper. "Much to be thankful for," he said to Mayberry. "Your kindness are quite overwhelming—"

"Anything doing?" asked Mayberry eagerly.

Chan shook his head. "Presently speaking, no. Our motions just now must be blackly clouded in secrecy."

"Well," said the reporter, "when it comes time to roll them clouds away, don't forget me."

"Impossibility," protested Chan. "Good night."

They left Mayberry bending over his typewriter, and at Chan's suggestion went to the All American Restaurant, where he ordered two cups of "your inspeakable coffee." While they waited to be served, he spread out on the table his complete copy of the newspaper, and laying the torn page on its counterpart, carefully removed the upper right-hand corner.

"The missing fragment," he explained. For a time he studied it thoughtfully, and finally shook his head. "I apprehend nothing to startle," he admitted. He handed it across the table. "If you will condescend greatly—"

John Quincy took the bit of newspaper. On one side was the advertisement of a Japanese dealer in shirtings who wrote his own publicity. Any one might carry off, he said, six yards for the price of five. John Quincy laughed aloud.

"Ah," said Chan, "you are by rights mirthful. Kikuchi, purveyor of skirting cloth, seize on grand English language and make it into a jumble. On that side are nothing to detain us. But humbly hinting you reverse the fragment—"

John Quincy reversed it. The other side was a part of the shipping page. He read it carefully, news of sailings and arrivals, there would be places for five passengers to the Orient on the Shinyo Maru, leaving Wednesday, the Wilhelmina was six hundred and forty miles east of Makupuu Point, the brig Mary Jane from the Treaty Ports—

John Quincy started, and caught his breath. A small item in tiny print had met his eye.

"Among the passengers who will arrive here on the Sonoma from Australia a week from Saturday are: Mr. and Mrs. Thomas Macan Brade, of Calcutta—"

John Quincy sat staring at the unwashed window of the All American Restaurant. His mind went back to the deck of the PRESIDENT TYLER, to a lean old missionary telling a tale of a bright morning on Apiang, a grave under a palm tree. "Mr. and Mrs. Thomas Macan Brade, of Calcutta." He heard again the missionary's high-pitched voice. "A callous brute, a pirate and adventurer. Tom Brade, the blackbirder."

But Brade had been buried in a long pine box on Apiang. Even at the Crossroads of the Pacific, his path and that of Dan Winterslip could hardly have crossed again.

The waiter brought the coffee. Chan said nothing, watching John Quincy closely. Finally he spoke: "You have much to tell me."

John Quincy looked around quickly, he had forgotten Chan's presence.

His dilemma was acute. Must he here in this soiled restaurant in a far town reveal to this man that ancient blot on the Winterslip name? What would Aunt Minerva say? Well, only a short time ago she had remarked that she was resolved to have no more secrets from the police. However, there was family pride—

John Quincy's eye fell on the Japanese waiter. What were those lines from The Mikado? "But family pride must be denied and mortified and set aside."

The boy smiled. "Yes, Charlie," he admitted, "I have much to tell you." And over the inspeakable coffee of the All American Restaurant he repeated to the detective the story the Reverend Frank Upton had told on the PRESIDENT TYLER.

Chan beamed. "Now," he cried, "we arrive in the neighborhood of something! Brade the blackbirder, master Maid of Shiloh boat, on which Mr. Dan Winterslip are first officer—"

"But Brade was buried on Apiang," protested John Quincy.

"Yes, indeed. And who saw him, pardon me? Was it then an unsealed box? Oh, no!" Chan's eyes were dancing. "Please recollect something more. The strong box of ohia wood. Initials on it are T.M.B. Mysteries yet, but we move, we advance!"

"I guess we do," admitted John Quincy.

"This much we grasp," Chan continued. "Dan Winterslip repose for quiet hour on lanai, in peaceful reading. This news assault his eye. He now leaps up, paces about, flees to dock to send letter requesting, please, the ohia wood box must be buried deep in Pacific. Why?" Fumbling in his pocket, Chan took out a sheaf of papers, evidently lists of steamer arrivals. "On Saturday just gone by, the Sonoma make this port. Among passengers—yes—yes—Thomas Macan Brade and honorable wife, Calcutta. It is here inscribed they arrive to stay, not being present when Sonoma persist on journey. On the night of Monday, Mr. Dan Winterslip are foully slain."

"Which makes Mr. Brade an important person to locate," said John Quincy.

"How very true. But the hurry are not intense. No boats sailing now. Before sleeping, I will investigate downtown hotels, Waikiki to-morrow. Where are you, Mr. Brade?" Chan seized the check. "No—pardon me—the honor of paying for this poison-tasting beverage must be mine."

Out in the street, he indicated an approaching trolley. "It bears imprint of your destination," he pointed out. "You will require sleep. We meet to-morrow. Congratulations on most fruitful evening."

Once more John Quincy was on a Waikiki car. Weary but thrilled, he took out his pipe and filling it, lighted up. What a day! He seemed to have lived a lifetime since he landed that very morning. He perceived that his smoke was blowing in the face of a tired little Japanese woman beside him. "Pardon me," he remarked, and knocking the pipe against the side rail, put it in his pocket. The woman stared at him in meek startled wonder; no one had ever asked her pardon before.

On the seat behind John Quincy a group of Hawaiian boys with yellow leis about their necks twanged on steel guitars and sang a plaintive love song. The trolley rattled on through the fragrant night; above the clatter of the wheels the music rose with a sweet intensity. John Quincy leaned back and closed his eyes.

A clock struck the hour of midnight. Another day—Wednesday—it flashed through his mind that to-day his firm in Boston would offer that preferred stock for the shoe people in Lynn. Would the issue be over-subscribed? No matter.

Here he was, out in the middle of the Pacific on a trolley-car. Behind him brown-skinned boys were singing a melancholy love song of long ago, and the moon was shining on crimson poinciana trees. And somewhere on this tiny island a man named Thomas Macan Brade slept under a mosquito netting. Or lay awake, perhaps, thinking of Dan Winterslip.

XIII

The Luggage in Room Nineteen

John Quincy emerged from sleep the next morning with a great effort, and dragged his watch from under the pillow. Eight-thirty! Good lord, he was due at the office at nine! A quick bath and shave, a brief pause at the breakfast table, a run past the Public Gardens and the Common and down to School Street—

He sat up in bed. Why was he imprisoned under mosquito netting? What was the meaning of the little lizard that sported idly outside the cloth? Oh, yes—Honolulu. He was in Hawaii, and he'd never reach his office by nine. It was five thousand miles away.

The low murmur of breakers on the beach confirmed him in this discovery and stepping to his window, he gazed out at the calm sparkling morning. Yes, he was in Honolulu entangled in a murder mystery, consorting with Chinese detectives and Waikiki Widows, following clues. The new day held interesting promise. He must hurry to find what it would bring forth.

Haku informed him that his aunt and Barbara had already breakfasted, and set before him a reddish sort of cantaloupe which was, he explained in answer to the boy's question, a papaia. When he had eaten, John Quincy went out on the lanai. Barbara stood there, staring at the beach. A new Barbara, with the old vivacity, the old joy of living, submerged; a pale girl with sorrow in her eyes.

John Quincy put his arm about her shoulder; she was a Winterslip and the family was the family. Again he felt in his heart that flare of anger against the "person or persons unknown" who had brought this grief upon her. The guilty must pay—Egan or whoever, Brade or Leatherbee or the chorus girl. Pay and pay dearly—he was resolved on that.

"My dear girl," he began. "What can I say to you—"

"You've said it all, without speaking," she answered. "See, John Quincy, this is my beach. When I was only five I swam alone to that first float. He—he was so proud of me."

"It's a lovely spot, Barbara," he told her.

"I knew you'd think so. One of these days we'll swim together out to the reef, and I'll teach you to ride a surfboard. I want your visit to be a happy one."

He shook his head. "It can't be that," he said, "because of you. But because of you, I'm mighty glad I came."

She pressed his hand. "I'm going out to sit by the water. Will you come?"

The bamboo curtain parted, and Miss Minerva joined them. "Well, John Quincy," she said sharply, "this is a pretty hour for you to appear. If you're going to rescue me from lotus land, you'll have to be immune yourself."

He smiled. "Just getting acclimated," he explained. "I'll follow you in a moment, Barbara," he added, and held open the door for her.

"I waited up," Miss Minerva began, when the girl had gone, "until eleven-thirty. But I'd had very little sleep the night before, and that was my limit. I make no secret of it—I'm very curious to know what happened at the police station."

He repeated to her the story told by Mrs. Compton and Leatherbee. "I wish I'd been present," she said. "A pretty woman can fool all the men in Christendom. Lies, probably."

"Maybe," admitted John Quincy. "But wait a minute. Later on, Chan and I followed up your newspaper clue. And it led us to a startling discovery."

"Of course it did," she beamed. "What was it?"

"Well," he said, "first of all, I met a missionary on the boat." He told her the Reverend Frank Upton's tale of that morning on Apiang, and added the news that a man named Thomas Macan Brade was now in Honolulu.

She was silent for a time. "So Dan was a blackbirder," she remarked at last. "How charming! Such a pleasant man, too. But then, I learned that lesson early in life—the brighter the smile, the darker the past. All this will make delightful reading in the Boston papers, John Quincy."

"Oh, they'll never get it," her nephew said.

"Don't deceive yourself. Newspapers will go to the ends of the earth for a good murder. I once wrote letters to all the editors in Boston urging them to print no more details about homicides. It hadn't the slightest effect—though I did get an acknowledgment of my favor from the Herald."

John Quincy glanced at his watch. "Perhaps I should go down to the station. Anything in the morning paper?"

"A very hazy interview with Captain Hallet. The police have unearthed important clues, and promise early results. You know—the sort of thing they always give out just after a murder."

The boy looked at her keenly. "Ah," he said, "then you read newspaper accounts of the kind you tried to suppress?"

"Certainly I do," snapped his aunt. "There's little enough excitement in my life. But I gladly gave up my port wine because I felt intoxicants were bad for the lower classes, and—"

Haku interrupted with the news that John Quincy was wanted on the telephone. When the boy returned to the lanai there was a brisk air of business about him.

"That was Charlie," he announced. "The day's work is about to get under way. They've located Mr. and Mrs. Brade at the Reef and Palm Hotel, and I'm to meet Charlie there in fifteen minutes."

"The Reef and Palm," repeated Miss Minerva. "You see, it keeps coming back to Egan. I'd wager a set of Browning against a modern novel that he's the man who did it."

"You'd lose your Browning, and then where would you be when the lecture season started?" laughed John Quincy. "I never knew you to be so stupid before." His face became serious. "By the way, will you explain to Barbara that I can't join her, after all?"

Miss Minerva nodded. "Go along," she said. "I envy you all this. First time in my life I ever wished I were a man."

John Quincy approached the Reef and Palm by way of the beach. The scene was one of bright serenity. A few languid tourists lolled upon the sand; others, more ambitious, were making picture post-card history out where the surf began. A great white steamer puffed blackly into port. Standing in water up to their necks, a group of Hawaiian women paused in their search for luncheon delicacies to enjoy a moment's gossip.

John Quincy passed Arlene Compton's cottage and entered the grounds of the Reef and Palm. On the beach not far from the hotel, an elderly Englishwoman sat on a camp stool with an easel and canvas before her. She was seeking to capture something of that exotic scene— vainly seeking, for John Quincy, glancing over her shoulder, perceived that her work was terrible. She turned and looked at him, a weary look of protest against his intrusion, and he was sorry she had caught him in the act of smiling at her inept canvas.

Chan had not yet arrived at the hotel, and the clerk informed John Quincy that Miss Carlota had gone to the city. For that interview with her father, no doubt. He hoped that the evidence of the check would bring about Egan's release. It seemed to him that the man was being held on a rather flimsy pretext, anyhow.

He sat down on the lanai at the side, where he could see both the path that led in from the street and the restless waters of the Pacific. On the beach near by a man in a purple bathing suit reclined dejectedly, and John Quincy smiled in recollection. Mr. Saladine, alone with his tragedy, peering out at the waters that had robbed him—waiting, no doubt, for the tide to yield up its loot.

Some fifteen or twenty minutes passed, and then John Quincy heard voices in the garden. He saw that Hallet and Chan were coming up the walk and went to meet them at the front door.

"Splendid morning," said Chan. "Nice day to set out on new path leading unevitably to important discovery."

John Quincy accompanied them to the desk. The Japanese clerk regarded them with sullen unfriendliness; he had not forgotten the events of the day before. Information had to be dragged from him bit by bit. Yes, there was a Mr. and Mrs. Brade stopping there. They arrived last Saturday, on the steamship Sonoma. Mr. Brade was not about at the moment. Mrs. Brade was on the beach painting pretty pictures.

"Good," said Hallet, "I'll have a look around their room before I question them. Take us there."

The clerk hesitated. "Boy!" he called. It was only a bluff; the Reef and Palm had no bell-boys. Finally, with an air of injured dignity, he led the way down a long corridor on the same floor as the office and unlocked the door of nineteen, the last room on the right. Hallet strode in and went to the window.

"Here—wait a minute," he called to the clerk. He pointed to the elderly woman painting on the beach. "That Mrs. Brade?"

"Yes-s," hissed the clerk.

"All right—go along." The clerk went out. "Mr. Winterslip, I'll ask you to sit here in the window and keep an eye on the lady. If she starts to come in, let me know." He stared eagerly about the poorly furnished bedroom. "Now, Mr. Brade, I wonder what you've got?"

John Quincy took the post assigned him, feeling decidedly uncomfortable. This didn't seem quite honorable to him. However, he probably wouldn't be called upon to do any searching himself, and if policemen were forced to do disagreeable things—well, they should have thought of that before they became policemen. Not that either Hallet or Chan appeared to be embarrassed by the task before them.

There was a great deal of luggage in the room—English luggage, which is usually large and impressive. John Quincy noted a trunk, two enormous bags, and a smaller case. All were plastered with labels of the Sonoma, and beneath were the worn fragments of earlier labels, telling a broken story of other ships and far hotels.

Hallet and Chan were old hands at this game; they went through Brade's trunk rapidly and thoroughly, but without finding anything of note. The captain turned his attention to the small traveling case. With every evidence of delight he drew forth a packet of letters, and sat down with them at a table. John Quincy was shocked. Reading other people's mail was, in his eyes, something that simply wasn't done.

It was done by Hallet, however. In a moment the captain spoke. "Seems to have been in the British civil service in Calcutta, but he's resigned," he announced to Chan. "Here's a letter from his superior in London referring to Brade's thirty-six years on the job, and saying he's sorry to lose him." Hallet took up another letter, his face brightened as he read. "Say—this is more like it!" He handed the typewritten page to Chan. Chan looked at it, and his eyes sparkled. "Most interesting," he cried, and turned it over to John Quincy.

The boy hesitated. The standards of a lifetime are not easily abandoned. But the others had read it first, so he put aside his scruples. The letter was several months old, and was addressed to Brade in Calcutta.

DEAR SIR

In reply to your inquiry of the sixth instant, would say that Mr. Daniel Winterslip is alive and is a resident of this city. His address is 3947 Kalia Road, Waikiki, Honolulu, T.H.

The signature was that of the British consul at Honolulu. John Quincy returned the epistle to Hallet, who put it in his pocket. At that instant Chan, who had been exploring one of the larger bags, emitted a little grunt of satisfaction.

"What is it, Charlie?" Hallet asked.

Chan set out on the table before his chief a small tin box, and removed the lid. It was filled with cigarettes. "Corsican brand," he announced cheerfully.

"Good," said Hallet. "It begins to look as though Mr. Thomas Macan Brade would have a lot to explain."

They continued their researches, while John Quincy sat silent by the window. Presently Carlota Egan appeared outside. She walked slowly to a chair on the lanai, and sat down. For a moment she stared at the breakers, then she began to weep.

John Quincy turned uncomfortably away. It came to him that here in this so-called paradise sorrow was altogether too rampant. The only girls he knew were given to frequent tears, and not without reason.

"If you'll excuse me—" he said. Hallet and Chan, searching avidly, made no reply, and climbing over the sill, he stepped on to the lanai. The girl looked up as he approached.

"Oh," she said, "I thought I was alone."

"You'd like to be, perhaps," he answered. "But it might help if you told me what has happened. Did you speak to your father about that check?"

She nodded. "Yes, I showed it to him. And what do you think he did? He snatched it out of my hand and tore it into a hundred pieces. He gave me the pieces to—to throw away. And he said I was never to mention it to a soul."

"I don't understand that," frowned John Quincy.

"Neither do I. He was simply furious—not like himself at all. And when I told him you knew about it, he lost his temper again."

"But you can rely on me. I shan't tell any one."

"I know that. But of course father wasn't so sure of you as—as I am. Poor dad—he's having a horrible time of it. They don't give him a moment's rest—keep after him constantly—trying to make him tell. But all the policemen in the world couldn't—Oh, poor old dad!"

She was weeping again, and John Quincy felt toward her as he had felt toward Barbara. He wanted to put his arm about her, just by way of comfort and cheer. But alas, Carlota Maria Egan was not a Winterslip.

"Now, now," he said, "that won't do a bit of good."

She looked at him through her tears. "Won't it? I—I don't know. It seems to help a little. But"—she dried her eyes—"I really haven't time for it now. I must go in and see about lunch."

She rose, and John Quincy walked with her along the balcony. "I wouldn't worry if I were you," he said. "The police are on an entirely new trail this morning."

"Really?" she answered eagerly.

"Yes. There's a man named Brade stopping at your hotel. You know him, I suppose?"

She shook her head. "No, I don't."

"What! Why, he's a guest here."

"He was. But he isn't here now."

"Wait a minute!" John Quincy laid his hand on her arm, and they stopped. "This is interesting. Brade's gone, you say?"

"Yes. I understand from the clerk that Mr. and Mrs. Brade arrived here last Saturday. But early Tuesday morning, before my boat got in, Mr. Brade disappeared and he hasn't been seen since."

"Mr. Brade gets better all the time," John Quincy said. "Hallet and Chan are in his room now, and they've unearthed some rather intriguing facts. You'd better go in and tell Hallet what you've just told me."

They entered the lobby by a side door. As they did so, a slim young Hawaiian boy was coming in through the big door at the front. Something in his manner caught the attention of John Quincy, and he stopped. At that instant a purple bathing suit slipped by him, and Mr. Saladine also approached the desk. Carlota Egan went on down the corridor toward room nineteen, but John Quincy remained in the lobby.

The Hawaiian boy moved rather diffidently toward the clerk. "Excuse me, please," he said. "I come to see Mr. Brade. Mr. Thomas Brade."

"Mr. Brade not here," replied the clerk.

"Then I will wait till he comes."

The clerk frowned. "No good. Mr. Brade not in Honolulu now."

"Not in Honolulu!" The Hawaiian seemed startled by the news.

"Mrs. Brade outside on the beach," continued the clerk.

"Oh, then Mr. Brade returns," said the boy with evident relief. "I call again."

He turned away, moving rapidly now. The clerk addressed Mr. Saladine, who was hovering near the cigar case. "Yes, sir, please?"

"Thigarettes," said the bereft Mr. Saladine.

The clerk evidently knew the brand desired, and handed over a box.

"Juth put it on my bill," said Saladine. He stood for a moment staring after the Hawaiian, who was disappearing through the front door. As he swung round his eyes encountered those of John Quincy. He looked quickly away and hurried out.

The two policemen and the girl entered from the corridor. "Well, Mr. Winterslip," said Hallet, "the bird has flown."

"So I understand," John Quincy answered.

"But we'll find him," continued Hallet. "I'll go over these islands with a drag-net. First of all, I want a talk with his wife." He turned to Carlota Egan. "Get her in here," he ordered. The girl looked at him. "Please," he added.

She motioned to the clerk, who went out the door.

"By the way," remarked John Quincy, "someone was just here asking for Brade."

"What's that!" Hallet was interested.

"A young Hawaiian, about twenty, I should say. Tall and slim. If you go to the door, you may catch a glimpse of him."

Hallet hurried over and glanced out into the garden. In a second he returned. "Humph," he said. "I know him. Did he say he'd come again?"

"He did."

Hallet considered. "I've changed my mind," he announced. "I won't question Mrs. Brade, after all. For the present, I don't want her to know we're looking for her husband. I'll trust you to fix that up with your clerk," he added to the girl. She nodded. "Lucky we left things as we found them in nineteen," he went on. "Unless she misses that letter and the cigarettes, which isn't likely, we're all right. Now, Miss Egan, we three will go into your father's office there behind the desk, and leave the door open. When Mrs. Brade comes in, I want you to question her about her husband's absence. Get all you can out of her. I'll be listening."

"I understand," the girl said.

Hallet, Chan and John Quincy went into Jim Egan's sanctum. "You found nothing else in the room?" the latter inquired of the Chinese man.

Chan shook his head. "Even so, fates are in smiling mood. What we have now are plentiful."

"Sh!" warned Hallet.

"Mrs. Brade, a young man was just here inquiring for your husband." It was Carlota Egan's voice.

"Really?" The accent was unmistakably British.

"He wanted to know where he could find him. We couldn't say."

"No—of course not."

"Your husband has left town, Mrs. Brade?"

"Yes. I fancy he has."

"You know when he will return, perhaps?"

"I really couldn't say. Is the mail in?"

"Not yet. We expect it about one."

"Thank you so much."

"Go to the door," Hallet directed John Quincy.

"She's gone to her room," announced the boy.

The three of them emerged from Egan's office.

"Oh, Captain?" said the girl. "I'm afraid I wasn't very successful."

"That's all right," replied Hallet. "I didn't think you would be." The clerk was again at his post behind the desk. Hallet turned to him. "Look here," he said. "I understand some one was here a minute ago asking for Brade. It was Dick Kaohla, wasn't it?"

"Yes-s," answered the clerk.

"Had he been here before to see Brade?"

"Yes-s. Sunday night. Mr. Brade and him have long talk on the beach."

Hallet nodded grimly. "Come on, Charlie," he said. "We've got our work cut out for us. Wherever Brade is, we must find him."

John Quincy stepped forward. "Pardon me, Captain," he remarked. "But if you don't mind—just who is Dick Kaohla?"

Hallet hesitated. "Kaohla's father—he's dead now—was a sort of confidential servant to Dan Winterslip. The boy's just plain no good. And oh, yes—he's the grandson of that woman who's over at your place now. Kamaikui—is that her name?"

XIV

What Kaohla Carried

Several Days slipped by so rapidly John Quincy scarcely noted their passing. Dan Winterslip was sleeping now under the royal palms of the lovely island where he had been born. Sun and moon shone brightly in turn on his last dwelling place, but those who sought the person he had encountered that Monday night on his lanai were still groping in the dark.

Hallet had kept his word, he was combing the Islands for Brade. But Brade was nowhere. Ships paused at the crossroads and sailed again; the name of Thomas Macan Brade was on no sailing list. Through far settlements that were called villages but were nothing save clusters of Japanese huts, in lonely coves where the surf moaned dismally, over pineapple and sugar plantations, the emissaries of Hallet pursued their quest. Their efforts came to nothing.

John Quincy drifted idly with the days. He knew now the glamour of Waikiki waters; he had felt their warm embrace. Every afternoon he experimented with a board in the malihini surf, and he was eager for the moment when he could dare the big rollers farther out. Boston seemed like a tale that is told, State Street and Beacon memories of another more active existence now abandoned. No longer was he at a loss to understand his aunt's reluctance to depart these friendly shores.

Early Friday afternoon Miss Minerva found him reading a book on the lanai. Something in the nonchalance of his manner irritated her. She had always been for action, and the urge was on her even in Hawaii.

"Have you seen Mr. Chan lately?" she inquired.

"Talked with him this morning. They're doing their best to find Brade."

"Humph," sniffed Miss Minerva. "Their best is none too good. I'd like to have a few Boston detectives on this case."

"Oh, give them time," yawned John Quincy.

"They've had three days," she snapped. "Time enough. Brade never left this island of Oahu, that's certain. And when you consider that you can drive across it in a motor in two hours, and around it in about six,

Mr. Hallet's brilliance does not impress. I'll have to end by solving this thing myself."

John Quincy laughed. "Yes, maybe you will."

"Well, I've given them the two best clues they have. If they'd keep their eyes open the way I do—"

"Charlie's eyes are open," protested John Quincy.

"Think so? They look pretty sleepy to me."

Barbara appeared on the lanai, dressed for a drive. Her eyes were somewhat happier; a bit of color had come back to her cheeks. "What are you reading, John Quincy?" she asked.

He held up the book. "The City by the Golden Gate," he told her.

"Oh, really? If you're interested, I believe dad had quite a library on San Francisco. I remember there was a history of the stock exchange—he wanted me to read it, but I couldn't."

"You missed a good one," John Quincy informed her. "I finished it this morning. I've read five other books on San Francisco since I came."

His aunt stared at him. "What for?" she asked.

"Well—" He hesitated. "I've taken sort of a fancy to the town. I don't know—sometimes I think I'd rather like to live there."

Miss Minerva smiled grimly. "And they sent you out to take me back to Boston," she remarked.

"Boston's all right," said her nephew hastily. "It's Winterslip headquarters—but its hold has never been strong enough to prevent an occasional Winterslip from hitting the trail. You know, when I came into San Francisco harbor, I had the oddest feeling." He told them about it. "And the more I saw of the city, the better I liked it. There's a snap and sparkle in the air, and the people seem to know how to get the most out of life."

Barbara smiled on him approvingly. "Follow that impulse, John Quincy," she advised.

"Maybe I will. All this reminds me—I must write a letter." He rose and left the lanai.

"Does he really intend to desert Boston?" Barbara asked.

Miss Minerva shook her head. "Just a moment's madness," she explained. "I'm glad he's going through it—he'll be more human in the future. But as for leaving Boston! John Quincy! As well expect Bunker Hill Monument to emigrate to England."

In his room up-stairs, however, John Quincy's madness was persisting. He had never completed that letter to Agatha Parker, but he now plunged into his task with enthusiasm. San Francisco was his topic, and he wrote well. He pictured the city in words that glowed with life, and he wondered—just a suggestion—how she'd like to live there.

Agatha was now, he recalled, on a ranch in Wyoming—her first encounter with the West—and that was providential. She had felt for herself the lure of the wide open spaces. Well, the farther you went the wider and opener they got. In California life was all color and light. Just a suggestion, of course.

As he sealed the flap of the envelope, he seemed to glimpse Agatha's thin patrician face, and his heart sank. Her gray eyes were cool, so different from Barbara's, so very different from those of Carlota Maria Egan.

On Saturday afternoon John Quincy had an engagement to play golf with Harry Jennison. He drove up Nuuanu Valley in Barbara's roadster—for Dan Winterslip's will had been read and everything he possessed was Barbara's now. In that sheltered spot a brisk rain was falling, as is usually the case, though the sun was shining brightly. John Quincy had grown accustomed to this phenomenon; "liquid sunshine" the people of Hawaii call such rain, and pay no attention to it. Half a dozen different rainbows added to the beauty of the Country Club links.

Jennison was waiting on the veranda, a striking figure in white. He appeared genuinely glad to see his guest, and they set out on a round of golf that John Quincy would long remember. Never before had he played amid such beauty. The low hills stood on guard, their slopes bright with tropical colors—the yellow of kukui trees, the gray of ferns, the emerald of ohia and banana trees, here and there a splotch of brick-red earth. The course was a green velvet carpet beneath their feet, the showers came and went. Jennison was a proficient driver, but the boy was his superior on approaches, and at the end of the match John Quincy was four up. They putted through a rainbow and returned to the locker room.

In the roadster going home, Jennison brought up the subject of Dan Winterslip's murder. John Quincy was interested to get the reaction of a lawyer to the evidence.

"I've kept more or less in touch with the case," Jennison said. "Egan is still my choice."

Somehow, John Quincy resented this. A picture of Carlota Egan's lovely but unhappy face flashed through his mind. "How about Leatherbee and the Compton woman?" he asked.

"Well, of course, I wasn't present when they told their story," Jennison replied. "But Hallet claims it sounded perfectly plausible. And it doesn't seem likely that if he'd had anything to do with the murder, Leatherbee would have been fool enough to keep that page from the guest book."

"There's Brade, too," John Quincy suggested.

"Yes—Brade complicates things. But when they run him down—if they do—I imagine the result will be nil."

"You know that Kamaikui's grandson is mixed up somehow with Brade?"

"So I understand. It's a matter that wants looking into. But mark my words, when all these trails are followed to the end, everything will come back to Jim Egan."

"What have you against Egan?" inquired John Quincy, swerving to avoid another car.

"I have nothing against Egan," Jennison replied. "But I can't forget the look on Dan Winterslip's face that day he told me he was afraid of the man. Then there is the stub of the Corsican cigarette. Most important of all, Egan's silence regarding his business with Winterslip. Men who are facing a charge of murder, my boy, talk, and talk fast. Unless it so happens that what they have to say would further incriminate them."

They drove on in silence into the heart of the city. "Hallet tells me you're doing a little detective work yourself," smiled Jennison.

"I've tried, but I'm a duffer," John Quincy admitted. "Just at present my efforts consist of a still hunt for that watch Aunt Minerva saw on the murderer's wrist. Whenever I see a wrist watch I get as close to it as I can, and stare. But as most of my sleuthing is done in the day time, it isn't so easy to determine whether the numeral two is bright or dim."

"Persistence," urged Jennison. "That's the secret of a good detective. Stick to the job and you may succeed yet."

The lawyer was to dine with the family at Waikiki. John Quincy set him down at his office, where he had a few letters to sign, and then drove him out to the beach. Barbara was gowned in white; she was slim and wistful and beautiful, and considering the events of the immediate past, the dinner was a cheerful one.

They had coffee on the lanai. Presently Jennison rose and stood by Barbara's chair. "We've something to tell you," he announced. He looked down at the girl. "Is that right, my dear?"

Barbara nodded.

"Your cousin and I"—the lawyer turned to the two from Boston—"have been fond of each other for a long time. We shall be married very quietly in a week or so—"

"Oh, Harry—not a week," said Barbara.

"Well, as you wish. But very soon."

"Yes, very soon," she repeated.

"And leave Honolulu for a time," Jennison continued. "Naturally, Barbara feels she can not stay here for the present—so many memories—you both understand. She has authorized me to put this house up for sale—"

"But, Harry," Barbara protested, "you make me sound so inhospitable. Telling my guests that the house is for sale and I am leaving—"

"Nonsense, my dear," said Aunt Minerva. "John Quincy and I understand, quite. I sympathize with your desire to get away." She rose.

"I'm sorry," said Jennison. "I did sound a little abrupt. But I'm naturally eager to take care of her now."

"Of course," John Quincy agreed.

Miss Minerva bent over and kissed the girl. "If your mother were here, dear child," she said, "she couldn't wish for your happiness any more keenly than I do." Barbara reached up impulsively and put her arms about the older woman.

John Quincy shook Jennison's hand. "You're mighty lucky."

"I think so," Jennison answered.

The boy went over to Barbara. "All—all good wishes," he said. She nodded, but did not reply. He saw there were tears in her eyes.

Presently Miss Minerva withdrew to the living-room, and John Quincy, feeling like a fifth wheel, made haste to leave the two together. He went out on the beach. The pale moon rode high amid the golden stars; romance whispered through the cocoanut palms. He thought of the scene he had witnessed that breathless night on the PRESIDENT TYLER—only two in the world, love quick and overwhelming—well, this was the setting for it. Here on this beach they had walked two and two since the beginning of time, whispering the same vows, making the same promises, whatever their color and creed. Suddenly the boy felt lonely.

Barbara was a Winterslip, and not for him. Why then did he feel again that frustrated pang in his heart? She had chosen and her choice was fitting; what affair was it of his?

He found himself moving slowly toward the Reef and Palm Hotel. For a chat with Carlota Egan? But why should he want to talk with this girl, whose outlook was so different from that of the world he knew? The girls at home were on a level with the men in brains—often, indeed, they were superior, seemed to be looking down from a great height. They discussed that article in the latest Atlantic, Shaw's grim philosophy, the new Sargent at the Art Gallery. Wasn't that the sort of talk he should be seeking here? Or was it? Under these palms on this romantic beach, with the moon riding high over Diamond Head?

Carlota Egan was seated behind the desk in the deserted lobby of the Reef and Palm, a worried frown on her face.

"You've come at the psychological moment," she cried, and smiled. "I'm having the most awful struggle."

"Arithmetic?" John Quincy inquired.

"Compound fractions, it seems to me. I'm making out the Brades' bill."

He came round the desk and stood at her side. "Let me help you."

"It's so fearfully involved." She looked up at him, and he wished they could do their sums on the beach. "Mr. Brade has been away since Tuesday morning, and we don't charge for any absence of more than three days. So that comes out of it. Maybe you can figure it—I can't."

"Charge him anyhow," suggested John Quincy.

"I'd like to—that would simplify everything. But it's not dad's way."

John Quincy took up a pencil. "What rate are they paying?" he inquired. She told him, and he began to figure. It wasn't a simple matter, even for a bond expert. John Quincy frowned too.

Some one entered the front door of the Reef and Palm. Looking up, John Quincy beheld the Hawaiian boy, Dick Kaohla. He carried a bulky object, wrapped in newspapers.

"Mr. Brade here now?" he asked.

Carlota Egan shook her head. "No, he hasn't returned."

"I will wait," said the boy.

"But we don't know where he is, or when he will come back," the girl protested.

"He will be here soon," the Hawaiian replied. "I wait on the lanai." He went out the side door, still carrying his clumsy burden. John Quincy and the girl stared at each other.

"'We move, we advance!'" John Quincy quoted in a low voice. "Brade will be here soon! Would you mind going out on the lanai and telling me where Kaohla is now?"

Quickly the girl complied. She returned in a few seconds. "He's taken a chair at the far end."

"Out of earshot?"

"Quite. You want the telephone—"

But John Quincy was already in the booth. Charlie Chan's voice came back over the wire.

"Most warm congratulations. You are number one detective yourself. Should my self-starter not indulge in stubborn spasm, I will make immediate connection with you."

John Quincy returned to the desk, smiling. "Charlie's flying to us in his Ford. Begins to look as though we were getting somewhere now. But about this bill. Mrs. Brade's board and room I make sixteen dollars. The charge against Mr. Brade—one week's board and room minus four days' board—totals nine dollars and sixty-two cents."

"How can I ever thank you?" said the girl.

"By telling me again about your childhood on this beach." A shadow crossed her face. "Oh, I'm sorry I've made you unhappy."

"Oh, no—you couldn't." She shook her head. "I've never been—so very happy. Always an 'if' in it, as I told you before. That morning on the ferry I think I was nearest to real happiness. I seemed to have escaped from life for a moment."

"I remember how you laughed at my hat."

"Oh—I hope you've forgiven me."

"Nonsense. I'm mighty glad I was able to make you laugh like that." Her great eyes stared into the future, and John Quincy pitied her. He had known others like her, others who loved their fathers, built high hopes for them, then saw them drift into a baffled old age. One of the girl's slender, tanned hands lay on the desk, John Quincy put his own upon it. "Don't be unhappy," he urged. "It's such a wonderful night. The moon—you're a what-you-may-call-it—a kamaaina, I know, but I'll bet you never saw the moon looking so well before. It's like a thousand-dollar gold piece, pale but negotiable. Shall we go out and spend it?"

Gently she drew her hand away. "There were seven bottles of charged water sent to the room. Thirty-five cents each—"

"What? Oh, the Brades' bill. Yes, that means two forty-five more. I'd like to mention the stars too. Isn't it odd how close the stars seem in the tropics—"

She smiled. "We mustn't forget the trunks and bags. Three dollars for bringing them up from the dock."

"Say—that's rather steep. Well, it goes down on the record. Have I ever told you that all this natural beauty out here has left its imprint on your face? In the midst of so much loveliness, one couldn't be anything but—"

"Mrs. Brade had three trays to the room. That's seventy-five cents more."

"Extravagant lady! Brade will be sorry he came back, for more reasons than one. Well, I've got that. Anything else?"

"Just the laundry. Ninety-seven cents."

"Fair enough. Adding it all up, I get thirty-two dollars and sixty-nine cents. Let's call it an even thirty-three."

She laughed. "Oh, no. We can't do that."

Mrs. Brade came slowly into the lobby from the lanai. She paused at the desk. "Has there been a message?" she inquired.

"No, Mrs. Brade," the girl answered. She handed over the slip of paper. "Your bill."

"Ah, yes. Mr. Brade will attend to this the moment he returns."

"You expect him soon?"

"I really can't say." The Englishwoman moved on into the corridor leading to nineteen.

"Full of information, as usual," smiled John Quincy. "Why, here's Charlie now."

Chan came briskly to the desk, followed by another policeman, also in plain clothes.

"Automobile act noble," he announced, "having fondly feeling for night air." He nodded toward his companion. "Introducing Mr. Spencer. Now, what are the situation? Humbly hinting you speak fast."

John Quincy told him Kaohla was waiting on the lanai, and mentioned the unwieldy package carried by the boy. Chan nodded.

"Events are turning over rapidly," he said. He addressed the girl. "Please kindly relate to this Kaohla that Brade has arrived and would wish to encounter him here." She hesitated. "No, no," added Chan hastily, "I forget nice heathen delicacy. It is not pretty I should ask a lady to scatter false lies from ruby lips. I humbly demand forgiveness. Content yourself with a veiled pretext bringing him here."

The girl smiled and went out. "Mr. Spencer," said Chan, "I make bold to suggest you interrogate this Hawaiian. My reckless wanderings among words of unlimitable English language often fail to penetrate sort of skulls plentiful round here."

Spencer nodded and went to the side door, standing where he would not be seen by any one entering there. In a moment Kaohla appeared, followed by the girl. The Hawaiian came in quickly but seeing Chan, stopped, and a frightened look crossed his face. Spencer startled him further by seizing his arm.

"Come over here," said the detective. "We want to talk to you." He led the boy to a far corner of the room. Chan and John Quincy followed. "Sit down—here, I'll take that." He removed the heavy package from under the boy's arm. For a moment the Hawaiian seemed about to protest, but evidently he thought better of it. Spencer placed the package on a table and stood over Kaohla.

"Want to see Brade, eh?" he began in a threatening tone.

"Yes."

"What for?"

"Business is private."

"Well, I'm telling you to come across. You're in bad. Better change your mind and talk."

"No."

"All right. We'll see about that. What have you got in that package?" The boy's eyes went to the table, but he made no answer.

Chan took out a pocket knife. "Simple matter to discover," he said. He cut the rough twine, unwound several layers of newspapers. John Quincy pressed close, he felt that something important was about to be divulged.

The last layer of paper came off. "Hot dog!" cried Chan. He turned quickly to John Quincy. "Oh, I am so sorry—I pick up atrocious phrase like that from my cousin Mr. Willie Chan, Captain of All Chinese baseball team—"

But John Quincy did not hear, his eyes were glued to the object that lay on the table. An ohia wood box, bound with copper—the initials T.M.B.

"We will unlatch it," said Chan. He made an examination. "No, locked most strongly. We will crash into it at police station, where you and I and this silent Hawaiian will now hasten. Mr. Spencer, you will remain on spot here. Should Brade appear, you know your duty."

"I do," said Spencer.

"Mr. Kaohla, do me the honor to accompany," continued Chan. "At police headquarters much talk will be extracted out of you."

They turned toward the door. As they did so, Carlota Egan came up. "May I speak to you a moment?" she said to John Quincy.

"Surely." He walked with her to the desk.

"I went to the lanai just now," she whispered breathlessly. "Some one was crouching outside the window near where you were talking. I went closer and it was—Mr. Saladine!"

"Aha," said John Quincy. "Mr. Saladine had better drop that sort of thing, or he'll get himself in trouble."

"Should we tell Chan?"

"Not yet. You and I will do a little investigating ourselves first. Chan has other things to think about. And we don't want any of our guests to leave unless it's absolutely necessary."

"We certainly don't," she smiled. "I'm glad you've got the interests of the house at heart."

"That's just where I've got them—" John Quincy began, but Chan cut in.

"Humbly begging pardon," he said, "we must speed. Captain Hallet will have high delight to encounter this Kaohla, to say nothing of ohia wood box."

In the doorway, Kaohla crowded close to John Quincy, and the latter was startled by the look of hate he saw in the boy's stormy eyes. "You did this," muttered the Hawaiian. "I don't forget."

XV

THE MAN FROM INDIA

They clattered along Kalakaua Avenue in Chan's car. John Quincy sat alone on the rear seat; at the detective's request he held the ohia wood box on his knees.

He rested his hands upon it. Once it had eluded him, but he had it now. His mind went back to that night in the attic two thousand miles away, the shadow against the moonlit window, the sting of a jewel cutting across his cheek. Roger's heartfelt cry of "Poor old Dan!" Did they hold at last, in this ohia wood box, the answer to the mystery of Dan's death?

Hallet was waiting in his room. With him was a keen-eyed, efficient looking man evidently in his late thirties.

"Hello, boys," said the captain. "Mr. Winterslip, meet Mr. Greene, our district court prosecutor."

Greene shook hands cordially. "I've been wanting to meet you, sir," he said. "I know your city rather well. Spent three years at your Harvard Law School."

"Really?" replied John Quincy with enthusiasm.

"Yes. I went there after I got through at New Haven. I'm a Yale man, you know."

"Oh," remarked John Quincy, without any enthusiasm at all. But Greene seemed a pleasant fellow, despite his choice of college.

Chan had set the box on the table before Hallet, and was explaining how they had come upon it. The captain's thin face had brightened perceptibly. He inspected the treasure. "Locked, eh?" he remarked. "You got the key, Kaohla?"

The Hawaiian shook his head sullenly. "No."

"Watch your step, boy," warned Hallet. "Go over him, Charlie."

Chan went over him, rapidly and thoroughly. He found a key ring, but none of the keys fitted the lock on the box. He also brought to light a fat roll of bills.

"Where'd you get all that money, Dick?" Hallet inquired.

"I got it," glowered the boy.

But Hallet was more interested in the box. He tapped it lovingly.

"This is important, Mr. Greene. We may find the solution of our puzzle in here." He took a small chisel from his desk, and after a brief struggle, pried open the lid.

John Quincy, Chan and the prosecutor pressed close, their eyes staring eagerly as the captain lifted the lid. The box was empty.

"Filled with nothing," murmured Chan. "Another dream go smash against stone wall."

The disappointment angered Hallet. He turned on Kaohla. "Now, my lad," he said. "I want to hear from you. You've been in touch with Brade, you talked with him last Sunday night, you've heard he's returning to-night. You've got some deal on with him. Come across and be quick about it."

"Nothing to tell," said the Hawaiian stubbornly.

Hallet leaped to his feet. "Oh, yes you have. And by heaven, you're going to tell it. I'm not any too patient tonight and I warn you if you don't talk and talk quick I'm likely to get rough." He stopped suddenly and turned to Chan. "Charlie, that Inter-Island boat is due from Maui about now. Get down to the dock and watch for Brade. You've got his description?"

"Sure," answered Chan. "Thin pale face, one shoulder descended below other, gray mustaches that droop in saddened mood."

"That's right. Keep a sharp lookout. And leave this lad to us. He won't have any secrets when we get through with him, eh, Mr. Greene?"

The prosecutor, more discreet, merely smiled.

"Mr. Winterslip," said Chan. "The night is delicious. A little stroll to moonly dock—"

"I'm with you," John Quincy replied. He looked back over his shoulder as he went, and reflected that he wouldn't care to be in Kaohla's shoes.

The pier-shed was dimly lighted and a small but diversified group awaited the incoming boat. Chan and John Quincy walked to the far end and there, seated on a packing-case, they found the water-front reporter of the evening paper.

"Hello, Charlie," cried Mr. Mayberry. "What you doing here?"

"Maybe friend arrive on boat," grinned Chan.

"Is that so?" responded Mayberry. "You boys over at the station have certainly become pretty mysterious all of a sudden. What's doing, Charlie?"

"All pronouncements come from captain," advised Chan.

"Yeah, we've heard his pronouncements," sneered Mayberry. "The police have unearthed clues and are working on them. Nothing to report at present. It's sickening. Well, sit down, Charlie. Oh— Mr. Winterslip—good evening. I didn't recognize you at first."

"How are you," said John Quincy. He and Chan also found packing-cases. There was a penetrating odor of sugar in the air. Through a wide opening in the pier-shed they gazed along the water-front and out upon the moonlit harbor. A rather exotic and intriguing scene, John Quincy reflected, and he said as much.

"Think so?" answered Mayberry. "Well, I don't. To me it's just like Seattle or Galveston or any of those stereotyped ports. But you see—I knew it when—"

"I think you mentioned that before," John Quincy smiled.

"I'm likely to mention it at any moment. As far as I'm concerned, the harbor of Honolulu has lost its romance. Once this was the most picturesque water-front in the world, my boy. And now look at the damned thing!" The reporter relighted his pipe. "Charlie can tell you— he remembers. The old ramshackle, low-lying wharves. Old Naval Row with its sailing ships. The wooden-hulled steamers with a mast or two— not too proud to use God's good winds occasionally. The bright little row-boats, the Aloha, the Manu, the Emma. Eh, Chan?"

"All extinct," agreed Chan.

"You wouldn't see a Rotary Club gang like this on a pier in those days," Mayberry continued. "Just Hawaiian stevedores with leis on their hats and ukuleles in their hands. Fishermen with their nets, and maybe a breezy old-time purser—a glad-hander and not a mere machine." He puffed a moment in sad silence. "Those were the days, Mr. Winterslip, the days of Hawaii's isolation, and her charm. The cable and the radio hadn't linked us up with the so-called civilization of the mainland. Every boat that came in we'd scamper over it, hunting a newspaper with the very latest news of the outside world. Remember those steamer days, Charlie, when everybody went down to the wharf in the good old hacks of yesteryear, when the women wore holokus and lauhala hats, and Berger was there with his band, and maybe a prince or two—"

"And the nights," suggested Charlie.

"Yeah, old-timer, I was coming to the nights. The soft nights when the serenaders drifted about the harbor in row-boats, and the lanterns speared long paths on the water—"

He seemed about to weep. John Quincy's mind went back to books he had read in his boyhood.

"And occasionally," he said, "I presume somebody went aboard a ship against his will?"

"I'll say he did," replied Mr. Mayberry, brightening at the thought. "Why, it was only in the 'nineties I was sitting one night on a dock a few yards down, when I saw a scuffle near the landing, and one of my best friends shouted to me: 'Good-by, Pete!' I was up and off in a minute, and I got him away from them—I was younger in those days. He was a good fellow, a sailorman, and he wasn't intending to take the journey that bunch had planned for him. They'd got him into a saloon and drugged him, but he pulled out of it just in time—oh, well, those days are gone for ever now. Just like Galveston or Seattle. Yes, sir, this harbor of Honolulu has lost its romance."

The little Inter-Island boat was drawing up to the pier, and they watched it come. As the gangplank went down, Chan rose.

"Who you expecting, Charlie?" asked Mayberry.

"We grope about," said Chan. "Maybe on this boat are Mr. Brade."

"Brade!" Mayberry leaped to his feet.

"Not so sure," warned Chan. "Only a matter we suppose. If correct, humbly suggest you follow to the station. You might capture news."

John Quincy and Chan moved up to the gangplank as the passengers descended. There were not many aboard. A few Island business men, a scattering of tourists, a party of Japanese in western clothes, ceremoniously received by friends ashore—a quaint little group all bowing from the waist. John Quincy was watching them with interest when Chan touched his arm.

A tall stooped Englishman was coming down the plank. Thomas Macan Brade would have been easily spotted in any crowd. His mustache was patterned after that of the Earl of Pawtucket, and to make identification even simpler, he wore a white pith helmet. Pith helmets are not necessary under the kindly skies of Hawaii; this was evidently a relic of Indian days.

Chan stepped forward. "Mr. Brade?"

The man had a tired look in his eyes. He started nervously. "Y—yes," he hesitated.

"I am Detective-Sergeant Chan. Honolulu police. You will do me the great honor to accompany me to the station, if you please."

Brade stared at him, then shook his head. "It's quite impossible," he said.

"Pardon me, please," answered Chan. "It are unevitable."

"I—I have just returned from a journey," protested the man. "My wife may be worried regarding me. I must have a talk with her, and after that—"

"Regret," purred Chan, "are scorching me. But duty remains duty. Chief's words are law. Humbly suggest we squander valuable time."

"Am I to understand that I'm under arrest?" flared Brade.

"The idea is preposterous," Chan assured him. "But the captain waits eager for statement from you. You will walk this way, I am sure. A moment's pardon. I introduce my fine friend, Mr. John Quincy Winterslip, of Boston."

At mention of the name, Brade turned and regarded John Quincy with deep interest. "Very good," he said. "I'll go with you."

They went out to the street, Brade carrying a small hand-bag. The flurry of arrival was dying fast. Honolulu would shortly return to its accustomed evening calm.

When they reached the police station, Hallet and the prosecutor seemed in high good humor. Kaohla sat in a corner, hopeless and defeated; John Quincy saw at a glance that the boy's secret was his no longer.

"Introducing Mr. Brade," said Chan.

"Ah," cried Hallet, "we're glad to see you, Mr. Brade. We'd been getting pretty worried about you."

"Really, sir," said Brade, "I am completely at a loss—"

"Sit down," ordered Hallet. The man sank into a chair. He too had a hopeless, defeated air. No one can appear more humble and beaten than a British civil servant, and this man had known thirty-six years of baking under the Indian sun, looked down on by the military, respected by none. Not only his mustache but his whole figure drooped "in saddened mood." Yet now and then, John Quincy noted, he flashed into life, a moment of self-assertion and defiance.

"Where have you been, Mr. Brade?" Hallet inquired.

"I have visited one of the other islands. Maui."

"You went last Tuesday morning?"

"Yes. On the same steamer that brought me back."

"Your name was not on the sailing list," Hallet said.

"No. I went under another name. I had—reasons."

"Indeed?"

The flash of life. "Just why am I here, sir?" He turned to the prosecutor. "Perhaps you will tell me that?"

Greene nodded toward the detective. "Captain Hallet will enlighten you," he said.

"You bet I will," Hallet announced. "As perhaps you know, Mr. Brade, Mr. Dan Winterslip has been murdered."

Brade's washed-out eyes turned to John Quincy. "Yes," he said. "I read about it in a Hilo newspaper."

"You didn't know it when you left last Tuesday morning?" Hallet asked.

"I did not. I sailed without seeing a paper here."

"Ah, yes. When did you see Mr. Dan Winterslip last?"

"I never saw him."

"What! Be careful, sir."

"I never saw Dan Winterslip in my life."

"All right. Where were you last Tuesday morning at twenty minutes past one?"

"I was asleep in my room at the Reef and Palm Hotel. I'd retired at nine-thirty, as I had to rise early in order to board my boat. My wife can verify that."

"A wife's testimony, Mr. Brade, is not of great value—"

Brade leaped to his feet. "Look here, sir! Do you mean to insinuate—"

"Take it easy," said Hallet smoothly. "I have a few matters to call to your attention, Mr. Brade. Mr. Dan Winterslip was murdered at one-twenty or thereabouts last Tuesday morning. We happen to know that in his youth he served as first officer aboard the Maid of Shiloh, a blackbirder. The master of that vessel had the same name as yourself. An investigation of your room at the Reef and Palm—"

"How dare you!" cried Brade. "By what right—"

"I am hunting the murderer of Dan Winterslip," broke in Hallet coolly. "And I follow the trail wherever it leads. In your room I found a letter from the British Consul here addressed to you, and informing you that Winterslip was alive and in Honolulu. I also found this tin of Corsican cigarettes. Just outside the living-room door of Winterslip's house, we picked up the stub of a Corsican cigarette. It's a brand not on sale in Honolulu."

Brade had dropped back into his chair, and was staring in a dazed way at the tin box in Hallet's hand. Hallet indicated the Hawaiian boy in the corner. "Ever see this lad before, Mr. Brade?" Brade nodded.

"You had a talk with him last Sunday night on the beach?"

"Yes."

"The boy's told us all about it. He read in the paper that you were coming to Honolulu. His father was a confidential servant in Dan Winterslip's employ and he himself was brought up in the Winterslip household. He could make a pretty good guess at your business with Winterslip, and he figured you'd be pleased to lay hands on this ohia wood box. In his boyhood he'd seen it in a trunk in the attic of Winterslip's San Francisco house. He went down to the PRESIDENT TYLER and arranged with a friend aboard that boat, the quartermaster, to break into the house and steal the box. When he saw you last Sunday night he told you he'd have the box as soon as the PRESIDENT TYLER got in, and he arranged to sell it to you for a good sum. Am I right so far, Mr. Brade?"

"You are quite right," said Brade.

"The initials on the box are T.M.B." Hallet persisted. "They are your initials, are they not?"

"They happen to be," said Brade. "But they were also the initials of my father. My father died aboard ship in the South Seas many years ago, and that box was stolen from his cabin after his death. It was stolen by the first officer of the Maid of Shiloh—by Mr. Dan Winterslip."

For a moment no one spoke. A cold shiver ran down the spine of John Quincy Winterslip and a hot flush suffused his cheek. Why, oh, why, had he strayed so far from home? In Boston he traveled in a rut, perhaps, but ruts were safe, secure. There no one had ever brought a charge such as this against a Winterslip, no whisper of scandal had ever sullied the name. But here Winterslips had run amuck, and there was no telling what would next be dragged into the light.

"I think, Mr. Brade," said the prosecutor slowly, "you had better make a full statement."

Brade nodded. "I intend to do so. My case against Winterslip is not complete and I should have preferred to remain silent for a time. But under the circumstances, of course I must speak out. I'll smoke, if you don't mind." He took a cigarette from his case and lighted it. "I'm a bit puzzled just how to begin. My father disappeared from England in the 'seventies, leaving my mother and me to shift for ourselves. For a time we heard nothing of him, then letters began to arrive from various points in Australia and the South Seas. Letters with money in them, money we badly needed. I have since learned that he had gone into the blackbirding trade; it is nothing to be proud of, God knows, but I like to recall in his favor that he did not entirely abandon his wife and boy.

"In the 'eighties we got word of his death. He died aboard the Maid of Shiloh and was buried on the island of Apiang in the Gilbert Group—buried by Dan Winterslip, his first officer. We accepted the fact of his death, the fact of no more letters with remittances, and took up our struggle again. Six months later we received, from a friend of my father in Sydney, a brother captain, a most amazing letter.

"This letter said that, to the writer's certain knowledge, my father had carried a great deal of money in his cabin on the Maid of Shiloh. He had done no business with banks, instead he had had this strong box made of ohia wood. The man who wrote us said that he had seen the inside of it, and that it contained jewelry and a large quantity of gold. My father had also shown him several bags of green hide, containing gold coins from many countries. He estimated that there must have been close to twenty thousand pounds, in all. Dan Winterslip, the letter said, had brought the Maid of Shiloh back to Sydney and turned over to the proper authorities my father's clothing and personal effects, and a scant ten pounds in money. He had made no mention of anything further. He and the only other white man aboard the Maid, an Irishman named Hagin, had left at once for Hawaii. My father's friend suggested that we start an immediate investigation.

"Well, gentlemen"—Brade looked about the circle of interested faces—"what could we do? We were in pitiful circumstances, my mother and I. We had no money to employ lawyers, to fight a case thousands of miles away. We did make a few inquiries through a relative in Sydney, but nothing came of them. There was talk for a time, but the talk died out, and the matter was dropped. But I—I have never forgotten.

"Dan Winterslip returned here, and prospered. He built on the foundation of the money he found in my father's cabin a fortune that inspired the admiration of Honolulu. And while he prospered, we were close to starvation. My mother died, but I carried on. For years it has been my dream to make him pay. I have not been particularly successful, but I have saved, scrimped. I have the money now to fight this case.

"Four months ago I resigned my post in India and set out for Honolulu. I stopped over in Sydney—my father's friend is dead, but I have his letter. I have the depositions of others who knew about that money—about the ohia wood box. I came on here, ready to face Dan Winterslip at last. But I never faced him. As you know, gentlemen"—Brade's hand trembled slightly as he put down his cigarette—"some one robbed me of that privilege. Some unknown hand removed from my path the man I have hated for more than forty years."

"You arrived last Saturday—a week ago," said Hallet, after a pause. "On Sunday evening Kaohla here called on you. He offered you the strong box?"

"He did," Brade replied. "He'd had a cable from his friend, and expected to have the box by Tuesday. I promised him five thousand dollars for it—a sum I intended Winterslip should pay. Kaohla also told me that Hagin was living on a ranch in a remote part of the Island of Maui. That explains my journey there—I took another name, as I didn't want Winterslip to follow my movements. I had no doubt he was watching me."

"You didn't tell Kaohla you were going, either?"

"No, I didn't think it advisable to take him completely into my confidence. I found Hagin, but could get nothing out of him. Evidently Winterslip had bought his silence long ago. I realized the box was of great importance to me, and I cabled Kaohla to bring it to me immediately on my return. It was then that the news of Winterslip's death came through. It was a deep disappointment, but it will not deter me." He turned to John Quincy. "Winterslip's heirs must pay. I am determined they shall make my old age secure."

John Quincy's face flushed again. A spirit of rebellion, of family pride outraged, stirred within him. "We'll see about that, Mr. Brade," he said. "You have unearthed the box, but so far as any proof about valuables—money—"

"One moment," cut in Greene, the prosecutor. "Mr. Brade, have you a description of any article of value taken from your father?"

Brade nodded. "Yes. In my father's last letter to us—I was looking through it only the other day—he spoke of a brooch he had picked up in Sydney. A tree of emeralds, rubies and diamonds against an onyx background. He said he was sending it to my mother—but it never came."

The prosecutor looked at John Quincy. John Quincy looked away. "I'm not one of Dan Winterslip's heirs, Mr. Brade," he explained. "As a matter of fact, he was a rather distant relative of mine. I can't presume to speak for his daughter, but I'm reasonably sure that when she knows your story, this matter can be settled out of court. You'll wait, of course?"

"I'll wait," agreed Brade. "And now, Captain—"

Hallet raised his hand. "Just a minute. You didn't call on Winterslip? You didn't go near his house?"

"I did not," said Brade.

"Yet just outside the door of his living-room we found, as I told you, the stub of a Corsican cigarette. It's a matter still to be cleared up."

Brade considered briefly. "I don't want to get any one into trouble," he said. "But the man is nothing to me, and I must clear my own name. In the course of a chat with the proprietor of the Reef and Palm Hotel, I offered him a cigarette. He was delighted when he recognized the brand—said it had been years since he'd seen one. So I gave him a handful, and he filled his case—"

"You're speaking of Jim Egan," suggested Hallet delightedly.

"Of Mr. James Egan, yes," Brade replied.

"That's all I want to know," said Hallet. "Well, Mr. Greene—"

The prosecutor addressed Brade. "For the present, we can't permit you to leave Honolulu," he said. "But you are free to go to your hotel. This box will remain here until we can settle its final disposition."

"Naturally." Brade rose.

John Quincy faced him. "I'll call on you very soon," he promised.

"What? Oh, yes—yes, of course." The man stared nervously about him. "If you'll pardon me, gentlemen, I must run—I really must—"

He went out. The prosecutor looked at his watch. "Well, that's that. I'll have a conference with you in the morning, Hallet. My wife's waiting for me at the Country Club. Good night, Mr. Winterslip." He saw the look on John Quincy's face, and smiled. "Don't take those revelations about your cousin too seriously. The 'eighties are ancient history, you know."

As Greene disappeared, Hallet turned to John Quincy. "What about this Kaohla?" he inquired. "It will be a pretty complicated job to prosecute him and his housebreaking friend on the President Tyler, but it can be done—"

A uniformed policeman appeared at the door, summoning Chan outside.

"Oh, no," said John Quincy. "Let the boy go. We don't want any publicity about this. I'll ask you, Captain, to keep Brade's story out of the papers."

"I'll try," Hallet replied. He turned to the Hawaiian. "Come here!" The boy rose. "You heard what this gentleman said. You ought to be sent up for this, but we've got more important things to attend to now. Run along—beat it—"

Chan came in just in time to hear the last. At his heels followed a sly little Japanese man and a young Chinese boy. The latter was attired in the extreme of college-cut clothes; he was an American and he emphasized the fact.

"Only one moment," Chan cried. "New and interesting fact emerge into light. Gentlemen, my Cousin Willie Chan, captain All Chinese baseball team and demon back-stopper of the Pacific!"

"Pleased to meetchu," said Willie Chan.

"Also Okamoto, who have auto stand on Kalakaua Avenue, not far from Winterslip household—"

"I know Okamoto," said Hallet. "He sells okolehau on the side."

"No, indeed," protested Okamoto. "Auto stand, that is what."

"Willie do small investigating to help out crowded hours," went on Chan. "He have dug up strange event out of this Okamoto here. On early morning of Tuesday, July first, Okamoto is roused from slumber by fierce knocks on door of room. He go to door—"

"Let him tell it," suggested Hallet. "What time was this?"

"Two of the morning," said Okamoto. "Knocks were as described. I rouse and look at watch, run to door. Mr. Dick Kaohla here is waiting. Demand I drive him to home over in Iwilei district. I done so."

"All right," said Hallet. "Anything else? No? Charlie—take them out and thank them—that's your specialty." He waited until the Orientals had left the room, then turned fiercely on Kaohla. "Well, here you are back in the limelight," he cried. "Now, come across. What were you doing out near Winterslip's house the night of the murder?"

"Nothing," said the Hawaiian.

"Nothing! A little late to be up doing nothing, wasn't it? Look here, my boy, I'm beginning to get you. For years Dan Winterslip gave you money, supported you, until he finally decided you were no good. So he stopped the funds and you and he had a big row. Now, didn't you?"

"Yes," admitted Dick Kaohla.

"On Sunday night Brade offered you five thousand for the box. You thought it wasn't enough. The idea struck you that maybe Dan Winterslip would pay more. You were a little afraid of him, but you screwed up your courage and went to his house—"

"No, no," the boy cried. "I did not go there."

"I say you did. You'd made up your mind to double-cross Brade. You and Dan Winterslip had another big scrap, you drew a knife—"

"Lies, all lies," the boy shouted, terrified.

"Don't tell me I lie! You killed Winterslip and I'll get it out of you! I got the other and I'll get this." Hallet rose threateningly from his chair.

Chan suddenly reentered the room, and handed Hallet a note. "Arrive this moment by special messenger," he explained.

Hallet ripped open the envelope and read. His expression altered. He turned disgustedly to Kaohla. "Beat it!" he scowled.

The boy fled gratefully. John Quincy and Chan looked wonderingly at the captain. Hallet sat down at his desk. "It all comes back to Egan," he said. "I've known it from the first."

"Wait a minute," cried John Quincy. "What about that boy?"

Hallet crumpled the letter in his hand. "Kaohla? Oh, he's out of it now."

"Why?"

"That's all I can tell you. He's out of it."

"That's not enough," John Quincy said. "I demand to know—"

Hallet glared at him. "You know all you're going to," he answered angrily. "I say Kaohla's out, and that settles it. Egan killed Winterslip, and before I get through with him—"

"Permit me to say," interrupted John Quincy, "that you have the most trusting nature I ever met. Everybody's story goes with you. The Compton woman and that rat Leatherbee come in here and spin a yarn, and you bow them out. And Brade! What about Brade! In bed at one-twenty last Tuesday morning, eh? Who says so? He does. Who can prove it? His wife can. What was to prevent his stepping out on the balcony of the Reef and Palm and walking along the beach to my cousin's house? Answer me that!"

Hallet shook his head. "It's Egan. That cigarette—"

"Yes—that cigarette. Has it occurred to you that Brade may have given him those cigarettes purposely—"

"Egan did it," cut in Hallet stubbornly. "All I need now is his story; I'll get it. I have ways and means—"

"I congratulate you on your magnificent stupidity," cried John Quincy. "Good night, sir."

He walked along Bethel Street, Chan at his side.

"You are partly consumed by anger," said the Chinaman. "Humbly suggest you cool. Calm heads needed."

"But what was in that note? Why wouldn't he tell us?"

"In good time, we know. Captain honest man. Be patient."

"But we're all at sea again," protested John Quincy. "Who killed Cousin Dan? We get nowhere."

"So very true," agreed Chan. "More clues lead us into presence of immovable stone wall. We sway about, seeking still other path."

"I'll say we do," answered John Quincy. "There comes my car. Good night!"

Not until the trolley was half-way to Waikiki did he remember Mr. Saladine. Saladine crouching outside that window at the Reef and Palm. What did that mean? But Saladine was a comic figure, a lisping searcher after bridge-work in the limpid waters of Waikiki. Even so, perhaps his humble activities should be investigated.

XVI

The Return of Captain Cope

After breakfast on Sunday morning, John Quincy followed Miss Minerva to the lanai. It was a neat world that lay outside the screen, for Dan Winterslip's yard boy had been busy until a late hour the night before, sweeping the lawn with the same loving thoroughness a housewife might display on a precious Oriental rug.

Barbara had not come down to breakfast, and John Quincy had seized the opportunity to tell his aunt of Brade's return, and repeat the man's story of Dan Winterslip's theft on board the Maid of Shiloh. Now he lighted a cigarette and sat staring seriously out at the distant water.

"Cheer up," said Miss Minerva. "You look like a judge. I presume you're thinking of poor Dan."

"I am."

"Forgive and forget. None of us ever suspected Dan of being a saint."

"A saint! Far from it! He was just a plain—"

"Never mind," put in his aunt sharply. "Remember, John Quincy, man is a creature of environment. And the temptation must have been great. Picture Dan on that ship in these easy-going latitudes, wealth at his feet and not a soul in sight to claim it. Ill-gotten wealth, at that. Even you—"

"Even I," said John Quincy sternly, "would have recalled I am a Winterslip. I never dreamed I'd live to hear you offering apologies for that sort of conduct."

She laughed. "You know what they say about white women who go to the tropics. They lose first their complexion, then their teeth, and finally their moral sense." She hesitated. "I've had to visit the dentist a good deal of late," she added.

John Quincy was shocked. "My advice to you is to hurry home," he said.

"When are you going?"

"Oh, soon—soon."

"That's what we all say. Returning to Boston, I suppose?"

"Of course."

"How about San Francisco?"

"Oh, that's off. I did suggest it to Agatha, but I'm certain she won't hear of it. And I'm beginning to think she'd be quite right." His aunt rose. "You'd better go to church," said John Quincy severely.

"That's just where I am going," she smiled. "By the way, Amos is coming to dinner to-night, and he'd best hear the Brade story from us, rather than in some garbled form. Barbara must hear it too. If it proves to be true, the family ought to do something for Mr. Brade."

"Oh, the family will do something for him, all right," John Quincy remarked. "Whether it wants to or not."

"Well, I'll let you tell Barbara about him," Miss Minerva promised.

"Thank you so much," replied her nephew sarcastically.

"Not at all. Are you coming to church?"

"No," he said. "I don't need it the way you do."

She left him there to face a lazy uneventful day. By five in the afternoon Waikiki was alive with its usual Sunday crowd—not the unsavory holiday throng seen on a mainland beach, but a scattering of good-looking people whose tanned straight bodies would have delighted the heart of a physical culture enthusiast. John Quincy summoned sufficient energy to don a bathing suit and plunge in.

There was something soothing in the warm touch of the water, and he was becoming more at home there every day. With long powerful strokes he drew away from the malihini breakers to dare the great rollers beyond. Surfboard riders flashed by him; now and then he had to alter his course to avoid an outrigger canoe.

On the farthest float of all he saw Carlota Egan. She sat there, a slender lovely figure vibrant with life, and awaited his coming. As he climbed up beside her and looked into her eyes he was—perhaps from his exertion in the water—a little breathless.

"I rather hoped I'd find you," he panted.

"Did you?" She smiled faintly. "I hoped it too. You see, I need a lot of cheering up."

"On a perfect day like this!"

"I'd pinned such hopes on Mr. Brade," she explained. "Perhaps you know he's back—and from what I can gather, his return hasn't meant a thing so far as dad's concerned. Not a thing."

"Well, I'm afraid it hasn't," John Quincy admitted. "But we mustn't get discouraged. As Chan puts it, we sway about, seeking a new path. You and I have a bit of swaying to do. How about Mr. Saladine?"

"I've been thinking about Mr. Saladine. But I can't get excited about him, somehow. He's so ridiculous."

"We mustn't pass him up on that account," admonished John Quincy. "I caught a glimpse of his purple bathing suit on the first float. Come on—we'll just casually drop in on him. I'll race you there."

She smiled again, and leaped to her feet. For a second she stood poised, then dived in a way that John Quincy could never hope to emulate. He slipped off in pursuit, and though he put forth every effort, she reached Saladine's side five seconds before he did.

"Hello, Mr. Saladine," she said. "This is Mr. Winterslip, of Boston."

"Ah, yeth," responded Mr. Saladine, gloomily. "Mr. Winterthlip." He regarded the young man with interest.

"Any luck, sir?" inquired John Quincy sympathetically.

"Oh—you heard about my accthident?"

"I did, sir, and I'm sorry."

"I am, too," said Mr. Saladine feelingly. "Not a thrath of them tho far. And I muth go home in a few deth."

"I believe Miss Egan said you lived in Des Moines?"

"Yeth. Deth—Deth—I can't they it."

"In business there?" inquired John Quincy nonchalantly.

"Yeth. Wholethale grothery buthineth," answered Mr. Saladine, slowly but not very successfully.

John Quincy turned away to hide a smile. "Shall we go along?" he said to the girl. "Good luck to you, sir." He dove off, and as they swam toward the shore, he reflected that they were on a false trail there—a trail as spurious as the teeth. That little business man was too conventional a figure to have any connection with the murder of Dan Winterslip. He kept these thoughts to himself, however.

Half-way to the beach, they encountered an enormous figure floating languidly on the water. Just beyond the great stomach John Quincy perceived the serene face of Charlie Chan.

"Hello, Charlie," he cried. "It's a small ocean, after all! Got your Ford with you?"

Chan righted himself and grinned. "Little pleasant recreation," he explained. "Forget detective worries out here floating idle like leaf on stream."

"Please float ashore," suggested John Quincy. "I have something to tell you."

"Only too happy," agreed Chan.

He followed them in and they sat, an odd trio, on the white sand. John Quincy told the detective about Saladine's activities outside the window the night before, and repeated the conversation he had just had with the middle westerner. "Of course, the man seems almost too foolish to mean anything," he added.

Chan shook his head. "Begging most humble pardon," he said, "that are wrong attitude completely. Detective business made up of unsignificant trifles. One after other our clues go burst in our countenance. Wise to pursue matter of Mr. Saladine."

"What do you suggest?" John Quincy asked.

"To-night I visit city for night work to drive off my piled tasks," Chan replied. "After evening meal, suggest you join with me at cable office. We despatch message to postmaster of this Des Moines, inquiring what are present locality of Mr. Saladine, expert in wholeselling provisions. Your name will be signed to message, much better than police meddling."

"All right," John Quincy agreed, "I'll meet you there at eight-thirty."

Carlota Egan rose. "I must get back to the Reef and Palm. You've no idea all I have to do—"

John Quincy stood beside her. "If I can help, you know—"

"I know," she smiled. "I'm thinking of making you assistant manager. They'd be so proud of you—in Boston."

She moved off toward the water for her homeward swim, and John Quincy dropped down beside Chan. Chan's amber eyes followed the girl. "Endeavoring to make English language my slave," he said, "I pursue poetry. Who were the great poet who said—'She walks in beauty like the night?'"

"Why, that was—er—who was it?" remarked John Quincy helpfully.

"Name is slippery," went on Chan. "But no matter. Lines pop into brain whenever I see this Miss Egan. Beauty like the night, Hawaiian night maybe, lovely as purest jade. Most especially on this beach. Spot of heartbreaking charm, this beach."

"Surely is," agreed John Quincy, amused at Chan's obviously sentimental mood.

"Here on gleaming sand I first regard my future wife," continued Chan. "Slender as the bamboo is slender, beautiful as blossom of the plum—"

"Your wife," repeated John Quincy. The idea was a new one.

"Yes, indeed." Chan rose. "Recalls I must hasten home where she attends the children who are now, by actual count, nine in number." He looked down at John Quincy thoughtfully. "Are you well-fitted with the armor of preparation?" he said. "Consider. Some night the moon has splendor in this neighborhood, the cocoa-palms bow lowly and turn away their heads so they do not see. And the white man kisses without intending to do so."

"Oh, don't worry about me," John Quincy laughed. "I'm from Boston, and immune."

"Immune," repeated Chan. "Ah, yes, I grasp meaning. In my home I have idol brought from China with insides of solid stone. He would think he is—immune. But even so I would not entrust him on this beach. As my cousin Willie Chan say with vulgarity, see you later."

John Quincy sat for a time on the sand, then rose and strolled toward home. His path lay close to the lanai of Arlene Compton's cottage, and he was surprised to hear his name called from behind the screen. He stepped to the door and looked in. The woman was sitting there alone.

"Come in a minute, Mr. Winterslip," she said.

John Quincy hesitated. He did not care to make any social calls on this lady, but he did not have it in him to be rude. He went inside and sat down gingerly, poised for flight. "Got to hurry back for dinner," he explained.

"Dinner? You'll want a cocktail."

"No, thanks. I'm—I'm on the wagon."

"You'll find it hard to stick out here," she said a little bitterly. "I won't keep you long. I just want to know—are those boneheads down at the station getting anywhere, or ain't they?"

"The police," smiled John Quincy. "They seem to be making progress. But it's slow. It's very slow."

"I'll tell the world it's slow. And I got to stick here till they pin it on somebody. Pleasant outlook, ain't it?"

"Is Mr. Leatherbee still with you?" inquired John Quincy.

"What do you mean is he still with me?" she flared.

"Pardon me. Is he still in town?"

"Of course he's in town. They won't let him go, either. But I ain't worrying about him. I got troubles of my own. I want to go home." She nodded toward a newspaper on the table. "I just got hold of an old Variety and seen about a show opening in Atlantic City. A lot of the gang is in it, working like dogs, rehearsing night and day, worrying themselves sick over how long the thing will last. Gee, don't I envy them. I was near to bawling when you came along."

"You'll get back all right," comforted John Quincy.

"Say—if I ever do! I'll stop everybody I meet on Broadway and promise never to leave 'em again." John Quincy rose. "You tell that guy Hallet to get a move on," she urged.

"I'll tell him," he agreed.

"And drop in to see me now and then," she added wistfully. "Us easterners ought to stick together out here."

"That's right, we should," John Quincy answered. "Good-by."

As he walked along the beach, he thought of her with pity. The story she and Leatherbee had told might be entirely false; even so, she was a human and appealing figure and her homesickness touched his heart.

Later that evening when John Quincy came downstairs faultlessly attired for dinner, he encountered Amos Winterslip in the living-room. Cousin Amos's lean face was whiter than ever; his manner listless. He had been robbed of his hate; his evenings beneath the algaroba tree had lost their savor; life was devoid of spice.

Dinner was not a particularly jolly affair. Barbara seemed intent on knowing now the details of the search the police were conducting, and it fell to John Quincy to enlighten her. Reluctantly he came at last to the story of Brade. She listened in silence. After dinner she and John Quincy went out into the garden and sat on a bench under the hau tree, facing the water.

"I'm terribly sorry I had to tell you that about Brade," John Quincy said gently. "But it seemed necessary."

"Of course," she agreed. "Poor dad! He was weak—weak—"

"Forgive and forget," John Quincy suggested. "Man is a creature of environment." He wondered dimly where he had heard that before. "Your father was not entirely to blame—"

"You're terribly kind, John Quincy," she told him.

"No—but I mean it," he protested. "Just picture the scene to yourself. That lonely ocean, wealth at his feet for the taking, no one to see or know."

She shook her head. "Oh, but it was wrong, wrong. Poor Mr. Brade. I must make things right with him as nearly as I can. I shall ask Harry to talk with him to-morrow—"

"Just a suggestion," interposed John Quincy. "Whatever you agree to do for Brade must not be done until the man who killed your father is found."

She stared at him. "What! You don't think that Brade—"

"I don't know. Nobody knows. Brade is unable to prove where he was early last Tuesday morning."

They sat silent for a moment; then the girl suddenly collapsed and buried her face in her hands. Her slim shoulders trembled convulsively and John Quincy, deeply sympathetic, moved closer. He put his arm about her. The moonlight shone on her bright hair, the trades whispered in the hau tree, the breakers murmured on the beach. She lifted her face, and he kissed her. A cousinly kiss he had meant it to be, but somehow it wasn't—it was a kiss he would never have been up to on Beacon Street.

"Miss Minerva said I'd find you here," remarked a voice behind them.

John Quincy leaped to his feet and found himself staring into the cynical eyes of Harry Jennison. Even though you are the girl's cousin, it is a bit embarrassing to have a man find you kissing his fiancee. Particularly if the kiss wasn't at all cousinly—John Quincy wondered if Jennison had noticed that.

"Come in—I mean, sit down," stammered John Quincy. "I was just going."

"Good-by," said Jennison coldly.

John Quincy went hastily through the living-room, where Miss Minerva sat with Amos. "Got an appointment down-town," he explained, and picking up his hat in the hall, fled into the night.

He had intended taking the roadster, but to reach the garage he would have to pass that bench under the hau tree. Oh, well, the colorful atmosphere of a trolley was more interesting, anyhow.

In the cable office on the ground floor of the Alexander Young Hotel, Chan was waiting, and they sent off their inquiry to the postmaster at Des Moines, signing John Quincy's name and address. That attended to, they returned to the street. In the park across the way an unseen group of young men strummed steel guitars and sang in soft haunting voices; it was the only sign of life in Honolulu.

"Kindly deign to enter hotel lobby with me," suggested Chan. "It is my custom to regard names in register from time to time."

At the cigar stand just inside the door, the boy paused to light his pipe, while Chan went on to the desk. As John Quincy turned he saw a man seated alone in the lobby, a handsome, distinguished man who wore immaculate evening clothes that bore the stamp of Bond Street. An old acquaintance, Captain Arthur Temple Cope.

At sight of John Quincy, Cope leaped to his feet and came forward. "Hello, I'm glad to see you," he cried, with a cordiality that had not been evident at former meetings. "Come over and sit down."

John Quincy followed him. "Aren't you back rather soon?" he inquired.

"Sooner than I expected," Cope rejoined. "Not sorry, either."

"Then you didn't care for your little flock of islands?"

"My boy, you should visit there. Thirty-five white men, two hundred and fifty natives, and a cable station. Jolly place of an evening, what?"

Chan came up, and John Quincy presented him. Captain Cope was the perfect host. "Sit down, both of you," he urged. "Have a cigarette." He extended a silver case.

"Thanks, I'll stick to the pipe," John Quincy said. Chan gravely accepted a cigarette and lighted it.

"Tell me, my boy," Cope said when they were seated, "is there anything new on the Winterslip murder? Haven't run down the guilty man, by any chance."

"No, not yet," John Quincy replied.

"That's a great pity. I—er—understand the police are holding a chap named Egan?"

"Yes—Jim Egan, of the Reef and Palm Hotel."

"Just what evidence have they against Egan, Mr. Winterslip?"

John Quincy was suddenly aware of Chan looking at him in a peculiar way. "Oh, they've dug up several things," he answered vaguely.

"Mr. Chan, you are a member of the police force," Captain Cope went on. "Perhaps you can tell me?"

Chan's little eyes narrowed. "Such matters are not yet presented to public," he replied.

"Ah, yes, naturally." Captain Cope's tone suggested disappointment.

"You have interest in this murder, I think?" Chan said.

"Why, yes—every one out this way is puzzling about it, I fancy. The thing has so many angles."

"Is it possible that you were an acquaintance with Mr. Dan Winterslip?" the detective persisted.

"I—I knew him slightly. But that was many years ago."

Chan stood. "Humbly begging pardon to be so abrupt," he said. He turned to John Quincy. "The moment of our appointment is eminent—"

"Of course," agreed John Quincy. "See you again, Captain." Perplexed, he followed Chan to the street. "What appointment—" he began, and stopped. Chan was carefully extinguishing the light of the cigarette against the stone facade of the hotel. That done, he dropped the stub into his pocket.

"You will see," he promised. "First we visit police station. As we journey, kindly relate all known facts concerning this Captain Cope."

John Quincy told of his first meeting with Cope in the San Francisco club, and repeated the conversation as he recalled it.

"Evidence of warm dislike for Dan Winterslip were not to be concealed?" inquired Chan.

"Oh, quite plain, Charlie. He certainly had no love for Cousin Dan. But what—"

"Immediately he was leaving for Hawaii—pardon the interrupt. Does it happily chance you know his date of arrival here?"

"I do. I saw him in the Alexander Young Hotel last Tuesday evening when I was looking for you. He was rushing off to the Fanning Islands, and he told me he had got in the previous day at noon—"

"Monday noon to put it lucidly."

"Yes—Monday noon. But Charlie—what are you trying to get at?"

"Groping about," Chan smiled. "Seeking to seize truth in my hot hands."

They walked on in silence to the station, where Chan led the way into the deserted room of Captain Hallet. He went directly to the safe and opened it. From a drawer he removed several small objects, which he carried over to the captain's table.

"Property Mr. Jim Egan," he announced, and laid a case of tarnished silver before John Quincy. "Open it—what do you find now? Corsican cigarettes." He set down another exhibit. "Tin box found in room of Mr. Brade. Open that, also. You find more Corsican cigarettes."

He removed an envelope from his pocket and taking out a charred stub, laid that too on the table. "Fragment found by walk outside door of Dan Winterslip's mansion," he elucidated. "Also Corsican brand."

Frowning deeply, he removed a second charred stub from his pocket and laid it some distance from the other exhibits. "Cigarette offered just now with winning air of hospitality by Captain Arthur Temple Cope. Lean close and perceive. More Corsican brand!"

"Good lord!" John Quincy cried.

"Can it be you are familiar with these Corsicans?" inquired Chan.

"Not at all."

"I am more happily located. This afternoon before the swim I pause at public library for listless reading. In Australian newspaper I encounter advertising talk of Corsican cigarette. It are assembled in two distinct fashions, one, labeled on tin 222, holds Turkish tobacco. Note 222 on tin of Brade. Other labeled 444 made up from Virginia weeds. Is it that you are clever to know difference between Turkish and Virginia tobacco?"

"Well, I think so—" began John Quincy.

"Same with me, but thinking are not enough now. The moment are serious. We will interrogate expert opinion. Honor me by a journey to smoking emporium."

He took a cigarette from Brade's tin, put it in an envelope and wrote something on the outside, then did the same with one from Egan's case. The two stubs were similarly classified.

They went in silence to the street. John Quincy, amazed by this new turn of events, told himself the idea was absurd. But Chan's face was grave, his eyes awake and eager.

John Quincy was vastly more amazed when they emerged from the tobacco shop after a brisk interview with the young man in charge. Chan was jubilant now.

"Again we advance! You hear what he tells us. Cigarette from Brade's tin and little brother from Egan's case are of identical contents, both being of Turkish tobacco. Stub found near walk are of Virginia stuff. So also are remnant received by me from the cordial hand of Captain Arthur Temple Cope!"

"It's beyond me," replied John Quincy. "By gad—that lets Egan out. Great news for Carlota. I'll hurry to the Reef and Palm and tell her—"

"Oh, no, no," protested Chan. "Please to let that happy moment wait. For the present, indulge only in silence. Before asking Captain Cope for statement we spy over his every move. Much may be revealed by the unsuspecting. I go to station to make arrangements—"

"But the man's a gentleman," John Quincy cried. "A captain in the British Admiralty. What you suggest is impossible."

Chan shook his head. "Impossible in Rear Bay at Boston," he said, "but here at moonly crossroads of Pacific, not so much so. Twenty-five years of my life are consumed in Hawaii, and I have many times been witness when the impossible roused itself and occurred."

XVII

Night Life in Honolulu

Monday brought no new developments, and John Quincy spent a restless day. Several times he called Chan at the police station, but the detective was always out.

Honolulu, according to the evening paper, was agog. This was not, as John Quincy learned to his surprise, a reference to the Winterslip case. An American fleet had just left the harbor of San Pedro bound for Hawaii. This was the annual cruise of the graduating class at Annapolis; the war-ships were overflowing with future captains and admirals. They would linger at the port of Honolulu for several days and a gay round of social events impended—dinners, dances, moonlight swimming parties.

John Quincy had not seen Barbara all day; the girl had not appeared at breakfast and had lunched with a friend down the beach. They met at dinner, however, and it seemed to him that she looked more tired and wan than ever. She spoke about the coming of the warships.

"It's always such a happy time," she said wistfully. "The town simply blooms with handsome boys in uniform. I don't like to have you miss all the parties, John Quincy. You're not seeing Honolulu at its best."

"Why—that's all right," John Quincy assured her.

She shook her head. "Not with me. You know, we're not such slaves to convention out here. If I should get you a few invitations—what do you think, Cousin Minerva?"

"I'm an old woman," said Miss Minerva. "According to the standards of your generation, I suppose it would be quite the thing. But it's not the sort of conduct I can view approvingly. Now, in my day—"

"Don't you worry, Barbara," John Quincy broke in. "Parties mean nothing to me. Speaking of old women, I'm an old man myself—thirty my next birthday. Just my pipe and slippers by the fire—or the electric fan—that's all I ask of life now."

She smiled and dropped the matter. After dinner, she followed John Quincy to the lanai. "I want you to do something for me," she began.

"Anything you say."

"Have a talk with Mr. Brade, and tell me what he wants."

"Why, I thought that Jennison—" said John Quincy.

"No, I didn't ask him to do it," she replied. For a long moment she was silent. "I ought to tell you—I'm not going to marry Mr. Jennison, after all."

A shiver of apprehension ran down John Quincy's spine. Good lord—that kiss! Had she misunderstood? And he hadn't meant a thing by it. Just a cousinly salute—at least, that was what it had started out to be. Barbara was a sweet girl, yes, but a relative, a Winterslip, and relatives shouldn't marry, no matter how distant the connection. Then, too, there was Agatha. He was bound to Agatha by all the ties of honor. What had he got himself into, anyhow?

"I'm awfully sorry to hear that," he said. "I'm afraid I'm to blame—"

"Oh, no," she protested.

"But surely Mr. Jennison understood. He knows we're related, and that what he saw last night meant—nothing." He was rather proud of himself. Pretty neat the way he'd got that over.

"If you don't mind," Barbara said, "I'd rather not talk about it any more. Harry and I will not be married—not at present, at any rate. And if you'll see Mr. Brade for me—"

"I certainly will," John Quincy promised. "I'll see him at once." He was glad to get away, for the moon was rising on that "spot of heart-breaking charm."

A fellow ought to be more careful, he reflected as he walked along the beach. Fit upon himself the armor of preparation, as Chan had said. Strange impulses came to one here in this far tropic land; to yield to them was weak. Complications would follow, as the night the day. Here was one now, Barbara and Jennison estranged, and the cause was clear. Well, he was certainly going to watch his step hereafter.

On the far end of the Reef and Palm's first floor balcony, Brade and his wife sat together in the dusk. John Quincy went up to them.

"May I speak with you, Mr. Brade?" he said.

The man looked up out of a deep reverie. "Ah, yes—of course—"

"I'm John Quincy Winterslip. We've met before."

"Oh, surely, surely sir." Brade rose and shook hands. "My dear—" he turned to his wife, but with one burning glance at John Quincy, the woman had fled. The boy tingled—in Boston a Winterslip was never snubbed. Well, Dan Winterslip had arranged it otherwise in Hawaii.

"Sit down, sir," said Brade, somewhat embarrassed by his wife's action. "I've been expecting some one of your name."

"Naturally. Will you have a cigarette, sir." John Quincy proffered his case, and when the cigarettes were lighted, seated himself at the man's side. "I'm here, of course, in regard to that story you told Saturday night."

"Story?" flashed Brade.

John Quincy smiled. "Don't misunderstand me. I'm not questioning the truth of it. But I do want to say this, Mr. Brade—you must be aware that you will have considerable difficulty establishing your claim in a court of law. The 'eighties are a long time back."

"What you say may be true," Brade agreed. "I'm relying more on the fact that a trial would result in some rather unpleasant publicity for the Winterslip family."

"Precisely," nodded John Quincy. "I am here at the request of Miss Barbara Winterslip, who is Dan Winterslip's sole heir. She's a very fine girl, sir—"

"I don't question that," cut in Brade impatiently.

"And if your demands are not unreasonable—" John Quincy paused, and leaned closer. "Just what do you want, Mr. Brade?"

Brade stroked those gray mustaches that drooped "in saddened mood." "No money," he said, "can make good the wrong Dan Winterslip did. But I'm an old man, and it would be something to feel financially secure for the rest of my life. I'm not inclined to be grasping—particularly since Dan Winterslip has passed beyond my reach. There were twenty thousand pounds involved. I'll say nothing about interest for more than forty years. A settlement of one hundred thousand dollars would be acceptable."

John Quincy considered. "I can't speak definitely for my cousin," he said, "but to me that sounds fair enough. I have no doubt Barbara will agree to give you that sum"—he saw the man's tired old eyes brighten in the semidarkness—"the moment the murderer of Dan Winterslip is found," he added quickly.

"What's that you say?" Brade leaped to his feet.

"I say she'll very likely pay you when this mystery is cleared up. Surely you don't expect her to do so before that time?" John Quincy rose too.

"I certainly do!" Brade cried. "Why, look here, this thing may drag on indefinitely. I want England again—the Strand, Piccadilly—it's twenty-five years since I saw London. Wait! Damn it, why should I wait! What's this murder to me—by gad, sir—" He came close, erect, flaming, the son of Tom Brade, the blackbirder, now. "Do you mean to insinuate that I—"

John Quincy faced him calmly. "I know you can't prove where you were early last Tuesday morning," he said evenly. "I don't say that incriminates you, but I shall certainly advise my cousin to wait. I'd not care to see her in the position of having rewarded the man who killed her father."

"I'll fight," cried Brade. "I'll take it to the courts—"

"Go ahead," John Quincy said. "But it will cost you every penny you've saved, and you may lose in the end. Good night, sir."

"Good night!" Brade answered, standing as his father might have stood on the Maid of Shiloh's deck.

John Quincy had gone half-way down the balcony when he heard quick footsteps behind him. He turned. It was Brade, Brade the civil servant, the man who had labored thirty-six years in the oven of India, a beaten, helpless figure.

"You've got me," he said, laying a hand on John Quincy's arm. "I can't fight. I'm too tired, too old—I've worked too hard. I'll take whatever your cousin wants to give me—when she's ready to give it."

"That's a wise decision, sir," John Quincy answered. A sudden feeling of pity gripped his heart. He felt toward Brade as he had felt toward that other exile, Arlene Compton. "I hope you see London very soon," he added, and held out his hand.

Brade took it. "Thank you, my boy. You're a gentleman, even if your name is Winterslip."

Which, John Quincy reflected as he entered the lobby of the Reef and Palm, was a compliment not without its flaw.

He didn't worry over that long, however, for Carlota Egan was behind the desk. She looked up and smiled, and it occurred to John Quincy that her eyes were happier than he had seen them since that day on the Oakland ferry.

"Hello," he said. "Got a job for a good bookkeeper?"

She shook her head. "Not with business the way it is now. I was just figuring my pay-roll. You know, we've no undertow at Waikiki, but all my life I've had to worry about the overhead."

He laughed. "You talk like a brother Kiwanian. By the way, has anything happened? You seem considerably cheered."

"I am," she replied. "I went to see poor dad this morning in that horrible place—and when I left some one else was going in to visit him. A stranger."

"A stranger?"

"Yes—and the handsomest thing you ever saw—tall, gray, capable-looking. He had such a friendly air, too—I felt better the moment I saw him."

"Who was he?" John Quincy inquired, with sudden interest.

"I'd never seen him before, but one of the men told me he was Captain Cope, of the British Admiralty."

"Why should Captain Cope want to see your father?"

"I haven't a notion. Do you know him?"

"Yes—I've met him," John Quincy told her.

"Don't you think he's wonderful-looking?" Her dark eyes glowed.

"Oh, he's all right," replied John Quincy without enthusiasm. "You know, I can't help feeling that things are looking up for you."

"I feel that too," she said.

"What do you say we celebrate?" he suggested. "Go out among 'em and get a little taste of night life. I'm a bit fed up on the police station. What do people do here in the evening? The movies?"

"Just at present," the girl told him, "everybody visits Punahou to see the night-blooming cereus. It's the season now, you know."

"Sounds like a big evening," John Quincy laughed. "Go and look at the flowers. Well, I'm for it. Will you come?"

"Of course." She gave a few directions to the clerk, then joined him by the door. "I can run down and get the roadster," he offered.

"Oh, no," she smiled. "I'm sure I'll never own a motor-car, and it might make me discontented to ride in one. The trolley's my carriage— and it's lots of fun. One meets so many interesting people."

On the stone walls surrounding the campus of Oahu College, the strange flower that blooms only on a summer night was heaped in snowy splendor. John Quincy had been a bit lukewarm regarding the expedition when they set out, but he saw his error now. For here was beauty, breath-taking and rare. Before the walls paraded a throng of sight-seers; they joined the procession. The girl was a charming companion, her spirits had revived and she chatted vivaciously. Not about Shaw and the art galleries, true enough, but bright human talk that John Quincy liked to hear.

He persuaded her to go to the city for a maidenly ice-cream soda, and it was ten o'clock when they returned to the beach. They left the trolley at a stop some distance down the avenue from the Reef and Palm, and strolled slowly toward the hotel. The sidewalk was lined to their right by dense foliage, almost impenetrable. The night was calm; the street lamps shone brightly; the paved street gleamed white in the moonlight. John Quincy was talking of Boston.

"I think you'd like it there. It's old and settled, but—"

From the foliage beside them came the flash of a pistol, and John Quincy heard a bullet sing close to his head. Another flash, another bullet. The girl gave a startled little cry.

John Quincy circled round her and plunged into the bushes. Angry branches stung his cheek. He stopped; he couldn't leave the girl alone. He returned to her side.

"What did that mean?" he asked, amazed. He stared in wonder at the peaceful scene before him.

"I—I don't know." She took his arm. "Come—hurry!"

"Don't be afraid," he said reassuringly.

"Not for myself," she answered.

They went on to the hotel, greatly puzzled. But when they entered the lobby, they had something else to think about. Captain Arthur Temple Cope was standing by the desk, and he came at once to meet them.

"This is Miss Egan, I believe. Ah, Winterslip, how are you?" He turned again to the girl, "I've taken a room here, if you don't mind."

"Why, not at all," she gasped.

"I talked with your father this morning. I didn't know about his trouble until I had boarded a ship for the Fanning Islands. I came back as quickly as I could."

"You came back—" She stared at him.

"Yes. I came back to help him."

"That's very kind of you," the girl said. "But I'm afraid I don't understand—"

"Oh, no, you don't understand. Naturally." The captain smiled down at her. "You see, Jim's my young brother. You're my niece, and your name is Carlota Maria Cope. I fancy I've persuaded old Jim to own up to us at last."

The girl's dark eyes were wide. "I—I think you're a very nice uncle," she said at last.

"Do you really?" The captain bowed. "I aim to be," he added.

John Quincy stepped forward. "Pardon me," he said. "I'm afraid I'm intruding. Good night, Captain."

"Good night, my boy," Cope answered.

The girl went with John Quincy to the balcony. "I—I don't know what to make of it," she said.

"Things are coming rather fast," John Quincy admitted. He remembered the Corsican cigarette. "I wouldn't trust him too far," he admonished.

"But he's so wonderful—"

"Oh, he's all right, probably. But looks are often deceptive. I'll go along now and let you talk with him."

She laid one slim tanned hand on his white-clad arm. "Do be careful!"

"Oh, I'm all right," he told her.

"But some one shot at you."

"Yes, and a very poor aim he had, too. Don't worry about me." She was very close, her eyes glowing in the dark. "You said you weren't afraid for yourself," he added. "Did you mean—"

"I meant—I was afraid—for you."

The moon, of course, was shining. The cocoa-palms turned their heads away at the suggestion of the trades. The warm waters of Waikiki murmured near by. John Quincy Winterslip, from Boston and immune, drew the girl to him and kissed her. Not a cousinly kiss, either—but why should it have been? She wasn't his cousin.

"Thank you, my dear," he said. He seemed to be floating dizzily in space. It came to him that he might reach out and pluck her a handful of stars.

It came to him a second later that, despite his firm resolve, he had done it again. Kissed another girl.

Three—that made three with whom he was sort of entangled.

"Good night," he said huskily, and leaping over the rail, fled hastily through the garden.

Three girls now—but he hadn't a single regret. He was living at last. As he hurried through the dark along the beach, his heart was light. Once he fancied he was being followed, but he gave it little thought. What of it?

On the bureau in his room he found an envelope with his name typewritten on the outside. The note within was typewritten too. He read:

"You are too busy out here. Hawaii can manage her affairs without the interference of a malihini. Boats sail almost daily. If you are still here forty-eight hours after you get this—look out! To-night's shots were fired into the air. The aim will quickly improve!"

Delighted, John Quincy tossed the note aside.

Threatening him, eh? His activities as a detective were bearing fruit. He recalled the glowering face of Kaohla when he said: "You did this. I don't forget." And a remark of Dan Winterslip's his aunt had quoted: "Civilized—yes. But far underneath there are deep dark waters flowing still."

Boats were sailing almost daily, were they? Well, let them sail. He would be on one some day—but not until he had brought Dan Winterslip's murderer to justice.

Life had a new glamour now. Look out? He'd be looking—and enjoying it, too. He smiled happily to himself as he took off his coat. This was better than selling bonds in Boston.

XVIII

A Cable From the Mainland

John Quincy awoke at nine the following morning and slipped from under his mosquito netting eager to face the responsibilities of a new day. On the floor near his bureau lay the letter designed to speed the parting guest. He picked it up and read it again with manifest enjoyment.

When he reached the dining-room Haku informed him that Miss Minerva and Barbara had breakfasted early and gone to the city on a shopping tour.

"Look here, Haku," the boy said. "A letter came for me late last night?"

"Yes-s," admitted Haku.

"Who delivered it?"

"Can not say. It were found on floor of hall close by big front door."

"Who found it?"

"Kamaikui."

"Oh, yes—Kamaikui."

"I tell her to put in your sleeping room."

"Did Kamaikui see the person who brought it?"

"Nobody see him. Nobody on place."

"All right," John Quincy said.

He spent a leisurely hour on the lanai with his pipe and the morning paper. At about half past ten he got out the roadster and drove to the police station.

Hallet and Chan, he was told, were in a conference with the prosecutor. He sat down to wait, and in a few moments word came for him to join them. Entering Greene's office, he saw the three men seated gloomily about the prosecutor's desk.

"Well, I guess I'm some detective," he announced.

Greene looked up quickly. "Found anything new?"

"Not precisely," John Quincy admitted. "But last night when I was walking along Kalakaua Avenue with a young woman, somebody took a couple of wild shots at me from the bushes. And when I got home I found this letter waiting."

He handed the epistle to Hallet, who read it with evident disgust, then passed it on to the prosecutor. "That doesn't get us anywhere," the captain said.

"It may get me somewhere, if I'm not careful," John Quincy replied. "However, I'm rather proud of it. Sort of goes to show that my detective work is hitting home."

"Maybe," answered Hallet, carelessly.

Greene laid the letter on his desk. "My advice to you," he said, "is to carry a gun. That's unofficial, of course."

"Nonsense, I'm not afraid," John Quincy told him. "I've got a pretty good idea who sent this thing."

"You have?" Greene said.

"Yes. He's a friend of Captain Hallet's. Dick Kaohla."

"What do you mean he's a friend of mine?" flared Hallet.

"Well, you certainly treated him pretty tenderly the other night."

"I knew what I was doing," said Hallet grouchily.

"I hope you did. But if he puts a bullet in me some lovely evening, I'm going to be pretty annoyed with you."

"Oh, you're in no danger," Hallet answered. "Only a coward writes anonymous letters."

"Yes, and only a coward shoots from ambush. But that isn't saying he can't take a good aim."

Hallet picked up the letter. "I'll keep this. It may prove to be evidence."

"Surely," agreed John Quincy. "And you haven't got any too much evidence, as I see it."

"Is that so?" growled Hallet. "We've made a rather important discovery about that Corsican cigarette."

"Oh, I'm not saying Charlie isn't good," smiled John Quincy. "I was with him when he worked that out."

A uniformed man appeared at the door. "Egan and his daughter and Captain Cope," he announced to Greene. "Want to see them now, sir?"

"Send them in," ordered the prosecutor.

"I'd like to stay, if you don't mind," John Quincy suggested.

"Oh, by all means," Greene answered. "We couldn't get along without you."

The policeman brought Egan to the door, and the proprietor of the Reef and Palm came into the room. His face was haggard and pale; his long siege with the authorities had begun to tell. But a stubborn light still flamed in his eyes. After him came Carlota Egan, fresh and beautiful, and with a new air of confidence about her. Captain Cope followed, tall, haughty, a man of evident power and determination.

"This is the prosecutor, I believe?" he said. "Ah, Mr. Winterslip, I find you everywhere I go."

"You don't mind my staying?" inquired John Quincy.

"Not in the least, my boy. Our business here will take but a moment." He turned to Greene. "Just as a preliminary," he continued, "I am Captain Arthur Temple Cope of the British Admiralty, and this gentleman"—he nodded toward the proprietor of the Reef and Palm—"is my brother."

"Really?" said Greene. "His name is Egan, as I understand it."

"His name is James Egan Cope," the captain replied. "He dropped the Cope many years ago for reasons that do not concern us now. I am here simply to say, sir, that you are holding my brother on the flimsiest pretext I have ever encountered in the course of my rather extensive travels. If necessary, I propose to engage the best lawyer in Honolulu and have him free by night. But I'm giving you this last chance to release him and avoid a somewhat painful expose of the sort of nonsense you go in for."

John Quincy glanced at Carlota Egan. Her eyes were shining but not on him. They were on her uncle.

Greene flushed slightly. "A good bluff, Captain, is always worth trying," he said.

"Oh, then you admit you've been bluffing," said Cope quickly.

"I was referring to your attitude, sir," Greene replied.

"Oh, I see," Cope said. "I'll sit down, if you don't mind. As I understand it, you have two things against old Jim here. One is that he visited Dan Winterslip on the night of the murder, and now refuses to divulge the nature of that call. The other is the stub of a Corsican cigarette which was found by the walk outside the door of Winterslip's living-room."

Greene shook his head. "Only the first," he responded. "The Corsican cigarette is no longer evidence against Egan." He leaned suddenly across his desk. "It is, my dear Captain Cope, evidence against you."

Cope met his look unflinchingly. "Really?" he remarked.

John Quincy noted a flash of startled bewilderment in Carlota Egan's eyes.

"That's what I said," Greene continued. "I'm very glad you dropped in this morning, sir. I've been wanting to talk to you. I've been told that you were heard to express a strong dislike for Dan Winterslip."

"I may have. I certainly felt it."

"Why?"

"As a midshipman on a British war-ship, I was familiar with Australian gossip in the 'eighties. Mr. Dan Winterslip had an unsavory reputation. It was rumored on good authority that he rifled the sea chest of his dead captain on the Maid of Shiloh. Perhaps we're a bit squeamish, but that is the sort of thing we sailors can not forgive. There were other quaint deeds in connection with his blackbirding activities. Yes, my dear sir, I heartily disliked Dan Winterslip, and if I haven't said so before, I say it now."

"You arrived in Honolulu a week ago yesterday," Greene continued. "At noon—Monday noon. You left the following day. Did you, by any chance, call on Dan Winterslip during that period?"

"I did not."

"Ah, yes. I may tell you, sir, that the Corsican cigarettes found in Egan's case were of Turkish tobacco. The stub found near the scene of Dan Winterslip's murder was of Virginia tobacco. So also, my dear Captain Cope, was the Corsican cigarette you gave our man Charlie Chan in the lobby of the Alexander Young Hotel last Sunday night."

Cope looked at Chan, and smiled. "Always the detective, eh?" he said.

"Never mind that!" Greene cried. "I'm asking for an explanation."

"The explanation is very simple," Cope replied. "I was about to give it to you when you launched into this silly cross-examination. The Corsican cigarette found by Dan Winterslip's door was, naturally, of Virginia tobacco. I never smoke any other kind."

"What!"

"There can be no question about it, sir. I dropped that cigarette there myself."

"But you just told me you didn't call on Dan Winterslip."

"That was true. I didn't. I called on Miss Minerva Winterslip, of Boston, who is a guest in the house. As a matter of fact, I had tea with her last Monday at five o'clock. You may verify that by telephoning the lady."

Greene glanced at Hallet, who glanced at the telephone, then turned angrily to John Quincy. "Why the devil didn't she tell me that?" he demanded.

John Quincy smiled. "I don't know, sir. Possibly because she never thought of Captain Cope in connection with the murder."

"She'd hardly be likely to," Cope said. "Miss Winterslip and I had tea in the living-room, then went out and sat on a bench in the garden, chatting over old times. When I returned to the house I was smoking a cigarette. I dropped it just outside the living-room door. Whether Miss Winterslip noted my action or not, I don't know. She probably didn't, it isn't the sort of thing one remembers. You may call her on the telephone if you wish, sir."

Again Greene looked at Hallet, who shook his head. "I'll talk with her later," announced the Captain of Detectives. Evidently Miss Minerva had an unpleasant interview ahead.

"At any rate," Cope continued to the prosecutor, "you had yourself disposed of the cigarette as evidence against old Jim. That leaves only the fact of his silence—"

"His silence, yes," Greene cut in, "and the fact that Winterslip had been heard to express a fear of Jim Egan."

Cope frowned. "Had he, really?" He considered a moment. "Well, what of it? Winterslip had good reason to fear a great many honest men. No, my dear sir, you have nothing save my brother's silence against him, and that is not enough. I demand—"

Greene raised his hand. "Just a minute. I said you were bluffing, and I still think so. Any other assumption would be an insult to your intelligence. Surely you know enough about the law to understand that your brother's refusal to tell me his business with Winterslip, added to the fact that he was presumably the last person to see Winterslip alive, is sufficient excuse for holding him. I can hold him on those grounds, I am holding him, and, my dear Captain, I shall continue to hold him until hell freezes over."

"Very good," said Cope, rising. "I shall engage a capable lawyer—"

"That is, of course, your privilege," snapped Greene. "Good morning."

Cope hesitated. He turned to Egan. "It means more publicity, Jim," he said. "Delay, too. More unhappiness for Carlota here. And since everything you did was done for her—"

"How did you know that?" asked Egan quickly.

"I've guessed it. I can put two and two together, Jim. Carlota was to return with me for a bit of schooling in England. You said you had the money, but you hadn't. That was your pride again, Jim. It's got you into a lifetime of trouble. You cast about for the funds, and you remembered Winterslip. I'm beginning to see it all now. You had something on Dan Winterslip, and you went to his house that night to—er—"

"To blackmail him," suggested Greene.

"It wasn't a pretty thing to do, Jim," Cope went on. "But you weren't doing it for yourself. Carlota and I know you would have died first. You did it for your girl, and we both forgive you." He turned to Carlota. "Don't we, my dear?"

The girl's eyes were wet. She rose and kissed her father. "Dear old dad," she said.

"Come on, Jim," pleaded Captain Cope. "Forget your pride for once. Speak up, and we'll take you home with us. I'm sure the prosecutor will keep the thing from the newspapers—"

"We've promised him that a thousand times," Greene said.

Egan lifted his head. "I don't care anything about the newspapers," he explained. "It's you, Arthur—you and Cary—I didn't want you two to know. But since you've guessed, and Cary knows too—I may as well tell everything."

John Quincy stood up. "Mr. Egan," he said. "I'll leave the room, if you wish."

"Sit down, my boy," Egan replied. "Cary's told me of your kindness to her. Besides, you saw the check—"

"What check was that?" cried Hallet. He leaped to his feet and stood over John Quincy.

"I was honor bound not to tell," explained the boy gently.

"You don't say so!" Hallet bellowed. "You're a fine pair, you and that aunt of yours—"

"One minute, Hallet," cut in Greene. "Now, Egan, or Cope, or whatever your name happens to be—I'm waiting to hear from you."

Egan nodded. "Back in the 'eighties I was teller in a bank in Melbourne, Australia," he said. "One day a young man came to my window—Williams or some such name he called himself. He had a green hide bag full of gold pieces—Mexican, Spanish and English coins, some of them crusted with dirt—and he wanted to exchange them for bank-notes. I made the exchange for him. He appeared several times with similar bags, and the transaction was repeated. I thought little of it at the time, though the fact that he tried to give me a large tip did rather rouse my suspicion.

"A year later, when I had left the bank and gone to Sydney, I heard rumors of what Dan Winterslip had done on the Maid of Shiloh. It occurred to me that Williams and Winterslip were probably the same man. But no one seemed to be prosecuting the case, the general feeling was that it was blood money anyhow, that Tom Brade had not come by it honestly himself. So I said nothing.

"Twelve years later I came to Hawaii, and Dan Winterslip was pointed out to me. He was Williams, right enough. And he knew me, too. But I'm not a blackmailer—I've been in some tight places, Arthur, but I've always played fair—so I let the matter drop. For more than twenty years nothing happened.

"Then, a few months ago, my family located me at last, and Arthur here wrote me that he was coming to Honolulu and would look me up. I'd always felt that I'd not done the right thing by my girl—that she was not taking the place in the world to which she was entitled. I wanted her to visit my old mother and get a bit of English training. I wrote to Arthur and it was arranged. But I couldn't let her go as a charity child—I couldn't admit I'd failed and was unable to do anything for her—I said I'd pay her way. And I—I didn't have a cent.

"And then Brade came. It seemed providential. I might have sold my information to him, but when I talked with him I found he had very little money, and I felt that Winterslip would beat him in the end. No, Winterslip was my man—Winterslip with his rotten wealth. I don't know just what happened—I was quite mad, I fancy—the world owed me that, I figured, just for my girl, not for me. I called Winterslip up and made an appointment for that Monday night.

"But somehow—the standards of a lifetime—it's difficult to change. The moment I had called him, I regretted it. I tried to slip out of it—I told myself there must be some other way—perhaps I could sell the Reef and Palm—anyhow, I called him again and said I wasn't coming. But he insisted, and I went.

"I didn't have to tell him what I wanted. He knew. He had a check ready for me—a check for five thousand dollars. It was Cary's happiness, her chance. I took it, and came away—but I was ashamed. I'm not trying to excuse my action; however, I don't believe I would ever have cashed it. When Cary found it in my desk and brought it to me, I tore it up. That's all." He turned his tired eyes toward his daughter. "I did it for you, Cary, but I didn't want you to know." She went over and put her arm about his shoulder, and stood smiling down at him through her tears.

"If you'd told us that in the first place," said Greene, "you could have saved everybody a lot of trouble, yourself included."

Cope stood up. "Well, Mr. Prosecutor, there you are. You're not going to hold him now?"

Greene rose briskly. "No. I'll arrange for his release at once." He and Egan went out together, then Hallet and Cope. John Quincy held out his hand to Carlota Egan—for by that name he thought of her still.

"I'm mighty glad for you," he said.

"You'll come and see me soon?" she asked. "You'll find a very different girl. More like the one you met on the Oakland ferry."

"She was very charming," John Quincy replied. "But then, she was bound to be—she had your eyes." He suddenly remembered Agatha Parker. "However, you've got your father now," he added. "You won't need me."

She looked up at him and smiled. "I wonder," she said, and went out.

John Quincy turned to Chan. "Well, that's that," he remarked. "Where are we now?"

"Speaking personally for myself," grinned Chan, "I am static in same place as usual. Never did have fondly feeling for Egan theory."

"But Hallet did," John Quincy answered. "A black morning for him."

In the small anteroom they encountered the Captain of Detectives. He appeared disgruntled.

"We were just remarking," said John Quincy pleasantly, "that there goes your little old Egan theory. What have you left?"

"Oh, I've got plenty," growled Hallet.

"Yes, you have. One by one your clues have gone up in smoke. The page from the guest book, the brooch, the torn newspaper, the ohia wood box, and now Egan and the Corsican cigarette."

"Oh, Egan isn't out of it. We may not be able to hold him, but I'm not forgetting Mr. Egan."

"Nonsense," smiled John Quincy. "I asked what you had left. A little button from a glove—useless. The glove was destroyed long ago. A wrist watch with an illuminated dial and a damaged numeral two—"

Chan's amber eyes narrowed. "Essential clue," he murmured. "Remember how I said it."

Hallet banged his fist on a table. "That's it—the wrist watch! If the person who wore it knows any one saw it, it's probably where we'll never find it now. But we've kept it pretty dark—perhaps he doesn't know. That's our only chance." He turned to Chan. "I've combed these islands once hunting that watch," he cried, "now I'm going to start all over again. The jewelry stores, the pawn shops, every nook and corner. You go out, Charlie, and start the ball rolling."

Chan moved with alacrity despite his weight. "I will give it one powerful push," he promised, and disappeared.

"Well, good luck," said John Quincy, moving on.

Hallet grunted. "You tell that aunt of yours I'm pretty sore," he remarked. He was not in the mood for elegance of diction.

John Quincy's opportunity to deliver the message did not come at lunch, for Miss Minerva remained with Barbara in the city. After dinner that evening he led his aunt out to sit on the bench under the hau tree.

"By the way," he said, "Captain Hallet is very much annoyed with you."

"I'm very much annoyed with Captain Hallet," she replied, "so that makes us even. What's his particular grievance now?"

"He believes you knew all the time the name of the man who dropped that Corsican cigarette."

She was silent for a moment. "Not all the time," she said at length. "What has happened?"

John Quincy sketched briefly the events of the morning at the police station. When he had finished he looked at her inquiringly.

"In the first excitement I didn't remember, or I should have spoken," she explained. "It was several days before the thing came to me. I saw it clearly then—Arthur—Captain Cope—tossing that cigarette aside as we reentered the house. But I said nothing about it."

"Why?"

"Well, I thought it would be a good test for the police. Let them discover it for themselves."

"That's a pretty weak explanation," remarked John Quincy severely. "You've been responsible for a lot of wasted time."

"It—it wasn't my only reason," said Miss Minerva softly.

"Oh—I'm glad to hear that. Go on."

"Somehow, I couldn't bring myself to link up that call of Captain Cope's with—a murder mystery."

Another silence. And suddenly—he was never dense—John Quincy understood.

"He told me you were very beautiful in the 'eighties," said the boy gently. "The captain, I mean. When I met him in that San Francisco club."

Miss Minerva laid her own hand on the boy's. When she spoke her voice, which he had always thought firm and sharp, trembled a little. "On this beach in my girlhood," she said, "happiness was within my grasp. I had only to reach out and take it. But somehow—Boston—Boston held me back. I let my happiness slip away."

"Not too late yet," suggested John Quincy.

She shook her head. "So he tried to tell me that Monday afternoon. But there was something in his tone—I may be in Hawaii, but I'm not quite mad. Youth, John Quincy, youth doesn't return, whatever they may say out here." She pressed his hand, and stood. "If your chance comes, dear boy," she added, "don't be such a fool."

She moved hastily away through the garden, and John Quincy looked after her with a new affection in his eyes.

Presently he saw the yellow glare of a match beyond the wire. Amos again, still loitering under his algaroba tree. John Quincy rose and strolled over to him.

"Hello, Cousin Amos," he said. "When are you going to take down this fence?"

"Oh, I'll get round to it some time," Amos answered. "By the way, I wanted to ask you. Any new developments?"

"Several," John Quincy told him. "But nothing that gets us anywhere. So far as I can see, the case has blown up completely."

"Well, I've been thinking it over," Amos said. "Maybe that would be the best outcome, after all. Suppose they do discover who did for Dan—it may only reveal a new scandal, worse than any of the others."

"I'll take a chance on that," replied John Quincy. "For my part, I intend to see this thing through—"

Haku came briskly through the garden. "Cable message for Mr. John Quincy Winterslip. Boy say collect. Requests money."

John Quincy followed quickly to the front door. A bored small boy awaited him. He paid the sum due and tore open the cable. It was signed by the postmaster at Des Moines, and it read:

"No one named Saladine ever heard of here."

John Quincy dashed to the telephone. Some one on duty at the station informed him that Chan had gone home, and gave him an address on Punchbowl Hill. He got out the roadster, and in five minutes more was speeding toward the city.

XIX

"Good-By, Pete!"

Charlie Chan lived in a bungalow that clung precariously to the side of Punchbowl Hill. Pausing a moment at the gate, John Quincy looked down on Honolulu, one great gorgeous garden set in an amphitheater of mountains. A beautiful picture, but he had no time for beauty now. He hurried up the brief walk that lay in the shadow of the palm trees.

A Chinese woman—a servant, she seemed—ushered him into Chan's dimly-lighted living-room. The detective was seated at a table playing chess; he rose with dignity when he saw his visitor. In this, his hour of ease, he wore a long loose robe of dark purple silk, which fitted closely at the neck and had wide sleeves. Beneath it showed wide trousers of the same material, and on his feet were shoes of silk, with thick felt soles. He was all Oriental now, suave and ingratiating but remote, and for the first time John Quincy was really conscious of the great gulf across which he and Chan shook hands.

"You do my lowly house immense honor," Charlie said. "This proud moment are made still more proud by opportunity to introduce my eldest son." He motioned for his opponent at chess to step forward, a slim sallow boy with amber eyes—Chan himself before he put on weight. "Mr. John Quincy Winterslip, of Boston, kindly condescend to notice Henry Chan. When you appear I am giving him lesson at chess so he may play in such manner as not to tarnish honored name."

The boy bowed low; evidently he was one member of the younger generation who had a deep respect for his elders. John Quincy also bowed. "Your father is my very good friend," he said. "And from now on, you are too."

Chan beamed with pleasure. "Condescend to sit on this atrocious chair. Is it possible you bring news?"

"It certainly is," smiled John Quincy. He handed over the message from the postmaster at Des Moines.

"Most interesting," said Chan. "Do I hear impressive chug of rich automobile engine in street?"

"Yes, I came in the car," John Quincy replied.

"Good. We will hasten at once to home of Captain Hallet, not far away. I beg of you to pardon my disappearance while I don more appropriate costume."

Left alone with the boy, John Quincy sought a topic of conversation. "Play baseball?" he asked.

The boy's eyes glowed. "Not very good, but I hope to improve. My cousin Willie Chan is great expert at that game. He has promised to teach me."

John Quincy glanced about the room. On the back wall hung a scroll with felicitations, the gift of some friend of the family at New Year's. Opposite him, on another wall, was a single picture, painted on silk, representing a bird on an apple bough. Charmed by its simplicity, he went over to examine it. "That's beautiful," he said.

"Quoting old Chinese saying, a picture is a voiceless poem," replied the boy.

Beneath the picture stood a square table, flanked by straight, low-backed armchairs. On other elaborately carved teakwood stands distributed about the room were blue and white vases, porcelain wine jars, dwarfed trees. Pale golden lanterns hung from the ceiling; a soft-toned rug lay on the floor. John Quincy felt again the gulf between himself and Charlie Chan.

But when the detective returned, he wore the conventional garb of Los Angeles or Detroit, and the gulf did not seem so wide. They went out together and entering the roadster, drove to Hallet's house on Iolani Avenue.

The captain lolled in pajamas on his lanai. He greeted his callers with interest.

"You boys are out late," he said. "Something doing?"

"Certainly is," replied John Quincy, taking a proffered chair. "There's a man named Saladine—"

At mention of the name, Hallet looked at him keenly. John Quincy went on to tell what he knew of Saladine, his alleged place of residence, his business, the tragedy of the lost teeth.

"Some time ago we got on to the fact that every time Kaohla figured in the investigation, Saladine was interested. He managed to be at the desk of the Reef and Palm the day Kaohla inquired for Brade. On the night Kaohla was questioned by your men, Miss Egan saw Mr. Saladine crouching outside the window. So Charlie and I thought it a good scheme to send a cable of inquiry to the postmaster at

Des Moines, where Saladine claimed to be in the wholesale grocery business." He handed an envelope to Hallet. "That answer arrived to-night," he added.

An odd smile had appeared on Hallet's usually solemn face. He took the cable and read it, then slowly tore it into bits.

"Forget it, boys," he said calmly.

"Wha—what!" gasped John Quincy.

"I said forget it. I like your enterprise, but you're on the wrong trail there."

John Quincy was greatly annoyed. "I demand an explanation," he cried.

"I can't give it to you," Hallet answered. "You'll have to take my word for it."

"I've taken your word for a good many things," said John Quincy hotly. "This begins to look rather suspicious to me. Are you trying to shield somebody?"

Hallet rose and laid his hand on John Quincy's shoulder. "I've had a hard day," he remarked, "and I'm not going to get angry with you. I'm not trying to shield anybody. I'm as anxious as you are to discover who killed Dan Winterslip. More anxious, perhaps."

"Yet when we bring you evidence you tear it up—"

"Bring me the right evidence," said Hallet. "Bring me that wrist watch. I can promise you action then."

John Quincy was impressed by the sincerity in his tone. But he was sadly puzzled, too. "All right," he said, "that's that. I'm sorry if we've troubled you with this trivial matter—"

"Don't talk like that," Hallet broke in. "I'm glad of your help. But as far as Mr. Saladine is concerned—" he looked at Chan—"let him alone."

Chan bowed. "You are undisputable chief," he replied.

They went back to Punchbowl Hill in the roadster, both rather dejected. As Chan alighted at his gate, John Quincy spoke: "Well, I'm pau. Saladine was my last hope."

Chan stared for a moment at the moonlit Pacific that lay beyond the water-front lamps. "Stone wall surround us," he said dreamily. "But we circle about, seeking loophole. Moment of discovery will come."

"I wish I thought so," replied John Quincy.

Chan smiled. "Patience are a very lovely virtue," he remarked. "Seem that way to me. But maybe that are my Oriental mind. Your race, I perceive, regard patience with ever-swelling disfavor."

It was with swelling disfavor that John Quincy regarded it as he drove back to Waikiki. Yet he had great need of patience in the days immediately following. For nothing happened.

The forty-eight-hour period given him to leave Hawaii expired, but the writer of that threatening letter failed to come forward and relieve the tedium. Thursday arrived, a calm day like the others; Thursday night, peaceful and serene.

On Friday afternoon Agatha Parker broke the monotony by a cable sent from the Wyoming ranch.

"You must be quite mad. I find the West crude and impossible."

John Quincy smiled; he could picture her as she wrote it, proud, haughty, unyielding. She must have been popular with the man who transmitted the message. Or was he, too, an exile from the East?

And perhaps the girl was right. Perhaps he was mad, after all. He sat on Dan Winterslip's lanai, trying to think things out. Boston, the office, the art gallery, the theaters. The Common on a winter's day, with the air bracing and full of life. The thrill of a new issue of bonds, like the thrill of a theatrical first night—would it get over big or flop at his feet? Tennis at Longwood, long evenings on the Charles, golf with people of his own kind at Magnolia. Tea out of exquisite cups in dim old drawing-rooms. Wasn't he mad to think of giving up all that? But what had Miss Minerva said? "If your chance ever comes—"

The problem was a big one, and big problems were annoying out here where the lotus grew. He yawned, and went aimlessly down-town. Drifting into the public library, he saw Charlie Chan hunched over a table that held an enormous volume. John Quincy went closer. The book was made up of back numbers of the Honolulu morning paper, and it was open at a time-yellowed sporting page.

"Hello, Chan. What are you up to?"

Chan gave him a smile of greeting. "Hello. Little bit of careless reading while I gallop about seeking loophole."

He closed the big volume casually. "You seem in the best of health."

"Oh, I'm all right."

"No more fierce shots out of bushes?"

"Not a trigger pulled. I imagine that was a big bluff—nothing more."

"What do you say—bluff?"

"I mean the fellow's a coward, after all."

Chan shook his head solemnly. "Pardon humble suggestion—do not lose carefulness. Hot heads plenty in hot climate."

"I'll look before I leap," John Quincy promised. "But I'm afraid I interrupted you."

"Ridiculous thought," protested Chan.

"I'll go along. Let me know if anything breaks."

"Most certainly. Up to present, everything are intact."

John Quincy paused at the door of the reference room. Charlie Chan had promptly opened the big book, and was again bending over it with every show of interest.

Returning to Waikiki, John Quincy faced a dull evening. Barbara had gone to the island of Kauai for a visit with old friends of the family. He had not been sorry when she went, for he didn't feel quite at ease in her presence. The estrangement between the girl and Jennison continued; the lawyer had not been at the dock to see her off. Yes, John Quincy had parted from her gladly, but her absence cast a pall of loneliness over the house on Kalia Road.

After dinner, he sat with his pipe on the lanai. Down the beach at the Reef and Palm pleasant company was available—but he hesitated. He had seen Carlota Egan several times by day, on the beach or in the water. She was very happy now, though somewhat appalled at thought of her approaching visit to England. They'd had several talks about that—daylight talks. John Quincy was a bit afraid to entrust himself—as Chan had said in speaking of his stone idol—of an evening. After all, there was Agatha, there was Boston. There was Barbara, too. Being entangled with three girls at once was a rather wearing experience. He rose, and went down-town to the movies.

On Saturday morning he was awakened early by the whir of aeroplanes above the house. The American fleet was in the offing, and the little brothers of the air service hastened out to hover overhead in friendly welcome. That day a spirit of carnival prevailed in Honolulu, flags floated from every masthead, and the streets bloomed, as Barbara had predicted, with handsome boys in spotless uniforms. They were everywhere, swarming in the souvenir stores, besieging the soda fountains, skylarking on the trolley-cars. Evening brought a great ball at the beach hotel, and John Quincy, out for a walk, saw that every spic and span uniform moved toward Waikiki, accompanied by a fair young thing who was only too happy to serve as sweetheart in that particular port.

John Quincy felt, suddenly, rather out of things. Each pretty girl he saw recalled Carlota Egan. He turned his wandering footsteps toward the Reef and Palm, and oddly enough, his pace quickened at once.

The proprietor himself was behind the desk, his eyes calm and untroubled now.

"Good evening, Mr. Egan—or should I say Mr. Cope," remarked John Quincy.

"Oh, we'll stick to the Egan, I guess," the man replied. "Sort of got out of the hang of the other. Mr. Winterslip, I'm happy to see you. Cary will be down in a moment."

John Quincy gazed about the big public room. It was a scene of confusion, spattered ladders, buckets of paint, rolls of new wall-paper. "What's going on?" he inquired.

"Freshening things up a bit," Egan answered. "You know, we're in society now." He laughed. "Yes, sir, the old Reef and Palm has been standing here a long time without so much as a glance from the better element of Honolulu. But now they know I'm related to the British Admiralty, they've suddenly discovered it's a quaint and interesting place. They're dropping in for tea. Just fancy. But that's Honolulu."

"That's Boston, too," John Quincy assured him.

"Yes—and precisely the sort of thing I ran away from England to escape, a good many years ago. I'd tell them all to go to the devil—but there's Cary. Somehow, women feel differently about those things. It will warm her heart a bit to have these dowagers smile upon her. And they're smiling—you know, they've even dug up the fact that my Cousin George has been knighted for making a particularly efficient brand of soap." He grimaced. "It's nothing I'd have mentioned myself—a family skeleton, as I see it. But society has odd standards. And I mustn't be hard on poor old George. As Arthur says, making soap is good clean fun."

"Is your brother still with you?"

"No. He's gone back to finish his job in the Fanning Group. When he returns, I'm sending Cary to England for a long stop. Yes, that's right—I'm sending her," he added quickly. "I'm paying for these repairs, too. You see, I've been able to add a second mortgage to the one already on the poor tottering Reef and Palm. That's another outcome of my new-found connection with the British Admiralty and the silly old soap business. Here's Cary now."

John Quincy turned. And he was glad he had, for he would not willingly have missed the picture of Carlota on the stairs. Carlota in an evening gown of some shimmering material, her dark hair dressed in a new and amazingly effective way, her white shoulders gleaming, her eyes happy at last. As she came quickly toward him he caught his

EARL DERR BIGGERS

breath, never had he seen her look so beautiful. She must have heard his voice in the office, he reflected, and with surprising speed arrayed herself thus to greet him. He was deeply grateful as he took her hand.

"Stranger," she rebuked. "We thought you'd deserted us."

"I'd never do that," he answered. "But I've been rather busy—"

A step sounded behind him. He turned, and there stood one of those ubiquitous navy boys, a tall, blond Adonis who held his cap in his hand and smiled in a devastating way.

"Hello, Johnnie," Carlota said. "Mr. Winterslip, of Boston, this is Lieutenant Booth, of Richmond, Virginia."

"How are you," nodded the boy, without removing his eyes from the girl's face. Just one of the guests, this Winterslip, no account at all—such was obviously the lieutenant's idea. "All ready, Cary? The car's outside."

"I'm frightfully sorry, Mr. Winterslip," said the girl, "but we're off to the dance. This week-end belongs to the navy, you know. You'll come again, won't you?"

"Of course," John Quincy replied. "Don't let me keep you."

She smiled at him and fled with Johnnie at her side. Looking after them, John Quincy felt his heart sink to his boots, an unaccountable sensation of age and helplessness. Youth, youth was going through that door, and he was left behind.

"A great pity she had to run," said Egan in a kindly voice.

"Why, that's all right," John Quincy assured him. "Old friend of the family, this Lieutenant Booth?"

"Not at all. Just a lad Cary met at parties in San Francisco. Won't you sit down and have a smoke with me?"

"Some other time, thanks," John Quincy said wearily. "I must hurry back to the house."

He wanted to escape, to get out into the calm lovely night, the night that was ruined for him now. He walked along the beach, savagely kicking his toes into the white sand. "Johnnie!" She had called him Johnnie. And the way she had looked at him, too! Again John Quincy felt that sharp pang in his heart. Foolish, foolish; better go back to Boston and forget. Peaceful old Boston, that was where he belonged. He was an old man out here—thirty, nearly. Better go away and leave these children to love and the moonlit beach.

Miss Minerva had gone in the big car to call on friends, and the house was quiet as the tomb. John Quincy wandered aimlessly about the rooms, gloomy and bereft. Down at the Moana an Hawaiian orchestra was playing and Lieutenant Booth, of Richmond, was holding Carlota close in the intimate manner affected these days by the young. Bah! If he hadn't been ordered to leave Hawaii, by gad, he'd go to-morrow.

The telephone rang. None of the servants appeared to answer it, so John Quincy went himself.

"Charlie Chan speaking," said a voice. "That is you, Mr. Winterslip? Good. Big events will come to pass very quick. Meet me drug and grocery emporium of Liu Yin, number 927 River Street, soon as you can do so. You savvy locality?"

"I'll find it," cried John Quincy, delighted.

"By bank of stream. I will await. Good-by."

Action—action at last! John Quincy's heart beat fast. Action was what he wanted to-night. As usually happens in a crisis, there was no automobile available; the roadster was at a garage undergoing repairs, and the other car was in use. He hastened over to Kalakaua Avenue intending to rent a machine, but a trolley approaching at the moment altered his plans and he swung aboard.

Never had a trolley moved at so reluctant a pace. When they reached the corner of Fort Street in the center of the city, he left it and proceeded on foot. The hour was still fairly early, but the scene was one of somnolent calm. A couple of tourists drifted aimlessly by. About the bright doorway of a shooting gallery loitered a group of soldiers from the fort, with a sprinkling of enlisted navy men. John Quincy hurried on down King Street, past Chinese noodle cafes and pawn shops, and turned presently off into River Street.

On his left was the river, on his right an array of shabby stores. He paused at the door of number 927, the establishment of Liu Yin. Inside, seated behind a screen that revealed only their heads, a number of Chinese were engrossed in a friendly little game. John Quincy opened the door; a bell tinkled, and he stepped into an odor of must and decay. Curious sights met his quick eye: dried roots and herbs, jars of sea-horse skeletons, dejected ducks flattened out and varnished to tempt the palate, gobbets of pork. An old Chinese man rose and came forward.

"I'm looking for Mr. Charlie Chan," said John Quincy.

The old man nodded and led the way to a red curtain across the rear of the shop. He lifted it, and indicated that John Quincy was to pass. The boy did so, and came into a bare room furnished with a cot, a table on which an oil lamp burned dimly behind a smoky chimney, and a couple of chairs. A man who had been sitting on one of the chairs rose suddenly—a huge red-haired man with the smell of the sea about him.

"Hello," he said.

"Is Mr. Chan here?" John Quincy inquired.

"Not yet. He'll be along in a minute. What say to a drink while we're waiting. Hey, Liu, a couple glasses that rotten rice wine!"

The Chinese man withdrew. "Sit down," said the man. John Quincy obeyed; the sailor sat too. One of his eyelids drooped wickedly; he rested his hands on the table—enormous hairy hands. "Charlie'll be here pretty quick," he said. "Then I got a little story to tell the two of you."

"Yes?" John Quincy replied. He glanced about the little vile-smelling room. There was a door, a closed door, at the back. He looked again at the red-haired man. He wondered how he was going to get out of there.

For he knew now that Charlie Chan had not called him on the telephone. It came to him belatedly that the voice was never Charlie's. "You savvy locality?" the voice had said. A clumsy attempt at Chan's style, but Chan was a student of English; he dragged his words painfully from the poets; he was careful to use nothing that savored of "pidgin." No, the detective had not telephoned; he was no doubt at home now bending over his chess-board, and here was John Quincy shut up in a little room on the fringe of the River District with a husky sailorman who leered at him knowingly.

The old Chinese man returned with two small glasses into which the liquor had already been poured. He set them on the table. The red-haired man lifted one of them. "Your health, sir," he said.

John Quincy took up the other glass and raised it to his lips. There was a suspicious eagerness in the sailor's one good eye. John Quincy put the glass back on the table. "I'm sorry," he said. "I don't want a drink, thank you."

The great face with its stubble of red beard leaned close to his. "Y' mean you won't drink with me?" said the red-haired man belligerently.

"That's just what I mean," John Quincy answered. Might as well get it over with, he felt; anything was better than this suspense. He stood up. "I'll be going along," he announced.

He took a step toward the red curtain. The sailor, evidently a fellow of few words, rose and got in his way. John Quincy, himself feeling the futility of talk, said nothing, but struck the man in the face. The sailor struck back with efficiency and promptness. In another second the room was full of battle, and John Quincy saw red everywhere, red curtain, red hair, red lamp flame, great red hairy hands cunningly seeking his face. What was it Roger had said? "Ever fought with a ship's officer—the old-fashioned kind with fists like flying hams?" No, he hadn't up to then, but that sweet experience was his now, and it came to John Quincy pleasantly that he was doing rather well at his new trade.

This was better than the attic; here he was prepared and had a chance. Time and again he got his hands on the red curtain, only to be dragged back and subjected to a new attack. The sailor was seeking to knock him out, and though many of his blows went home, that happy result—from the standpoint of the red-haired man—was unaccountably delayed. John Quincy had a similar aim in life; they lunged noisily about the room, while the surprising Orientals in the front of the shop continued their quiet game.

John Quincy felt himself growing weary; his breath came painfully; he realized that his adversary had not yet begun to fight. Standing with his back to the table in an idle moment while the red-haired man made plans for the future, the boy hit on a plan of his own. He overturned the table; the lamp crashed down; darkness fell over the world. In the final glimmer of light he saw the big man coming for him and dropping to his knees he tackled in the approved manner of Soldiers' Field, Cambridge, Massachusetts. Culture prevailed; the sailor went on his head with a resounding thump; John Quincy let go of him and sought the nearest exit. It happened to be the door at the rear, and it was unlocked.

He passed hurriedly through a cluttered back yard and climbing a fence, found himself in the neighborhood known as the River District. There in crazy alleys that have no names, no sidewalks, no beginning and no end, five races live together in the dark. Some houses were above the walk level, some below, all were out of alignment. John Quincy felt he had wandered into a futurist drawing. As he paused he heard the whine and clatter of Chinese music, the clicking of a typewriter, the rasp of a cheap phonograph playing American jazz, the distant scream of an auto horn, a child wailing Japanese lamentations. Footsteps in the yard beyond the fence roused him, and he fled.

He must get out of this mystic maze of mean alleys, and at once. Odd painted faces loomed in the dusk; pasty-white faces with just a suggestion of queer costumes beneath. A babel of tongues, queer eyes that glittered, once a lean hand on his arm. A group of moon-faced Chinese children under a lamp who scattered at his approach. And

EARL DERR BIGGERS

when he paused again, out of breath, the patter of many feet, bare feet, sandaled feet, the clatter of wooden clogs, the squeak of cheap shoes made in his own Massachusetts. Then suddenly the thump of large feet such as might belong to a husky sailor. He moved on.

Presently he came into the comparative quiet of River Street, and realized that he had traveled in a circle, for there was Liu Yin's shop again. As he hurried on toward King Street, he saw, over his shoulder, that the red-haired man still followed. A big touring car, with curtains drawn, waited by the curb. John Quincy leaped in beside the driver.

"Get out of here, quick!" he panted.

A sleepy Japanese face looked at him through the gloom. "Busy now."

"I don't care if you are—" began John Quincy, and glanced down at one of the man's arms resting on the wheel. His heart stood still. In the dusk he saw a wrist watch with an illuminated dial, and the numeral two was very dim.

Even as he looked, strong hands seized him by the collar and dragged him into the dark tonneau. At the same instant, the red-haired man arrived.

"Got him, Mike? Say, that's luck!" He leaped into the rear of the car. Quick able work went forward, John Quincy's hands were bound behind his back, a vile-tasting gag was put in his mouth. "Damned if this bird didn't land me one in the eye," said the red-haired man. "I'll pay him for it when we get aboard. Hey you—Pier 78. Show us some speed!"

The car leaped forward. John Quincy lay on the dusty floor, bound and helpless. To the docks? But he wasn't thinking of that, he was thinking of the watch on the driver's wrist.

A brief run, and they halted in the shadow of a pier-shed. John Quincy was lifted and propelled none too gently from the car. His cheek was jammed against one of the buttons holding the side curtain, and he had sufficient presence of mind to catch the gag on it and loosen it. As they left the car he tried to get a glimpse of its license plate, but he was able to ascertain only the first two figures—33—before it sped away.

His two huge chaperons hurried him along the dock. Some distance off he saw a little group of men, three in white uniforms, one in a darker garb. The latter was smoking a pipe. John Quincy's heart leaped. He maneuvered the loosened gag with his teeth, so that it dropped about his collar. "Good-by, Pete!" he shouted at the top of his lungs, and launched at once into a terrific struggle to break away from his startled captors.

There was a moment's delay, and then the clatter of feet along the dock. A stocky boy in a white uniform began an enthusiastic debate with Mike, and the other two were prompt to claim the attention of the red-haired man. Pete Mayberry was at John Quincy's back, cutting the rope on his wrists.

"Well, I'll be damned, Mr. Winterslip," he cried.

"Same here," laughed John Quincy. "Shanghaied in another minute but for you." He leaped forward to join the battle, but the red-haired man and his friend had already succumbed to youth and superior forces, and were in full retreat. John Quincy followed joyously along the dock, and planted his fist back of his old adversary's ear. The sailor staggered, but regained his balance and went on.

John Quincy returned to his rescuers. "The last blow is the sweetest," he remarked.

"I can place those guys," said Mayberry. "They're off that tramp steamer that's been lying out in the harbor the past week. An opium runner, I'll gamble on it. You go to the police station right away—"

"Yes," said John Quincy, "I must. But I want to thank you, Mr. Mayberry. And"—he turned to the white uniforms—"you fellows too."

The stocky lad was picking up his cap. "Why, that's all right," he said. "A real pleasure, if you ask me. But look here, old timer," he added, addressing Mayberry, "how about your Honolulu water-front and its lost romance? You go tell that to the marines."

As John Quincy hurried away Pete Mayberry was busily explaining that the thing was unheard of—not in twenty years—maybe more than that—his voice died in the distance.

Hallet was in his room, and John Quincy detailed his evening's adventure. The captain was incredulous, but when the boy came to the wrist watch on the driver of the car, he sat up and took notice.

"Now you're talking," he cried. "I'll start the force after that car to-night. First two figures 33, you say. I'll send somebody aboard that tramp, too. They can't get away with stuff like that around here."

"Oh, never mind them," said John Quincy magnanimously. "Concentrate on the watch."

Back in the quiet town he walked with his head up, his heart full of the joy of battle. And while he thought of it, he stepped into the cable office. The message he sent was addressed to Agatha Parker on that Wyoming ranch. "San Francisco or nothing," was all it said.

As he walked down the deserted street on his way to the corner to wait for his trolley, he heard quick footsteps on his trail again. Who now? He was sore and weary, a bit fed up on fighting for one evening. He quickened his pace. The steps quickened too. He went even faster. So did his pursuer. Oh, well, might as well stop and face him.

John Quincy turned. A young man rushed up, a lean young man in a cap.

"Mr. Winterslip, ain't it?" He thrust a dark brown object into John Quincy's hand. "Your July Atlantic, sir. Came in on the Maui this morning."

"Oh," said John Quincy limply. "Well, I'll take it. My aunt might like to look at it. Keep the change."

"Thank you, sir," said the newsman, touching his cap.

John Quincy rode out to Waikiki on the last seat of the car. His face was swollen and cut, every muscle ached. Under his arm, clasped tightly, he held the July Atlantic. But he didn't so much as look at the table of contents. "We move, we advance," he told himself exultantly. For he had seen the watch with the illuminated dial—the dial on which the numeral two was very dim.

XX

The Story of Lau Ho

Early Sunday morning John Quincy was awakened by a sharp knock on his door. Rising sleepily and donning dressing-gown and slippers, he opened it to admit his Aunt Minerva. She had a worried air.

"Are you all right, John Quincy?" she inquired.

"Surely. That is, I would be if I hadn't been dragged out of bed a full hour before I intended to get up."

"I'm sorry, but I had to have a look at you." She took a newspaper from under her arm and handed it to him. "What's all this?"

An eight-column head on the first page caught even John Quincy's sleepy eye. "Boston Man has Strange Adventure on Water-Front." Smaller heads announced that Mr. John Quincy Winterslip had been rescued from an unwelcome trip to China, "in the nick of time" by three midshipmen from the Oregon. Poor Pete Mayberry! He had been the real hero of the affair, but his own paper would not come out again until Monday evening, and rivals had beaten him to the story.

John Quincy yawned. "All true, my dear," he said. "I was on the verge of leaving you when the navy saved me. Life, you perceive, has become a musical comedy."

"But why should any one want to shanghai you?" cried Miss Minerva.

"Ah, I hoped you'd ask me that. It happens that your nephew has a brain. His keen analytical work as a detective is getting some one's goat. He admitted as much in a letter he sent me the night he took a few shots at my head."

"Some one shot at you!" gasped Miss Minerva.

"I'll say so. You rather fancy yourself as a sleuth, but is anybody taking aim at you from behind bushes? Answer me that."

Miss Minerva sat down weakly on a chair. "You're going home on the next boat," she announced.

He laughed. "About two weeks ago I made that suggestion to you. And what was your reply? Ah, my dear, the tables are turned. I'm not going home on the next boat. I may never go home. This gay, care-free, sudden country begins to appeal to me. Let me read about myself."

He returned to the paper. "The clock was turned back thirty years on the Honolulu water-front last night," began the somewhat imaginative account. It closed with the news that the tramp steamer Mary S. Allison had left port before the police could board her. Evidently she'd had steam up and papers ready, and was only awaiting the return of the red-haired man and his victim. John Quincy handed the newspaper back to his aunt.

"Too bad," he remarked. "They slipped through Hallet's fingers."

"Of course they did," she snapped. "Everybody does. I'd like a talk with Captain Hallet. If I could only tell him what I think of him, I'd feel better."

"Save that paper," John Quincy said. "I want to send it to mother."

She stared at him. "Are you mad? Poor Grace—she'd have a nervous breakdown. I only hope she doesn't hear of this until you're back in Boston safe and sound."

"Oh, yes—Boston," laughed John Quincy. "Quaint old town, they tell me. I must visit there some day. Now if you'll leave me a minute, I'll prepare to join you at breakfast and relate the story of my adventurous life."

"Very well," agreed Miss Minerva, rising. She paused at the door. "A little witch-hazel might help your face."

"The scars of honorable battle," said her nephew. "Why remove them?"

"Honorable fiddlesticks," Miss Minerva answered. "After all, the Back Bay has its good points." But in the hall outside she smiled a delighted little smile.

When John Quincy and his aunt were leaving the dining-room after breakfast Kamaikui, stiff and dignified in a freshly-laundered holoku, approached the boy.

"So very happy to see you safe this morning," she announced.

"Why, thank you, Kamaikui," he answered. He wondered. Was Kaohla responsible for his troubles, and if so, did this huge silent woman know of her grandson's activities?

"Poor thing," Miss Minerva said as they entered the living-room. "She's been quite downcast since Dan went. I'm sorry for her. I've always liked her."

"Naturally," smiled John Quincy. "There's a bond between you."

"What's that?"

"Two vanishing races, yours and hers. The Boston Brahman and the pure Hawaiian."

Later in the morning Carlota Egan telephoned him, greatly excited. She had just seen the Sunday paper.

"All true," he admitted. "While you were dancing your heart out, I was struggling to sidestep a Cook's tour of the Orient."

"I shouldn't have had a happy moment if I'd known."

"Then I'm glad you didn't. Big party, I suppose?"

"Yes. You know, I've been terribly worried about you ever since that night on the avenue. I want to talk with you. Will you come to see me?"

"Will I? I'm on my way already."

He hung up the receiver and hastened down the beach. Carlota was sitting on the white sand not far from the Reef and Palm, all in white herself. A serious wide-eyed Carlota quite different from the gay girl who had been hurrying to a party the night before.

John Quincy dropped down beside her, and for a time they talked of the dance and of his adventure. Suddenly she turned to him.

"I have no right to ask it, I know, but—I want you to do something for me."

"It will make me very happy—anything you ask."

"Go back to Boston."

"What! Not that. I was wrong—that wouldn't make me happy."

"Yes, it would. You don't think so now, perhaps. You're dazzled by the sun out here, but this isn't your kind of place. We're not your kind of people. You think you like us, but you'd soon forget. Back among your own sort—the sort who are interested in the things that interest you. Please go."

"It would be retreating under fire," he objected.

"But you proved your courage, last night. I'm afraid for you. Some one out here has a terrible grudge against you. I'd never forgive Hawaii if—if anything happened to you."

"That's sweet of you." He moved closer. But—confound it—there was Agatha. Bound to Agatha by all the ties of honor. He edged away again. "I'll think about it," he agreed.

"I'm leaving Honolulu too, you know," she reminded him.

"I know. You'll have a wonderful time in England."

She shook her head. "Oh, I dread the whole idea. Dad's heart is set on it, and I shall go to please him. But I shan't enjoy it. I'm not up to England."

"Nonsense."

"No, I'm not. I'm unsophisticated—crude, really—just a girl of the Islands."

"But you wouldn't care to stay here all your life?"

"No, indeed. It's a beautiful spot—to loll about in. But I've too much northern blood to be satisfied with that. One of these days I want dad to sell and we'll go to the mainland. I could get some sort of work—"

"Any particular place on the mainland?"

"Well, I haven't been about much, of course. But all the time I was at school I kept thinking I'd rather live in San Francisco than anywhere else in the world—"

"Good," John Quincy cried. "That's my choice too. You remember that morning on the ferry, how you held out your hand to me and said: 'Welcome to your city—'"

"But you corrected me at once. You said you belonged in Boston."

"I see my error now."

She shook her head. "A moment's madness, but you'll recover. You're an easterner, and you could never be happy anywhere else."

"Oh, yes, I could," he assured her. "I'm a Winterslip, a wandering Winterslip. Any old place we hang our hats—" This time he did lean rather close. "I could be happy anywhere—" he began. He wanted to add "with you." But Agatha's slim patrician hand was on his shoulder. "Anywhere," he repeated, with a different inflection. A gong sounded from the Reef and Palm.

Carlota rose. "That's lunch." John Quincy stood too. "It's beside the point—where you go," she went on. "I asked you to do something for me."

"I know. If you'd asked anything else in the world, I'd be up to my neck in it now. But what you suggest would take a bit of doing. To leave Hawaii—and say good-by to you—"

"I meant to be very firm about it," she broke in.

"But I must have a little time to consider. Will you wait?"

She smiled up at him. "You're so much wiser than I am," she said. "Yes—I'll wait."

He went slowly along the beach. Unsophisticated, yes—and charming. "You're so much wiser than I am." Where on the mainland could one encounter a girl nowadays who'd say that? He had quite forgotten that she smiled when she said it.

In the afternoon, John Quincy visited the police station. Hallet was in his room in rather a grouchy mood. Chan was out somewhere hunting the watch. No, they hadn't found it yet.

John Quincy was mildly reproving. "Well, you saw it, didn't you?" growled Hallet. "Why in Sam Hill didn't you grab it?"

"Because they tied my hands," John Quincy reminded him. "I've narrowed the search down for you to the taxi drivers of Honolulu."

"Hundreds of them, my boy."

"More than that, I've given you the first two numbers on the license plate of the car. If you're any good at all, you ought to be able to land that watch now."

"Oh, we'll land it," Hallet said. "Give us time."

Time was just what John Quincy had to give them. Monday came and went. Miss Minerva was bitterly sarcastic.

"Patience are a very lovely virtue," John Quincy told her. "I got that from Charlie."

"At any rate," she snapped, "it are a virtue very much needed with Captain Hallet in charge."

In another direction, too, John Quincy was called upon to exercise patience. Agatha Parker was unaccountably silent regarding that short peremptory cable he had sent on his big night in town. Was she offended? The Parkers were notoriously not a family who accepted dictation. But in such a vital matter as this, a girl should be willing to listen to reason.

Late Tuesday afternoon Chan telephoned from the station-house—unquestionably Chan this time. Would John Quincy do him the great honor to join him for an early dinner at the Alexander Young cafe?

"Something doing, Charlie?" cried the boy eagerly.

"Maybe it might be," answered Chan, "and maybe also not. At six o'clock in hotel lobby, if you will so far condescend."

"I'll be there," John Quincy promised, and he was.

He greeted Chan with anxious, inquiring eyes, but Chan was suave and entirely non-committal. He led John Quincy to the dining-room and carefully selected a table by a front window.

"Do me the great favor to recline," he suggested.

John Quincy reclined. "Charlie, don't keep me in suspense," he pleaded.

Chan smiled. "Let us not shade the feast with gloomy murder talk," he replied. "This are social meeting. Is it that you are in the mood to dry up plate of soup?"

"Why, yes, of course," John Quincy answered. Politeness, he saw, dictated that he hide his curiosity.

EARL DERR BIGGERS

"Two of the soup," ordered Chan of a white-jacketed waiter. A car drew up to the door of the Alexander Young. Chan half rose, staring at it keenly. He dropped back to his seat. "It is my high delight to entertain you thus humbly before you are restored to Boston. Converse at some length of Boston. I feel interested."

"Really?" smiled the boy.

"Undubitably. Gentleman I meet once say Boston are like China. The future of both, he say, lies in graveyards where repose useless bodies of honored guests on high. I am fogged as to meaning."

"He meant both places live in the past," John Quincy explained. "And he was right, in a way. Boston, like China, boasts a glorious history. But that's not saying the Boston of to-day isn't progressive. Why, do you know—"

He talked eloquently of his native city. Chan listened, rapt.

"Always," he sighed, when John Quincy finished, "I have unlimited yearning for travel." He paused to watch another car draw up before the hotel. "But it are unavailable. I am policeman on small remuneration. In my youth, rambling on evening hillside or by moonly ocean, I dream of more lofty position. Not so now. But that other American citizen, my eldest son, he are dreaming too. Maybe for him dreams eventuate. Perhaps he become second Baby Ruth, home run emperor, applause of thousands making him deaf. Who knows it?"

The dinner passed, unshaded by gloomy talk, and they went outside. Chan proffered a cigar of which he spoke in the most belittling fashion. He suggested that they stand for a time before the hotel door.

"Waiting for somebody?" inquired John Quincy, unable longer to dissemble.

"Precisely the fact. Barely dare to mention it, however. Great disappointment may drive up here any minute now."

An open car stopped before the hotel entrance. John Quincy's eyes sought the license plate, and he got an immediate thrill. The first two figures were 33.

A party of tourists, a man and two women, alighted. The doorman ran forward and busied himself with luggage. Chan casually strolled across the walk, and as the Japanese driver shifted his gears preparatory to driving away, put a restraining hand on the car door.

"One moment, please." The driver turned, fright in his eyes. "You are Okuda, from auto stand across way?"

"Yes-s," hissed the driver.

"You are now returned from exploring island with party of tourists? You leave this spot early Sunday morning?"

"Yes-s."

"Is it possible that you wear wrist watch, please?"

"Yes-s."

"Deign to reveal face of same."

The Jap hesitated. Chan leaned far over into the car and thrust aside the man's coat sleeve. He came back, a pleased light in his eyes, and held open the rear door. "Kindly embark into tonneau, Mr. Winterslip." Obediently John Quincy got in. Chan took his place by the driver's side. "The police station, if you will be so kind." The car leaped forward.

The essential clue! They had it at last. John Quincy's heart beat fast there in the rear of the car where, only a few nights before, he had been bound and gagged.

Captain Hallet's grim face relaxed into happy lines when he met them at the door of his room. "You got him, eh? Good work." He glanced at the prisoner's wrist. "Rip that watch off him, Charlie."

Charlie obeyed. He examined the watch for a moment, then handed it to his chief.

"Inexpensive time-piece of noted brand," he announced. "Numeral two faint and far away. One other fact emerge into light. This Japanese man have small wrist. Yet worn place on strap convey impression of being worn by man with wrist of vastly larger circumference."

Hallet nodded. "Yes, that's right. Some other man has owned this watch. He had a big wrist—but most men in Honolulu have, you know. Sit down, Okuda. I want to hear from you. You understand what it means to lie to me?"

"I do not lie, sir."

"No, you bet your sweet life you don't. First, tell me who engaged your car last Saturday night."

"Saturday night?"

"That's what I said!"

"Ah, yes. Two sailors from ship. Engage for evening paying large cash at once. I drive to shop on River Street, wait long time. Then off we go to dock with extra passenger in back."

"Know the names of those sailors?"

"Could not say."

"What ship were they from?"

"How can I know? Not told."

EARL DERR BIGGERS

"All right I'm coming to the important thing. Understand? The truth—that's what I want! Where did you get this watch?"

Chan and John Quincy leaned forward eagerly. "I buy him," said the Jap.

"You bought him? Where?"

"At jewel store of Chinese Lau Ho on Maunakea Street."

Hallet turned to Chan. "Know the place, Charlie?"

Chan nodded. "Yes, indeed."

"Open now?"

"Open until hour of ten, maybe more."

"Good," said Hallet. "Come along, Okuda. You can drive us there."

Lau Ho, a little wizened Chinese man, sat back of his work bench with a microscope screwed into one dim old eye. The four men who entered his tiny store filled it to overflowing, but he gave them barely a glance.

"Come on, Ho—wake up," Hallet cried. "I want to talk to you."

With the utmost deliberation Lau Ho descended from his stool and approached the counter. He regarded Hallet with a hostile eye. The captain laid the wrist watch on top of a showcase in which reposed many trays of jade.

"Ever see that before?" he inquired.

Lau Ho regarded it casually. Slowly he raised his eyes. "Maybe so. Can not say," he replied in a high squeaky voice.

Hallet reddened. "Nonsense. You had it here in the store, and you sold it to this fellow. Now, didn't you?"

Lau Ho dreamily regarded the taxi driver. "Maybe so. Can not say."

"Damn it!" cried Hallet. "You know who I am?"

"Policeman, maybe."

"Policeman maybe yes! And I want you to tell me about this watch. Now wake up and come across or by the Lord Harry—"

Chan laid a deferential hand on his chief's arm. "Humbly suggest I attempt this," he said.

Hallet nodded. "All right, he's your meat, Charlie." He drew back.

Chan bowed with a great show of politeness. He launched into a long story in Chinese. Lau Ho looked at him with slight interest. Presently he squeaked a brief reply. Chan resumed his flow of talk. Occasionally he paused, and Lau Ho spoke. In a few moments Chan turned beaming.

"Story are now completely extracted like aching tooth," he said. "Wrist watch was brought to Lau Ho on Thursday, same week as murder.

Offered him on sale by young man darkly colored with small knife scar marring cheek. Lau Ho buy and repair watch, interior works being in injured state. Saturday morning he sell at seemly profit to Japanese, presumably this Okuda here but Lau Ho will not swear. Saturday night dark young man appear much overwhelmed with excitement and demand watch again, please. Lau Ho say it is sold to Japanese. Which Japanese? Lau Ho is not aware of name, and can not describe, all Japanese faces being uninteresting outlook for him. Dark young man curse and fly. Appear frequently demanding any news, but Lau Ho is unable to oblige. Such are story of this jewel merchant here."

They went out on the street. Hallet scowled at the Japanese man. "All right—run along. I'll keep the watch."

"Very thankful," said the taxi driver, and leaped into his car.

Hallet turned to Chan. "A dark young man with a scar?" he queried.

"Clear enough to me," Chan answered. "Same are the Spaniard Jose Cabrera, careless man about town with reputation not so savory. Mr. Winterslip, is it that you have forgotten him?"

John Quincy started. "Me? Did I ever see him?"

"Recall," said Chan. "It are the night following murder. You and I linger in All American Restaurant engaged in debate regarding hygiene of pie. Door open, admitting Bowker, steward on President Tyler, joyously full of okolehau. With him are dark young man—this Jose Cabrera himself."

"Oh, I remember now," John Quincy answered.

"Well, the Spaniard's easy to pick up," said Hallet. "I'll have him inside an hour—"

"One moment, please," interposed Chan. "To-morrow morning at nine o'clock the President Tyler return from Orient. No gambler myself but will wager increditable sum Spaniard waits on dock for Mr. Bowker. If you present no fierce objection, I have a yearning to arrest him at that very moment."

"Why, of course," agreed Hallet. He looked keenly at Charlie Chan. "Charlie, you old rascal, you've got the scent at last."

"Who—me?" grinned Chan. "With your gracious permission I would alter the picture. Stone walls are crumbling now like dust. Through many loopholes light stream in like rosy streaks of dawn."

XXI

THE STONE WALLS CRUMBLE

The stone walls were crumbling and the light streaming through—but only for Chan. John Quincy was still groping in the dark, and his reflections were a little bitter as he returned to the house at Waikiki. Chan and he had worked together, but now that they approached the crisis of their efforts, the detective evidently preferred to push on alone, leaving his fellow-worker to follow if he could. Well, so be it—but John Quincy's pride was touched.

He had suddenly a keen desire to show Chan that he could not be left behind like that. If only he could, by some inspirational flash of deductive reasoning, arrive at the solution of the mystery simultaneously with the detective. For the honor of Boston and the Winterslips.

Frowning deeply, he considered all the old discarded clues again. The people who had been under suspicion and then dropped—Egan, the Compton woman, Brade, Kaohla, Leatherbee, Saladine, Cope. He even considered several the investigation had not touched. Presently he came to Bowker. What did Bowker's reappearance mean?

For the first time in two weeks he thought of the little man with the fierce pompadour and the gold-rimmed eyeglasses. Bowker with his sorrowful talk of vanished bar-rooms and lost friends behind the bar. How was the steward on the President Tyler connected with the murder of Dan Winterslip? He had not done it himself, that was obvious, but in some way he was linked up with the crime. John Quincy spent a long and painful period seeking to join Bowker up with one or another of the suspects. It couldn't be done.

All through that Tuesday evening the boy puzzled, so silent and distrait that Miss Minerva finally gave him up and retired to her room with a book. He awoke on Wednesday morning with the problem no nearer solution.

Barbara was due to arrive at ten o'clock from Kauai, and taking the small car, John Quincy went down-town to meet her. Pausing at the bank to cash a check, he encountered his old shipmate on the President Tyler, the sprightly Madame Maynard.

"I really shouldn't speak to you," she said. "You never come to see me."

"I know," he answered. "But I've been so very busy."

"So I hear. Running round with policemen and their victims. I have no doubt you'll go back to Boston and report we're all criminals and cutthroats out here."

"Oh, hardly that."

"Yes, you will. You're getting a very biased view of Honolulu. Why not stoop to associate with a respectable person now and then?"

"I'd enjoy it—if they're all like you."

"Like me? They're much more intelligent and charming than I am. Some of them are dropping in at my house tonight for an informal little party. A bit of a chat, and then a moonlight swim. Won't you come too?"

"I want to, of course," John Quincy replied. "But there's Cousin Dan—"

Her eyes flashed. "I'll say it, even if he was your relative. Ten minutes of mourning for Cousin Dan is ample. I'll be looking for you."

John Quincy laughed. "I'll come."

"Do," she answered. "And bring your Aunt Minerva. Tell her I said she might as well be dead as hog-tied by convention."

John Quincy went out to the corner of Fort and King Streets, near which he had parked the car. As he was about to climb into it, he paused. A familiar figure was jauntily crossing the street. The figure of Bowker, the steward, and with him was Willie Chan, demon backstopper of the Pacific.

"Hello, Bowker," John Quincy called.

Mr. Bowker came blithely to join him. "Well, well, well. My old friend Mr. Winterslip. Shake hands with William Chan, the local Ty Cobb."

"Mr. Chan and I have met before," John Quincy told him.

"Know all the celebrities, eh? That's good. Well, we missed you on the PRESIDENT TYLER."

Bowker was evidently quite sober. "Just got in, I take it," John Quincy remarked.

"A few minutes ago. How about joining us?" He came closer and lowered his voice. "This intelligent young man tells me he knows a taxi stand out near the beach where one may obtain a superior brand of fusel oil with a very pretty label on the bottle."

"Sorry," John Quincy answered. "My cousin's coming in shortly on an Inter-Island boat, and I'm elected to meet her."

"I'm sorry, too," said the graduate of Dublin University. "If my strength holds out I'm aiming to stage quite a little party, and I'd like to have you in on it. Yes, a rather large affair—in memory of Tim, and as a last long lingering farewell to the seven seas."

"What? You're pau?"

"Pau it is. When I sail out of here to-night at nine on the old P.T. I'm through for ever. You don't happen to know a good country newspaper that can be bought for—well, say ten grand."

"This is rather sudden, isn't it?" John Quincy inquired.

"This is sudden country out here, sir. Well, we must roll along. Sorry you can't join us. If the going's not too rough and I can find a nice smooth table top, I intend to turn down an empty glass. For poor old Tim. So long, sir—and happy days."

He nodded to Willie Chan, and they went on down the street. John Quincy stood staring after them, a puzzled expression on his face.

Barbara seemed paler and thinner than ever, but she announced that her visit had been an enjoyable one, and on the ride to the beach appeared to be making a distinct effort to be gay and sprightly. When they reached the house, John Quincy repeated to his aunt Mrs. Maynard's invitation.

"Better come along," he urged.

"Perhaps I will," she answered. "I'll see."

The day passed quietly, and it was not until evening that the monotony was broken. Leaving the dining-room with his aunt and Barbara, John Quincy was handed a cablegram. He hastily opened it. It had been sent from Boston; evidently Agatha Parker, overwhelmed by the crude impossibility of the West, had fled home again, and John Quincy's brief "San Francisco or nothing" had followed her there. Hence the delay.

The cablegram said simply: "Nothing. Agatha." John Quincy crushed it in his hand; he tried to suffer a little, but it was no use. He was a mighty happy man. The end of a romance—no. There had never been any nonsense of that kind between them—just an affectionate regard too slight to stand the strain of parting. Agatha was younger than he, she would marry some nice proper boy who had no desire to roam. And John Quincy Winterslip would read of her wedding—in the San Francisco papers.

He found Miss Minerva alone in the living-room. "It's none of my business," she said, "but I'm wondering what was in your cablegram."

"Nothing," he answered truthfully.

"All the same, you were very pleased to get it?"

He nodded. "Yes. I imagine nobody was ever so happy over nothing before."

"Good heavens," she cried. "Have you given up grammar, too?"

"I'm thinking of it. How about going down the beach with me?"

She shook her head. "Some one is coming to look at the house—a leading lawyer, I believe he is. He's thinking of buying, and I feel I should be here to show him about. Barbara appears so listless and disinterested. Tell Sally Maynard I may drop in later."

At a quarter to eight, John Quincy took his bathing suit and wandered down Kalia Road. It was another of those nights; a bright moon was riding high; from a bungalow buried under purple alamander came the soft croon of Hawaiian music. Through the hedges of flaming hibiscus he caught again the exquisite odors of this exotic island.

Mrs. Maynard's big house was a particularly unlovely type of New England architecture, but a hundred flowering vines did much to conceal that fact. John Quincy found his hostess enthroned in her great airy drawing-room, surrounded by a handsome laughing group of the best people. Pleasant people, too; as she introduced him he began to wonder if he hadn't been missing a great deal of congenial companionship.

"I dragged him here against his will," the old lady explained. "I felt I owed it to Hawaii. He's been associating with the riff-raff long enough."

They insisted that he take an enormous chair, pressed cigarettes upon him, showered him with hospitable attentions. As he sat down and the chatter was resumed, he reflected that here was as civilized a company as Boston itself could offer. And why not? Most of these families came originally from New England, and had kept in their exile the old ideals of culture and caste.

"It might interest Beacon Street to know," Mrs. Maynard said, "that long before the days of 'forty-nine the people of California were sending their children over here to be educated in the missionary schools. And importing their wheat from here, too."

"Go on, tell him the other one, Aunt Sally," laughed a pretty girl in blue. "That about the first printing press in San Francisco being brought over from Honolulu."

Madame Maynard shrugged her shoulders. "Oh, what's the use? We're so far away, New England will never get us straight."

John Quincy looked up to see Carlota Egan in the doorway. A moment later Lieutenant Booth, of Richmond, appeared at her side.

It occurred to the young man from Boston that the fleet was rather overdoing its stop at Honolulu.

Mrs. Maynard rose to greet the girl. "Come in, my dear. You know most of these people." She turned to the others. "This is Miss Egan, a neighbor of mine on the beach."

It was amusing to note that most of these people knew Carlota too. John Quincy smiled—the British Admiralty and the soap business. It must have been rather an ordeal for the girl, but she saw it through with a sweet graciousness that led John Quincy to reflect that she would be at home in England—if she went there.

Carlota sat down on a sofa, and while Lieutenant Booth was busily arranging a cushion at her back, John Quincy dropped down beside her. The sofa was, fortunately, too small for three.

"I rather expected to see you," he said in a low voice. "I was brought here to meet the best people of Honolulu, and the way I see it, you're the best of all."

She smiled at him, and again the chatter of small talk filled the room. Presently the voice of a tall young man with glasses rose above the general hubbub.

"They got a cable from Joe Clark out at the Country Club this afternoon," he announced.

The din ceased, and every one listened with interest. "Clark's our professional," explained the young man to John Quincy. "He went over a month ago to play in the British Open."

"Did he win?" asked the girl in blue.

"He was put out by Hagen in the semi-finals," the young man said. "But he had the distinction of driving the longest ball ever seen on the St. Andrews course."

"Why shouldn't he?" asked an older man. "He's got the strongest wrists I ever saw on anybody!"

John Quincy sat up, suddenly interested. "How do you account for that?" he asked.

The older man smiled. "We've all got pretty big wrists out here," he answered. "Surf-boarding—that's what does it. Joe Clark was a champion at one time—body-surfing and board-surfing too. He used to disappear for hours in the rollers out by the reef. The result was a marvelous wrist development. I've seen him drive a golf ball three hundred and eighty yards. Yes, sir, I'll bet he made those Englishmen sit up and take notice."

While John Quincy was thinking this over, some one suggested that it was time for the swim, and confusion reigned. A Chinese servant led the way to the dressing-rooms, which opened off the lanai, and the young people trouped joyously after him.

"I'll be waiting for you on the beach," John Quincy said to Carlota Egan.

"I came with Johnnie, you know," she reminded him.

"I know all about it," he answered. "But it was the week-end you promised to the navy. People who try to stretch their week-end through the following Wednesday night deserve all they get."

She laughed. "I'll look for you," she agreed.

He donned his bathing suit hastily in a room filled with flying clothes and great waving brown arms. Lieutenant Booth, he noted with satisfaction, was proceeding at a leisurely pace. Hurrying through a door that opened directly on the beach, he waited under a near-by hau tree. Presently Carlota came, slender and fragile-looking in the moonlight.

"Ah, here you are," John Quincy cried. "The farthest float."

"The farthest float it is," she answered.

They dashed into the warm silvery water and swam gaily off. Five minutes later they sat on the float together. The light on Diamond Head was winking; the lanterns of sampans twinkled out beyond the reef; the shore line of Honolulu was outlined by a procession of blinking stars controlled by dynamos. In the bright heavens hung a lunar rainbow, one colorful end in the Pacific and the other tumbling into the foliage ashore.

A gorgeous setting in which to be young and in love, and free to speak at last. John Quincy moved closer to the girl's side.

"Great night, isn't it?" he said.

"Wonderful," she answered softly.

"Cary, I want to tell you something, and that's why I brought you out here away from the others—"

"Somehow," she interrupted, "it doesn't seem quite fair to Johnnie."

"Never mind him. Has it ever occurred to you that my name's Johnnie, too."

She laughed. "Oh, but it couldn't be."

"What do you mean?"

"I mean, I simply couldn't call you that. You're too dignified and—and remote. John Quincy—I believe I could call you John Quincy—"

"Well, make up your mind. You'll have to call me something, because I'm going to be hanging round pretty constantly in the future. Yes, my dear, I'll probably turn out to be about the least remote person in the world. That is, if I can make you see the future the way I see it. Cary dearest—"

A gurgle sounded behind them, and they turned around. Lieutenant Booth was climbing on to the raft. "Swam the last fifty yards under water to surprise you," he sputtered.

"Well, you succeeded," said John Quincy without enthusiasm.

The lieutenant sat down with the manner of one booked to remain indefinitely. "I'll tell the world it's some night," he offered.

"Speaking of the world, when do you fellows leave Honolulu?" asked John Quincy.

"I don't know. To-morrow, I guess. Me, I don't care if we never go. Hawaii's not so easy to leave. Is it, Cary?"

She shook her head. "Hardest place I know of, Johnnie. I shall have to be sailing presently, and I know what a wrench it will be. Perhaps I'll follow the example of Waioli the swimmer, and leave the boat when it passes Waikiki."

They lolled for a moment in silence. Suddenly John Quincy sat up. "What was that you said?" he asked.

"About Waioli? Didn't I ever tell you? He was one of our best swimmers, and for years they tried to get him to go to the mainland to take part in athletic meets, like Duke Kahanamoku. But he was a sentimentalist—he couldn't bring himself to leave Hawaii. Finally they persuaded him, and one sunny morning he sailed on the Matsonia, with a very sad face. When the ship was opposite Waikiki he slipped overboard and swam ashore. And that was that. He never got on a ship again. You see—"

John Quincy was on his feet. "What time was it when we left the beach?" he asked in a low tense voice.

"About eight-thirty," said Booth.

John Quincy talked very fast. "That means I've got just thirty minutes to get ashore, dress, and reach the dock before the PRESIDENT TYLER sails. I'm sorry to go, but it's vital—vital. Cary, I'd started to tell you something. I don't know when I'll get back, but I must see you when I do, either at Mrs. Maynard's or the hotel. Will you wait up for me?"

She was startled by the seriousness of his tone. "Yes, I'll be waiting," she told him.

"That's great." He hesitated a moment; it is a risky business to leave the girl you love on a float in the moonlight with a handsome naval officer. But it had to be done. "I'm off," he said, and dove.

When he came up he heard the lieutenant's voice. "Say, old man, that dive was all wrong. You let me show you—"

"Go to the devil," muttered John Quincy wetly, and swam with long powerful strokes toward the shore. Mad with haste, he plunged into the dressing-room, donned his clothes, then dashed out again. No time for apologies to his hostess. He ran along the beach to the Winterslip house. Haku was dozing in the hall.

"Wikiwiki," shouted John Quincy. "Tell the chauffeur to get the roadster into the drive and start the engine. Wake up! Travel! Where's Miss Barbara?"

"Last seen on beach—" began the startled Haku.

On the bench under the hau tree he found Barbara sitting alone. He stood panting before her.

"My dear," he said. "I know at last who killed your father—"

She was on her feet. "You do?"

"Yes—shall I tell you?"

"No," she said. "No—I can't bear to hear. It's too horrible."

"Then you've suspected?"

"Yes—just suspicion—a feeling—intuition. I couldn't believe it—I didn't want to believe it. I went away to get it out of my mind. It's all too terrible—"

He put his hand on her shoulder. "Poor Barbara. Don't you worry. You won't appear in this in any way. I'll keep you out of it."

"What—what has happened?"

"Can't stop now. Tell you later." He ran toward the drive. Miss Minerva appeared from the house. "Haven't time to talk," he cried, leaping into the roadster.

"But John Quincy—a curious thing has happened—that lawyer who was here to look at the house—he said that Dan, just a week before he died, spoke to him about a new will—"

"That's good! That's evidence!" John Quincy cried.

"But why a new will? Surely Barbara was all he had—"

"Listen to me," cut in John Quincy. "You've delayed me already. Get the big car and go to the station—tell that to Hallet. Tell him too that I'm on the PRESIDENT TYLER and to send Chan there at once."

He stepped on the gas. By the clock in the automobile he had just seventeen minutes, to reach the dock before the PRESIDENT TYLER would sail. He shot like a madman through the brilliant Hawaiian night. Kalakaua Avenue, smooth and deserted, proved a glorious speedway. It took him just eight minutes to travel the three miles to the dock. A bit of traffic and an angry policeman in the center of the city caused the delay.

A scattering of people in the dim pier-shed waited for the imminent sailing of the liner. John Quincy dashed through them and up the gangplank. The second officer, Hepworth, stood at the top.

"Hello, Mr. Winterslip," he said. "You sailing?"

"No. But let me aboard!"

"I'm sorry. We're about to draw in the plank."

"No, no—you mustn't. This is life and death. Hold off just a few minutes. There's a steward named Bowker—I must find him at once. Life and death, I tell you."

Hepworth stood aside. "Oh, well, in that case. But please hurry, sir—"

"I will." John Quincy passed him on the run. He was on his way to the cabins presided over by Bowker when a tall figure caught his eye. A man in a long green ulster and a battered green hat—a hat John Quincy had last seen on the links of the Oahu Country Club.

The tall figure moved on up a stairway to the topmost deck. John Quincy followed. He saw the ulster disappear into one of the de luxe cabins. Still he followed, and pushed open the cabin door. The man in the ulster was back to, but he swung round suddenly.

"Ah, Mr. Jennison," John Quincy cried. "Were you thinking of sailing on this boat?"

For an instant Jennison stared at him. "I was," he said quietly.

"Forget it," John Quincy answered. "You're going ashore with me."

"Really? What is your authority?"

"No authority whatever," said the boy grimly. "I'm taking you, that's all."

Jennison smiled, but there was a gleam of hate behind it. And in John Quincy's heart, usually so gentle and civilized, there was hate too as he faced this man. He thought of Dan Winterslip, dead on his cot. He thought of Jennison walking down the gangplank with them that morning they landed, Jennison putting his arm about poor Barbara when she faltered under the blow. He thought of the shots fired at him from the bush, of the red-haired man battering him in that red room.

Well, he must fight again. No way out of it. The siren of the PRESIDENT TYLER sounded a sharp warning.

"You get out of here," said Jennison through his teeth. "I'll go with you to the gangplank—"

He stopped, as the disadvantages of that plan came home to him. His right hand went swiftly to his pocket. Inspired, John Quincy seized a filled water bottle and hurled it at the man's head. Jennison dodged; the bottle crashed through one of the windows. The clatter of glass rang through the night, but no one appeared. John Quincy saw Jennison leap toward him, something gleaming in his hand. Stepping aside, he threw himself on the man's back and forced him to his knees. He seized the wrist of Jennison's right hand, which held the automatic, in a firm grip. They kept that posture for a moment, and then Jennison began slowly to rise to his feet. The hand that held the pistol began to tear away. John Quincy shut his teeth and sought to maintain his grip. But he was up against a more powerful antagonist than the red-haired sailor, he was outclassed, and the realization of it crept over him with a sickening force.

Jennison was on his feet now, the right hand nearly free. Another moment—what then, John Quincy wondered? This man had no intention of letting him go ashore; he had changed that plan the moment he put it into words. A muffled shot, and later in the night when the ship was well out on the Pacific—John Quincy thought of Boston, his mother. He thought of Carlota waiting his return. He summoned his strength for one last desperate effort to renew his grip.

A serene, ivory-colored face appeared suddenly at the broken window. An arm with a weapon was extended through the jagged opening.

"Relinquish the firearms, Mr. Jennison," commanded Charlie Chan, "or I am forced to make fatal insertion in vital organ belonging to you."

Jennison's pistol dropped to the floor, and John Quincy staggered back against the berth. At that instant the door opened and Hallet, followed by the detective, Spencer, came in.

"Hello, Winterslip, what are you doing here?" the captain said. He thrust a paper into one of the pockets of the green ulster. "Come along, Jennison," he said. "We want you."

Limply John Quincy followed them from the stateroom. Outside they were joined by Chan. At the top of the gangplank Hallet paused. "We'll wait a minute for Hepworth," he said.

John Quincy put his hand on Chan's shoulder. "Charlie, how can I ever thank you? You saved my life."

Chan bowed. "My own pleasure is not to be worded. I have saved a life here and there, but never before one that had beginning in cultured city of Boston. Always a happy item on the golden scroll of memory."

Hepworth came up. "It's all right," he said. "The captain has agreed to delay our sailing one hour. I'll go to the station with you."

On the way down the gangplank, Chan turned to John Quincy. "Speaking heartily for myself, I congratulate your bravery. It is clear you leaped upon this Jennison with vigorous and triumphant mood of heart. But he would have pushed you down. He would have conquered. And why? The answer is, such powerful wrists."

"A great surf-boarder, eh?" John Quincy said.

Chan looked at him keenly. "You are no person's fool. Ten years ago this Harry Jennison are champion swimmer in all Hawaii. I extract that news from ancient sporting pages of Honolulu journal. But he have not been in the water much here lately. Pursuing the truth further, not since the night he killed Dan Winterslip."

XXII

The Light Streams Through

They moved on through the pier-shed to the street, where Hepworth, Jennison and the three policemen got into Hallet's car. The captain turned to John Quincy.

"You coming, Mr. Winterslip?" he inquired.

"I've got my own car," the boy explained. "I'll follow you in that."

The roadster was not performing at its best, and he reached the station house a good five minutes after the policemen. He noted Dan Winterslip's big limousine parked in the street outside.

In Hallet's room he found the captain and Chan closeted with a third man. It took a second glance at the latter to identify him as Mr. Saladine, for the little man of the lost teeth now appeared a great deal younger than John Quincy had thought him.

"Ah, Mr. Winterslip," remarked Hallet. He turned to Saladine. "Say, Larry, you've got me into a heap of trouble with this boy. He accused me of trying to shield you. I wish you'd loosen up for him."

Saladine smiled. "Why, I don't mind. My job out here is about finished. Of course, Mr. Winterslip will keep what I tell him under his hat?"

"Naturally," replied John Quincy. He noticed that the man spoke with no trace of a lisp. "I perceive you've found your teeth," he added.

"Oh, yes—I found them in my trunk, where I put them the day I arrived at Waikiki," answered Saladine. "When my teeth were knocked out twenty years ago in a football game, I was broken-hearted, but the loss has been a great help to me in my work. A man hunting his bridge work in the water is a figure of ridicule and mirth. No one ever thinks of connecting him with serious affairs. He can prowl about a beach to his heart's content. Mr. Winterslip, I am a special agent of the Treasury Department sent out here to break up the opium ring. My name, of course, is not Saladine."

"Oh," said John Quincy, "I understand at last."

"I'm glad you do," remarked Hallet. "I don't know whether you're familiar with the way our opium smugglers work. The dope is brought in from the Orient on tramp steamers—the Mary S. Allison, for example.

When they arrive off Waikiki they knock together a few small rafts and load 'em with tins of the stuff. A fleet of little boats, supposedly out there for the fishing, pick up these rafts and bring the dope ashore. It's taken downtown and hidden on ships bound for 'Frisco—usually those that ply only between here and the mainland, because they're not so closely watched at the other end. But it just happened that the quartermaster of the PRESIDENT TYLER is one of their go-betweens. We searched his cabin this evening and found it packed with the stuff."

"The quartermaster of the PRESIDENT TYLER," repeated John Quincy. "That's Dick Kaohla's friend."

"Yeah—I'm coming to Dick. He's been in charge of the pick-up fleet here. He was out on that business the night of the murder. Saladine saw him and told me all about it in that note, which was my reason for letting the boy go."

"I owe you an apology," John Quincy said.

"Oh, that's all right." Hallet was in great good humor. "Larry here has got some of the higher-ups, too. For instance, he's discovered that Jennison is the lawyer for the ring, defending any of them who are caught and brought before the commissioner. The fact has no bearing on Dan Winterslip's murder—unless Winterslip knew about it, and that was one of the reasons he didn't want Jennison to marry his girl."

Saladine stood up. "I'll turn the quartermaster over to you," he said. "In view of this other charge, you can of course have Jennison too. That's all for me. I'll go along."

"See you to-morrow, Larry," Hallet answered. Saladine went out, and the captain turned to John Quincy. "Well, my boy, this is our big night. I don't know what you were doing in Jennison's cabin, but if you'd picked him for the murderer, I'll say you're good."

"That's just what I'd done," John Quincy told him. "By the way, have you seen my aunt? She's got hold of a rather interesting bit of information—"

"I've seen her," Hallet said. "She's with the prosecutor now, telling it to him. By the way, Greene's waiting for us. Come along."

They went into the prosecutor's office. Greene was alert and eager, a stenographer was at his elbow, and Miss Minerva sat near his desk.

"Hello, Mr. Winterslip," he said. "What do you think of our police force now? Pretty good, eh, pretty good. Sit down, won't you?" He glanced through some papers on his desk while John Quincy, Hallet and Chan found chairs. "I don't mind telling you, this thing has knocked me all in a heap. Harry Jennison and I are old friends; I had lunch with him at the club only yesterday. I'm going to proceed a little differently than I would with an ordinary criminal."

John Quincy half rose from his chair. "Don't get excited," Greene smiled. "Jennison will get all that's coming to him, friendship or no friendship. What I mean is that if I can save the territory the expense of a long trial by dragging a confession out of him at once, I intend to do it. He's coming in here in a moment, and I propose to reveal my whole hand to him, from start to finish. That may seem foolish, but it isn't. For I hold aces, all aces, and he'll know it as quickly as any one."

The door opened. Spencer ushered Jennison into the room, and then withdrew. The accused man stood there, proud, haughty, defiant, a viking of the tropics, a blond giant at bay but unafraid.

"Hello, Jennison," Greene said. "I'm mighty sorry about this—"

"You ought to be," Jennison replied. "You're making an awful fool of yourself. What is this damned nonsense, anyhow—"

"Sit down," said the prosecutor sharply. He indicated a chair on the opposite side of the desk. He had already turned the shade on his desk lamp so the light would shine full in the face of any one sitting there. "That lamp bother you, Harry?" he asked.

"Why should it?" Jennison demanded.

"Good," smiled Greene. "I believe Captain Hallet served you with a warrant on the boat. Have you looked at it, by any chance?"

"I have."

The prosecutor leaned across the desk. "Murder, Jennison!"

Jennison's expression did not change. "Damned nonsense, as I told you. Why should I murder any one?"

"Ah, the motive," Greene replied. "You're quite right, we should begin with that. Do you wish to be represented here by counsel?"

Jennison shook his head. "I guess I'm lawyer enough to puncture this silly business," he replied.

"Very well." Greene turned to his stenographer. "Get this." The man nodded, and the prosecutor addressed Miss Minerva. "Miss Winterslip, we'll start with you."

Miss Minerva leaned forward. "Mr. Dan Winterslip's house on the beach has, as I told you, been offered for sale by his daughter. After dinner this evening a gentleman came to look at it—a prominent lawyer named Hailey. As we went over the house, Mr. Hailey mentioned that he had met Dan Winterslip on the street a week before his death, and that my cousin had spoken to him about coming in shortly to draw up a new will. He did not say what the provisions of the will were to be, nor did he ever carry out his intention."

"Ah yes," said Greene. "But Mr. Jennison here was your cousin's lawyer?"

"He was."

"If he wanted to draw a new will, he wouldn't ordinarily have gone to a stranger for that purpose."

"Not ordinarily. Unless he had some good reason."

"Precisely. Unless, for instance, the will had some connection with Harry Jennison."

"I object," Jennison cried. "This is mere conjecture."

"So it is," Greene answered. "But we're not in court. We can conjecture if we like. Suppose, Miss Winterslip, the will was concerned with Jennison in some way. What do you imagine the connection to have been?"

"I don't have to imagine," replied Miss Minerva. "I know."

"Ah, that's good. You know. Go on."

"Before I came down here to-night, I had a talk with my niece. She admitted that her father knew she and Jennison were in love, and that he had bitterly opposed the match. He had even gone so far as to say he would disinherit her if she went through with it."

"Then the new will Dan Winterslip intended to make would probably have been to the effect that in the event his daughter married Jennison, she was not to inherit a penny of his money?"

"There isn't any doubt of it," said Miss Minerva firmly.

"You asked for a motive, Jennison," Greene said. "That's motive enough for me. Everybody knows you're money mad. You wanted to marry Winterslip's daughter, the richest girl in the Islands. He said you couldn't have her—not with the money too. But you're not the sort to make a penniless marriage. You were determined to get both Barbara Winterslip and her father's property. Only one person stood in your way—Dan Winterslip. And that's how you happened to be on his lanai that Monday night—"

"Wait a minute," Jennison protested. "I wasn't on his lanai. I was on board the President Tyler, and everybody knows that ship didn't land its passengers until nine the following morning—"

"I'm coming to that," Greene told him. "Just now—by the way, what time is it?"

Jennison took from his pocket a watch on the end of a slender chain. "It's a quarter past nine."

"Ah, yes. Is that the watch you usually carry?"

"It is."

"Ever wear a wrist watch?"

Jennison hesitated. "Occasionally."

"Only occasionally." The prosecutor rose and came round his desk. "Let me see your left wrist, please."

Jennison held out his arm. It was tanned a deep brown, but on the wrist was etched in white the outline of a watch and its encircling strap.

Greene smiled. "Yes, you have worn a wrist watch—and you've worn it pretty constantly, from the look of things." He took a small object from his pocket and held it in front of Jennison. "This watch, perhaps?" Jennison regarded it stonily. "Ever see it before?" Greene asked. "No? Well, suppose we try it on, anyhow." He put the watch in position and fastened it. "I can't help noting, Harry," he continued, "that it fits rather neatly over that white outline on your wrist And the prong of the buckle falls naturally into the most worn of the holes on the strap."

"What of that?" asked Jennison.

"Oh, coincidence, probably. You have abnormally large wrists, however. Surf-boarding, swimming, eh? But that's something else I'll speak of later." He turned to Miss Minerva. "Will you please come over here, Miss Winterslip."

She came, and as she reached his side, the prosecutor suddenly bent over and switched off the light on his desk. Save for a faint glimmer through a transom, the room was in darkness. Miss Minerva was conscious of dim huddled figures, a circle of white faces, a tense silence. The prosecutor was lifting something slowly toward her startled eyes. A watch, worn on a human wrist—a watch with an illuminated dial on which the figure two was almost obliterated.

"Look at that and tell me," came the prosecutor's voice. "You have seen it before?"

"I have," she answered firmly.

"Where?"

"In the dark in Dan Winterslip's living-room just after midnight the thirtieth of June."

Greene flashed on the light. "Thank you, Miss Winterslip." He retired behind his desk and pressed a button. "You identify it by some distinguishing mark, I presume?"

"I do. The numeral two, which is pretty well obscured."

Spencer appeared at the door. "Send the Spaniard in," Greene ordered. "That is all for the present, Miss Winterslip."

Cabrera entered, and his eyes were frightened as they looked at Jennison. At a nod from the prosecutor, Chan removed the wrist watch and handed it to the Spaniard.

"You know that watch, Jose?" Greene asked.

"I—I—yes," answered the boy.

"Don't be afraid," Greene urged. "Nobody's going to hurt you. I want you to repeat the story you told me this afternoon. You have no regular job. You're a sort of confidential errand boy for Mr. Jennison here."

"I was."

"Yes—that's all over now. You can speak out. On the morning of Wednesday, July second, you were in Mr. Jennison's office. He gave you this wrist watch and told you to take it out and get it repaired. Something was the matter with it. It wasn't running. You took it to a big jewelry store. What happened?"

"The man said it is very badly hurt. To fix it would cost more than a new watch. I go back and tell Mr. Jennison. He laugh and say it is mine as a gift."

"Precisely." Greene referred to a paper on his desk. "Late in the afternoon of Thursday, July third, you sold the watch. To whom?"

"To Lau Ho, Chinese jeweler in Maunakea Street. On Saturday evening maybe six o'clock Mr. Jennison telephone my home, much excited. Must have watch again, and will pay any price. I speed to Lau Ho's store. Watch is sold once more, now to unknown Japanese. Late at night I see Mr. Jennison and he curse me with anger. Get the watch, he says. I have been hunting, but I could not find it."

Greene turned to Jennison. "You were a little careless with that watch, Harry. But no doubt you figured you were pretty safe—you had your alibi. Then, too, when Hallet detailed the clues to you on Winterslip's lanai the morning after the crime, he forgot to mention that some one had seen the watch. It was one of those happy accidents that are all we have to count on in this work. By Saturday night you realized your danger—just how you discovered it I don't know—"

"I do," John Quincy interrupted.

"What! What's that?" said Greene.

"On Saturday afternoon," John Quincy told him, "I played golf with Mr. Jennison. On our way back to town, we talked over the clues in this case, and I happened to mention the wrist watch. I can see now it was the first he had heard of it. He was to dine with us at the beach, but he asked to be put down at his office to sign a few letters. I waited below. It must have been then that he called up this young man in an effort to locate the watch."

"Great stuff," said Greene enthusiastically. "That finishes the watch, Jennison. I'm surprised you wore it, but you probably knew that it would be vital to you to keep track of the time, and you figured, rightly, that it would not be immediately affected by the salt water—"

"What the devil are you talking about?" demanded Jennison.

Again Greene pressed a button on his desk. Spencer appeared at once. "Take this Spaniard," the prosecutor directed, "and bring in Hepworth and the quartermaster." He turned again to Jennison. "I'll show you what I'm talking about in just a minute. On the night of June thirtieth you were a passenger on the PRESIDENT TYLER, which was lying by until dawn out near the channel entrance?"

"I was."

"No passengers were landed from that ship until the following morning?"

"That's a matter of record."

"Very well." The second officer of the PRESIDENT TYLER came in, followed by a big hulking sailorman John Quincy recognized as the quartermaster of that vessel. He was interested to note a ring on the man's right hand, and his mind went back to that encounter in the San Francisco attic.

"Mr. Hepworth," the prosecutor began, "on the night of June thirtieth your ship reached this port too late to dock. You anchored off Waikiki. On such an occasion, who is on deck—say, from midnight on?"

"The second officer," Hepworth told him. "In this case, myself. Also the quartermaster."

"The accommodation ladder is let down the night before?"

"Usually, yes. It was let down that night."

"Who is stationed near it?"

"The quartermaster."

"Ah, yes. You were in charge then on the night of June thirtieth. Did you notice anything unusual on that occasion?"

Hepworth nodded. "I did. The quartermaster appeared to be under the influence of liquor. At three o'clock I found him dozing near the accommodation ladder. I roused him. When I came back from checking

EARL DERR BIGGERS

up the anchor bearings before turning in at dawn—about four-thirty—he was dead to the world. I put him in his cabin, and the following morning I of course reported him."

"You noticed nothing else out of the ordinary?"

"Nothing, sir," Hepworth replied.

"Thank you very much. Now, you—" Greene turned to the quartermaster. "You were drunk on duty the night of June thirtieth. Where did you get the booze?" The man hesitated. "Before you say anything, let me give you a bit of advice. The truth, my man. You're in pretty bad already. I'm not making any promises, but if you talk straight here it may help you in that other matter. If you lie, it will go that much harder with you."

"I ain't going to lie," promised the quartermaster.

"All right. Where did you get your liquor?"

The man nodded toward Jennison. "He gave it to me."

"He did, eh? Tell me all about it."

"I met him on deck just after midnight—we was still moving. I knew him before—him and me—"

"In the opium game, both of you. I understand that. You met him on deck—"

"I did, and he says, you're on watch to-night, eh, and I says I am. So he slips me a little bottle an' says, this will help you pass the time. I ain't a drinking man, so help me I ain't, an' I took just a nip, but there was something in that whiskey, I'll swear to it. My head was all funny like, an' the next I knew I was waked up in my cabin with the bad news I was wanted above."

"What became of that bottle?"

"I dropped it overboard on my way to see the captain. I didn't want nobody to find it."

"Did you see anything the night of June thirtieth? Anything peculiar?"

"I seen plenty, sir—but it was that drink. Nothing you would want to hear about."

"All right." The prosecutor turned to Jennison. "Well, Harry—you drugged him, didn't you? Why? Because you were going ashore, eh? Because you knew he'd be on duty at that ladder when you returned, and you didn't want him to see you. So you dropped something into that whiskey—"

"Guess work," cut in Jennison, still unruffled. "I used to have some respect for you as a lawyer, but it's all gone now. If this is the best you can offer—"

"But it isn't," said Greene pleasantly. Again he pushed the button. "I've something much better, Harry, if you'll only wait." He turned to Hepworth. "There's a steward on your ship named Bowker," he began, and John Quincy thought that Jennison stiffened. "How has he been behaving lately?"

"Well, he got pretty drunk in Hong-kong," Hepworth answered. "But that, of course, was the money."

"What money?"

"It's this way. The last time we sailed out of Honolulu harbor for the Orient, over two weeks ago, I was in the purser's office. It was just as we were passing Diamond Head. Bowker came in, and he had a big fat envelope that he wanted to deposit in the purser's safe. He said it contained a lot of money. The purser wouldn't be responsible for it without seeing it, so Bowker slit the envelope—and there were ten one hundred dollar bills. The purser made another package of it and put it in the safe. He told me Bowker took out a couple of the bills when we reached Hong-kong."

"Where would a man like Bowker get all that money?"

"I can't imagine. He said he'd put over a business deal in Honolulu but—well, we knew Bowker."

The door opened. Evidently Spencer guessed who was wanted this time, for he pushed Bowker into the room. The steward of the President Tyler was bedraggled and bleary.

"Hello, Bowker," said the prosecutor. "Sober now, aren't you?"

"I'll tell the world I am," replied Bowker. "They've walked me to San Francisco and back. Can—can I sit down?"

"Of course," Greene smiled. "This afternoon, while you were still drunk, you told a story to Willie Chan, out at Okamoto's auto stand on Kalakaua Avenue. Later on, early this evening, you repeated it to Captain Hallet and me. I'll have to ask you to go over it again."

Bowker glanced toward Jennison, then quickly looked away. "Always ready to oblige," he answered.

"You're a steward on the President Tyler," Greene continued. "On your last trip over here from the mainland Mr. Jennison occupied one of your rooms—number 97. He was alone in it, I believe?"

"All alone. He paid extra for the privilege, I hear. Always traveled that way."

"Room 97 was on the main deck, not far from the accommodation ladder?"

"Yes, that's right."

"Tell us what happened after you anchored off Waikiki the night of June thirtieth."

Bowker adjusted his gold-rimmed glasses with the gesture of a man about to make an after-dinner speech. "Well, I was up pretty late that night. Mr. Winterslip here had loaned me some books—there was one I was particularly interested in. I wanted to finish it so I could give it to him to take ashore in the morning. It was nearly two o'clock when I finally got through it, and I was feeling stuffy, so I went on deck for a breath of air."

"You stopped not far from the accommodation ladder?"

"Yes sir, I did."

"Did you notice the quartermaster?"

"Yes—he was sound asleep in a deck chair. I went over and leaned on the rail, the ladder was just beneath me. I'd been standing there a few minutes when suddenly somebody came up out of the water and put his hands on the lowest rung. I drew back quickly and stood in a shadow.

"Well, pretty soon this man comes creeping up the ladder to the deck. He was barefooted, and all in black—black pants and shirt. I watched him. He went over and bent above the quartermaster, then started toward me down the deck. He was walking on tiptoe, but even then I didn't get wise to the fact anything was wrong.

"I stepped out of the shadow. 'Fine night for a swim, Mr. Jennison,' I said. And I saw at once that I'd made a social error. He gave one jump in my direction and his hands closed on my throat. I thought my time had come."

"He was wet, wasn't he?" Greene asked.

"Dripping. He left a trail of water on the deck."

"Did you notice a watch on his wrist?"

"Yes, but you can bet I didn't make any study of it. I had other things to think about just then. I managed to sort of ooze out of his grip, and I told him to cut it out or I'd yell. 'Look here,' he says, 'you and I can talk business, I guess. Come into my cabin.'

"But I wasn't wanting any tete-a-tete with him in any cabin, I said I'd see him in the morning, and after I'd promised to say nothing to anybody, he let me go. I went to bed, pretty much puzzled.

"The next morning, when I went into his cabin, there he was all fresh and rosy and smiling. If I'd had so much as a whiff of booze the night before, I'd have thought I never saw what I did. I went in there thinking I might get a hundred dollars out of the affair, but the minute he spoke I began to smell important money. He said no one must know about his swim the night before. How much did I want? Well, I held my breath and said ten thousand dollars. And I nearly dropped dead when he answered I could have it."

Bowker turned to John Quincy. "I don't know what you'll think of me. I don't know what Tim would think. I'm not a crook by nature. But I was fed up and choking over that steward job. I wanted a little newspaper of my own, and up to that minute I couldn't see myself getting it. And you must remember that I didn't know then what was in the air—murder. Later, when I did find out, I was scared to breathe. I didn't know what they could do to me." He turned to Greene. "That's all fixed," he said.

"I've promised you immunity," the prosecutor answered. "I'll keep my word. Go on—you agreed to accept the ten thousand?"

"I did. I went to his office at twelve. One of the conditions was that I could stay on the PRESIDENT TYLER until she got back to San Francisco, and after that I was never to show my face out this way again. It suited me. Mr. Jennison introduced me to this Cabrera, who was to chaperon me the rest of that day. I'll say he did. When I went aboard the ship, he handed me a thousand dollars in an envelope.

"When I came back this time, I was to spend the day with Cabrera and get the other nine grand when I sailed. This morning when we tied up I saw the Spaniard on the dock, but by the time I'd landed he had disappeared. I met this Willie Chan and we had a large day. This fusel oil they sell out here loosened my tongue, but I'm not sorry. Of course, the rosy dream has faded, and it's my flat feet on the deck from now to the end of time. But the shore isn't so much any more, with all the bar-rooms under cover, and this sea life keeps a man out in the open air. As I say, I'm not sorry I talked. I can look any man in the eye again and tell him to go to—" He glanced at Miss Minerva. "Madam, I will not name the precise locality."

Greene stood. "Well, Jennison, there's my case. I've tipped it all off to you, but I wanted you to see for yourself how air-tight it is. There are two courses open to you—you can let this go to trial with a plea of not guilty. A long humiliating ordeal for you. Or you can confess here and now and throw yourself on the mercy of the court. If you're the sensible man I think you are, that's what you'll do."

EARL DERR BIGGERS

Jennison did not answer, did not even look at the prosecutor. "It was a very neat idea," Greene went on. "I'll grant you that. Only one thing puzzles me—did it come as the inspiration of the moment or did you plan it all out in advance? You've been over to the mainland rather often of late—were you waiting your chance? Anyhow, it came, didn't it—it came at last. And for a swimmer like you, child's play. You didn't need that ladder when you left the vessel—perhaps you went overboard while the President Tyler was still moving. A quick silent dive, a little way under water in case any one was watching from the deck, and then a long but easy swim ashore. And there you were, on the beach at Waikiki. Not far away Dan Winterslip was asleep on his lanai, with not so much as a locked door between you. Dan Winterslip, who stood between you and what you wanted. A little struggle—a quick thrust of your knife. Come on, Jennison, don't be a fool. It's the best way out for you now. A full confession."

Jennison leaped to his feet, his eyes flashing. "I'll see you in hell first!" he cried.

"Very well—if you feel that way about it—" Greene turned his back upon him and began a low-toned conversation with Hallet. Jennison and Charlie Chan were together on one side of the desk. Chan took out a pencil and accidentally dropped it on the floor. He stooped to pick it up.

John Quincy saw that the butt of a pistol carried in Chan's hip pocket protruded from under his coat. He saw Jennison spring forward and snatch the gun. With a cry John Quincy moved nearer, but Greene seized his arm and held him. Charlie Chan seemed unaccountably oblivious to what was going on.

Jennison put the muzzle of the pistol to his forehead and pulled the trigger. A sharp click—and that was all. The pistol fell from his hand.

"That's it!" cried Greene triumphantly. "That's my confession, and not a word spoken. I've witnesses, Jennison—they all saw you—you couldn't stand the disgrace a man in your position—you tried to kill yourself. With an empty gun." He went over and patted Chan on the shoulder. "A great idea, Charlie," he said. "Chan thought of it," he added to Jennison. "The Oriental mind, Harry. Rather subtle, isn't it?"

But Jennison had dropped back into his chair and buried his face in his hands.

"I'm sorry," said Greene gently. "But we've got you. Maybe you'll talk now."

Jennison looked up slowly. The defiance was gone from his face; it was lined and old.

"Maybe I will," he said hoarsely.

XXIII

Moonlight at the Crossroads

They filed out, leaving Jennison with Greene and the stenographer. In the anteroom Chan approached John Quincy.

"You go home decked in the shining garments of success," he said. "One thought is tantalizing me. At simultaneous moment you arrive at same conclusion we do. To reach there you must have leaped across considerable cavity."

John Quincy laughed. "I'll say I did. It came to me to-night. First, some one mentioned a golf professional with big wrists who drove a long ball. I had a quick flash of Jennison on the links here, and his terrific drives. Big wrists, they told me, meant that a man was proficient in the water. Then some one else—a young woman—spoke of a champion swimmer who left a ship off Waikiki. That was the first time the idea of such a thing had occurred to me. I was pretty warm then, and I felt Bowker was the man who could verify my suspicion. When I rushed aboard the President Tyler to find him, I saw Jennison about to sail and that confirmed my theory. I went after him."

"A brave performance," commented Chan.

"But as you can see, Charlie, I didn't have an iota of real evidence. Just guesswork. You were the one who furnished the proof."

"Proof are essential in this business," Chan replied.

"I'm tantalized too, Charlie. I remember you in the library. You were on the crack long before I was. How come?"

Chan grinned. "Seated at our ease in All American Restaurant that first night, you will recall I spoke of Chinese people as sensitive, like camera film. A look, a laugh, a gesture, something go click. Bowker enters and hovering above, says with alcoholic accent, 'I'm my own mashter, ain't I?' In my mind, the click. He is not own master. I follow to dock, behold when Spaniard present envelope. But for days I am fogged. I can only learn Cabrera and Jennison are very close. Clues continue to burst in our countenance. The occasion remains suspensive. At the Library I read of Jennison the fine swimmer. After that, the watch, and triumph."

Miss Minerva moved on toward the door. "May I have great honor to accompany you to car?" asked Chan.

Outside, John Quincy directed the chauffeur to return alone to Waikiki with the limousine. "You're riding out with me," he told his aunt. "I want to talk with you."

She turned to Charlie Chan. "I congratulate you. You've got brains, and they count."

He bowed low. "From you that compliment glows rosy red. At this moment of parting, my heart droops. My final wish—the snowy chilling days of winter and the scorching windless days of summer— may they all be the springtime for you."

"You're very kind," she said softly.

John Quincy took his hand. "It's been great fun knowing you, Charlie," he remarked.

"You will go again to the mainland," Chan said. "The angry ocean rolling between us. Still I shall carry the memory of your friendship like a flower in my heart." John Quincy climbed into the car. "And the parting may not be eternal," Chan added cheerfully. "The joy of travel may yet be mine. I shall look forward to the day when I may call upon you in your home and shake a healthy hand."

John Quincy started the car and slipping away, they left Charlie Chan standing like a great Buddha on the curb.

"Poor Barbara," said Miss Minerva presently. "I dread to face her with this news. But then, it's not altogether news at that. She told me she'd been conscious of something wrong between her and Jennison ever since they landed. She didn't think he killed her father, but she believed he was involved in it somehow. She is planning to settle with Brade to-morrow and leave the next day, probably for ever. I've persuaded her to come to Boston for a long visit. You'll see her there."

John Quincy shook his head. "No, I shan't. But thanks for reminding me. I must go to the cable office at once."

When he emerged from the office and again entered the car, he was smiling happily.

"In San Francisco," he explained, "Roger accused me of being a Puritan survival. He ran over a little list of adventures he said had never happened to me. Well, most of them have happened now, and I cabled to tell him so. I also said I'd take that job with him."

Miss Minerva frowned. "Think it over carefully," she warned. "San Francisco isn't Boston. The cultural standard is, I fancy, much lower. You'll be lonely there—"

"Oh, no, I shan't. Some one will be there with me. At least, I hope she will."

"Agatha?"

"No, not Agatha. The cultural standard was too low for her. She's broken our engagement."

"Barbara, then?"

"Not Barbara, either."

"But I have sometimes thought—"

"You thought Barbara sent Jennison packing because of me. Jennison thought so too—it's all clear now. That was why he tried to frighten me into leaving Honolulu, and set his opium running friends on me when I wouldn't go. But Barbara is not in love with me. We understand now why she broke her engagement."

"Neither Agatha nor Barbara," repeated Miss Minerva. "Then who—"

"You haven't met her yet, but that happy privilege will be yours before you sleep. The sweetest girl in the Islands—or in the world. The daughter of Jim Egan, whom you have been heard to refer to as a glorified beachcomber."

Again Miss Minerva frowned. "It's a great risk, John Quincy. She hasn't our background—"

"No, and that's a pleasant change. She's the niece of your old friend—you knew that?"

"I did," answered Miss Minerva softly.

"Your dear friend of the 'eighties. What was it you said to me? If your chance ever comes—"

"I hope you will be very happy," his aunt said. "When you write it to your mother, be sure and mention Captain Cope of the British Admiralty. Poor Grace! That will be all she'll have to cling to—after the wreck."

"What wreck?"

"The wreck of all her hopes for you."

"Nonsense. Mother will understand. She knows I'm a roaming Winterslip, and when we roam, we roam."

They found Madame Maynard seated in her living-room with a few of her more elderly guests. From the beach came the sound of youthful revelry.

"Well my boy," the old woman cried, "it appears you couldn't stay away from your policemen friends one single evening, after all. I give you up."

John Quincy laughed. "I'm pau now. By the way, Carlota Egan—is she—"

"They're all out there somewhere," the hostess said. "They came in for a bit of supper—by the way, there are sandwiches in the dining-room and—"

"Not just now," said John Quincy. "Thank you so much. I'll see you again, of course—"

He dashed out on the sand. A group of young people under the hau tree informed him that Carlota Egan was on the farthest float. Alone? Well, no—that naval lieutenant—

He was, he reflected as he hurried on toward the water, a bit fed up with the navy. That was hardly the attitude he should have taken, considering all the navy had done for him. But it was human. And John Quincy was human at last.

For an instant he stood at the water's edge. His bathing suit was in the dressing-room, but he never gave it a thought. He kicked off his shoes, tossed aside his coat, and plunged into the breakers. The blood of the wandering Winterslips was racing through his veins; hot blood that tropical waters had ever been powerless to cool.

Sure enough, Carlota Egan and Lieutenant Booth were together on the float. John Quincy climbed up beside them.

"Well, I'm back," he announced.

"I'll tell the world you're back," said the lieutenant. "And all wet, too."

They sat there. Across a thousand miles of warm water the trade winds came to fan their cheeks. Just above the horizon hung the Southern Cross; the Island lights trembled along the shore; the yellow eye on Diamond Head was winking. A gorgeous setting. Only one thing was wrong with it. It seemed rather crowded.

John Quincy had an inspiration. "Just as I hit the water," he remarked, "I thought I heard you say something about my dive. Didn't you like it?"

"It was rotten," replied the lieutenant amiably.

"You offered to show me what was wrong with it, I believe?"

"Sure. If you want me to."

"By all means," said John Quincy. "Learn one thing every day. That's my motto."

Lieutenant Booth went to the end of the springboard. "In the first place, always keep your ankles close together—like this."

"I've got you," answered John Quincy.

"And hold your arms tight against your ears."

EARL DERR BIGGERS

"The tighter the better, as far as I'm concerned."

"Then double up like a jackknife," continued the instructor. He doubled up like a jackknife and rose into the air.

At the same instant John Quincy seized the girl's hands. "Listen to me. I can't wait another second. I want to tell you that I love you—"

"You're mad," she cried.

"Mad about you. Ever since that day on the ferry—"

"But your people?"

"What about my people? It's just you and I—we'll live in San Francisco—that is, if you love me—"

"Well, I—"

"In heaven's name, be quick. That human submarine is floating around here under us. You love me, don't you? You'll marry me?"

"Yes."

He took her in his arms and kissed her. Only the wandering Winterslips could kiss like that. The stay-at-homes had always secretly begrudged them the accomplishment.

The girl broke away at last, breathless. "Johnnie!" she cried.

A sputter beside them, and Lieutenant Booth climbed on to the float, moist and panting. "Wha's that?" he gurgled.

"She was speaking to me," cried John Quincy triumphantly.

The End

A Note About the Author

Earl Derr Biggers (1884–1933) was an American novelist and playwright. Born in Ohio, Biggers went on to graduate from Harvard University, where he was a member of *The Harvard Lampoon*, a humor publication for undergraduates. Following a brief career as a journalist, most significantly for Cleveland-based newspaper *The Plain Dealer*, Biggers turned to fiction, writing novels and plays for a popular audience. Many of his works have been adapted into film and theater productions, including the novel *Seven Keys to Baldpate* (1913), which was made into a Broadway stage play the same year it was published. Towards the end of his career, he produced a highly popular series of novels centered on Honolulu police detective Charlie Chan. Beginning with *The House Without a Key* (1925), Biggers intended his character as an alternative to Yellow Peril stereotypes prominent in the early twentieth century. His series of Charlie Chan novels inspired dozens of films in the United States and China, and has been recognized as an imperfect attempt to use popular media to depict Chinese Americans in a positive light.

A Note from the Publisher

Spanning many genres, from non-fiction essays to literature classics to children's books and lyric poetry, Mint Edition books showcase the master works of our time in a modern new package. The text is freshly typeset, is clean and easy to read, and features a new note about the author in each volume. Many books also include exclusive new introductory material. Every book boasts a striking new cover, which makes it as appropriate for collecting as it is for gift giving. Mint Edition books are only printed when a reader orders them, so natural resources are not wasted. We're proud that our books are never manufactured in excess and exist only in the exact quantity they need to be read and enjoyed. To learn more and view our library, go to minteditionbooks.com

bookfinity & MINT EDITIONS

Enjoy more of your favorite classics with Bookfinity,
a new search and discovery experience for readers.
With Bookfinity, you can discover more vintage
literature for your collection, find your Reader Type,
track books you've read or want to read,
and add reviews to your favorite books.
Visit www.bookfinity.com, and click on
Take the Quiz to get started.

Don't forget to follow us
@bookfinityofficial and @mint_editions